Acknowled

Many thanks to the people of Ic
knowingly or otherwise, in the creation of this novel. Without tneir
input, interest, and encouragement it would not have been
completed.

Thanks are also due to those tireless people who run the area's
pubs and have to suffer my constant thirst (for information).

Special thanks to Nicky Higgins for providing the image for the
book cover from the original idea by Andy Scott.

# CHAPTER 1

Acting DI Gary Ryan sat, head in hands, looking at the latest reported crime. A male PC in Keighley had been stabbed to death by a woman who was now in custody. He was reading her initial statement in which she claimed the PC was one of two men who raped her more than ten years ago. He looked at the whiteboard before deciding how he would assign the investigation before writing the names of Lynn and Jo-Jo against it after checking their availability. Everyone in the team was currently working on an active case but in all probability Lynn and Jo-Jo would soon be available to pick up the new case. He broke the news to them. They were less than delighted.

"I was hoping to take a couple of days off as soon as we'd wrapped up the current case. I've been working flat out for weeks."
"Sorry, Lynn. It's the same for everyone just now, but at least we've got reinforcements from next Monday."
"Thank God. So, Scoffer and Andy are permanent?"
"Yes. We don't know yet how long Brian will be off."
"Well, I hope he's back soon."
"He'll be back as soon as he's pronounced fit. It's out of our hands."
"I know. I miss him."
"We all do."

********

Brian Peters drove slowly into the car park and carefully pulled to a halt in his allotted parking space, marked with a white 16 painted on the wall facing him. He sat for a moment before getting out of the car and dragging the heavy cardboard box from the back seat, placing it on the ground before steeling himself for the first trip. He locked the car door, put the keys in his pocket and pulled out another set of keys which he gripped between his teeth as he picked up the box and carried it to the entrance door. He was lucky. A resident was just leaving as he neared the door. She recognised him and held the door open for him.

"Morning, Mr Peters."
"Morning, Mrs Metcalfe. Thank you."
"No problem. Do you need a hand with anything?"
"No. I'm fine, thanks."

"OK. Well, I'm just popping out to the shop. I'll be back in half an hour. Just give me a knock if you need any help."
"I will. Thank you."

Mrs Metcalfe. His new next-door neighbour. She'd introduced herself when he first looked at the property. He hoped she was just being polite and neighbourly. He wasn't looking for anything more.

He carried the box along the corridor to his new apartment and breathed a sigh of relief to see it was exactly as promised. It had been re-painted to his specification and new carpets and curtains fitted. The kitchen and bathroom had also been thoroughly cleaned. He checked his watch. 9.15. He had forty-five minutes to bring in the rest of his baggage before the furniture arrived. Until then, his belongings would remain in their boxes and suitcases.

He was about to return to the car to retrieve more of his belongings when he heard a buzzing sound. The door-entry system. He smiled. She promised she'd call to help him. He pressed the button and spoke.

"Come in, Teresa."

She heard the door release, and was soon walking through his front door, looking around at the unfamiliar surroundings.

"This is nice, Brian. I'm sure you'll love it here."
"I'm sure you're right. So, how are things at work?"
"We're run off our feet. Gary's been given the role of acting DI, but between you and me, he's struggling a bit."
"That's no surprise. It's difficult when you're thrown in at the deep end. The experience will be good for him, long term."
"Is there anything that needs doing before your stuff arrives?"
"No. It's all been left clean and tidy. I'd offer you a coffee, but I haven't got any milk."
"That's OK. I picked some up on my way. I hope you've got a kettle."
"Yes. In that big box. That's all stuff for the kitchen."
"OK. I'll start putting it away. You make a cuppa."

When their respective tasks were completed, Teresa forced Brian to take a good look at where she'd put everything.

"Memorise it, Brian. Make sure you put everything back where it goes after you've used it."

"Yes, mam."

"Don't be sarcastic. The sooner you settle into a routine, the better."

"I know. I'll have plenty time to memorise everything...."

"Don't be too despondent, Brian. It's not long until you have your review."

"Twelve more weeks. And there's no guarantee."

"No, but if you keep seeing your counsellor, you'll stay on track."

"It just doesn't get any easier."

"Moving here will help, Brian."

"I know."

He thought back to the day when his world was torn apart. The day when his wife and two young children were brutally murdered in their own home, and how their ghosts continued to inhabit the place. How, no matter how much it was cleaned and sanitised, the house still retained the stench of death. He *had to leave*. Hopefully, the move would aid his recovery, and his suspension from CID would be lifted. He felt it was his big chance, his only chance, to get his life back on track. He would never forget what had happened, but perhaps he would learn to cope. The doorbell interrupted his thoughts. The removal men were here. He let them in.

"Do you want me to stay for a while, Brian?"

"No, Teresa. You need to get back to HQ. You know they can't function without you."

"You're the one they need, Brian. The sooner you get back to work, the better. For all of us. I'll see myself out."

"Thanks for coming, Teresa. Give my regards to the team."

"Will do. Oh, by the way, we caught the guy who'd been running the minibus tours. He's due in court this week, and then he'll be deported."

"He's an illegal?"

"Yep. He's been here a long time. I can't believe he's never been picked up before. He used to run a tour of the places where the Yorkshire Ripper killed his victims, before turning his attention to your old house."

"Where are they holding him? I'd like a quiet word in his ear."

"You don't need to. Someone's already given him a good hammering while he's been in custody."

"Whoever did it deserves a medal. Who was it?"

"I can't tell you that, Brian."

"Well, pass on my thanks to whoever it was."

4

"OK. One other thing."

"What's that?"

"Where are you hiding the whisky?"

"It's OK, Teresa. It's under control. I'm allowed fourteen units of alcohol a week. I write it all down. I've been within the limit for the last three weeks, even though there's whisky in the house. I'm coping."

"OK. I trust you. Call me if you need me."

"Thanks, I will."

********

After the removal men had left, he drove up to Idle to stock up on food and the other items he'd never had to bother about when his wife was alive. Things such as bleach, washing powder and the rest of the necessities required to run a household. He'd learn. He'd adapt. He had no choice.

By the time he'd put everything in its place, and he was satisfied with his day's work, it was five o'clock. He put on his coat, checked his wallet and walked out of the building in search of somewhere to eat. He knew the area quite well, having had cause to conduct criminal investigations in and around the area, but had only rarely had any reason to check out a couple of the local pubs. Now was the time to rectify that omission, keeping in mind that it was not to be an excuse to get plastered. He needed a meal and was in no mood to cook for himself.

His first port of call was at the Ainsbury micropub, a small, welcoming bar, where snacks were set out free for the customers. It was tempting, but he really needed a substantial meal, so after a bottle of non-alcoholic lager and a chat with the owners, John and Nicky, he reluctantly left.

Two hours later, having been unable to find the kind of meal he was looking for, and finding it increasingly difficult being in a pub without sampling the beer, he bought a takeaway pizza and returned home.

"Get used to it, Brian," he told himself. "This is your life."

He ate the pizza while filling in his alcohol consumption daily record. It had been a good week so far; he could look forward to a small glass of malt before bed.

********

He was up early the following morning, adjusting the position of some of the furniture, re-hanging photo frames, all minor adjustments, but it made him feel in control. It was his apartment. He could have it exactly how *he* wanted it. He sat at the kitchen table eating a slice of toast and sipping a mug of coffee as he debated what to do with his day. That was soon to be decided for him when his mobile sounded. Teresa. He answered immediately.

"Morning, Brian. I hope I'm not disturbing you."
"Not at all, Teresa. How can I help you?"
"A man turned up at Reception this morning, asking if he could speak to you. The receptionist informed him you were on extended leave, and asked if there was anyone else he could speak to. He was adamant he'd only talk to you. Anyway, he kicked off a bit, saying lives were at stake, and getting quite agitated. Gary went down to talk to him, but he wouldn't discuss it with him. He would only deal with you."
"Did you get his name?"
"Terry Stanton."
"Mmm. I recognise the name but can't for the life of me place him."
"I looked him up in the database. His name came up several times in the records of ex-DI Hardcastle's criminal activity."
"I remember him now. He had his car nicked and traced the thieves. They were drug dealers. The investigation eventually led to Hardcastle's involvement in the trade. He put himself at significant risk, probably more than he ever realised. When it was all over, I went to thank him. Maybe he thinks we owe him. Give me his number. I'll call him."
"Thanks, Brian."

He dialled the number immediately.

"Is that Terry? It's Brian Peters."
"Oh, thank God! Thanks for calling me. I need your help."
"I'm sorry. I'm on leave now. Can I get another officer to help you?"
"No. I don't trust anyone else. Innocent people are at risk. You've got to help me."

"OK. Calm down. Where are you?"
"Skipton."
"Can you meet me in Keighley in half an hour?"
"Yeah. Where?"
"Wetherspoons. You know it?"
"Yeah."
"I'll see you there in half an hour."
"Thanks."
"OK. This had better be worth it."
"It will be."

Brian parked off Scott Street and made his way to the Livery Rooms. There were few customers at that time of day, apart from the regulars and he had no problem spotting Terry at the bar. He walked over and shook his hand.

"Good to see you, Mr Peters. How're you keeping?"
"I'm managing, Terry. But I'm busy so can we get straight down to business?"
"Of course. Do you want a drink?"
"Coffee, please."
"Find a table. I'll bring them over."

Brian sat impatiently at a corner table, as far away from the few customers as possible, until Terry brought the drinks over.

"Thanks, Terry. Now, what's the story!"
"Refugees."
"What about them?"
"They're being trafficked."
"That's a known fact, Terry. What makes it so important to you?"

Terry took a deep breath and launched into his story.

"My wife Linda has a brother, Tony. He's in his thirties and married to Nadia, a Ukrainian woman who worked and lived over here when they met. She has family back home. They were slap-bang in the middle of it. In real danger. Her mother and father, her brother and his wife and two children. They arranged to come over here. Tony and Nadia were going to house the parents and Tony had found a flat for his wife's brother's family."

He paused to gather his thoughts before continuing.

"It all seemed to be going well. They came over in two vehicles with volunteer drivers but once they got into England, and through immigration, one of the vans disappeared."

He stopped, trying desperately to conceal his anger.

"It just disappeared. Nobody's been able to contact the driver or any of the family since."
"I'm guessing the van which disappeared had the kids and their parents in it?"
"The kids and their mother."
"Do you have any photos of them?"
"Yes. I got them from my brother-in-law. You can take them but please let me have them back."
"I will. I'll get them copied. So, who have you told about this so far?"
"I phoned the Skipton police and they referred me to Bradford. Then I just got passed from pillar to post. Then I remembered you and asked if I could speak to you directly. They told me you were off sick. I persevered and got put through to someone who took the time to listen. Her name was Teresa. She said she'd speak to you. I'm desperate. Nobody will help me. You're my last hope. You're my only hope. Please help me."

Brian thought for a while before agreeing.

"OK. I'll see what I can do. But there's no guarantee. Give me the whole story. Names, dates, everything you can remember, and I'll look into it. Let me record the conversation and I'll take notes at the same time. OK?"
"OK. Thanks, Mr Peters."

********

An hour later, they parted company, but instead of going to the car park, Brian walked past it and headed for The Boltmakers, promising himself he'd just have one pint.

He sat in a corner, alone at a table on which he spread out the images and snippets of information he'd gathered from Terry. As he looked at everything spread out before him, he made copious notes and an action plan for himself to follow. He found the phone number for Terry's brother-in-law, called him and arranged to meet him the following morning at his home in Eccleshill. He ordered a second pint, again promising himself it would be the last and reminding himself he had to drive home.

Rather than adhering to the promises he'd made himself prior to deciding to live alone, he stopped for a takeaway on his way home to save himself the effort of cooking and washing up afterwards. Besides, the quicker the meal, the more time he could devote to his case.

He quickly realised that working from home had its disadvantages. He didn't have access to all the databases he could search from his desk at HQ. He would have to ask Teresa to find specific information for him, and he knew she could potentially be in trouble if she was found to be passing data to an unauthorised contact – after all, he was suspended. He looked around the room. It had never been designed as an office. He had a desktop PC as well as his laptop, but his inkjet printer was slow, and the second bedroom was never intended to be a workspace, having only one power point. Never mind. It would have to do. He would cope; he had a four-socket extension. There was also a closet where he had piled everything which didn't seem to have a natural place in an apartment. It contained suitcases, packing cases full of things collected over the years which he guessed would somehow prove useful, half-empty tins of paint, and off-cuts of wallpaper conveniently left by the decorators. He pulled out a roll and cut off a six-foot length, then checked every drawer in the apartment until he found a box of drawing pins which he used to fix the wallpaper, face-down, to the wall. He'd already found the marker pens which had belonged to his kids and used them to note the salient facts of his assignment on his makeshift wall chart. From this, he drew up an action plan for the following day. Point number 1 was his arranged meeting with Terry's brother-in-law. He quickly jotted down every question he could think of which might help him establish exactly what had happened. He was interrupted by a message on his mobile. Teresa.

"U OK, Brian? Did u meet Stanton?"

He replied.

"Yes. Might need your help soon."
"Just ask. I'll help if I can."
"Thanks."

He'd reached the point in the evening that his counsellor had warned him would be difficult. She was right. He really fancied a drink, but instead of reaching for the whisky, he got up and made a cup of tea before going to bed. He knew tomorrow would be a stressful day. No matter. He was focused. He would deal with it.

********

The alarm woke him at six-thirty. He'd slept well and showered, dressed and ate a light breakfast before driving the short distance to Eccleshill to interview Tony Broughton, Terry's brother-in-law.

He drove slowly along the road, checking the house numbers until he pulled up outside the address he'd been given. As he walked up the drive, the front door opened and a tall, casually dressed man beckoned him in. He looked up and down the road before closing the door behind him, ushering him into the lounge where his wife, Nadia, was seated. She'd been crying. Tony sat by her, holding her hand as he spoke.

"Thank you for coming, Mr Peters. Please sit down."
"Thank you. So, Terry told me about what happened. If you don't mind, I'd like to hear your version from the beginning."
"Don't you believe Terry?"
"Yes. Yes, I do. It's just that if I hear it from you, it's possible that the story might just differ slightly in some respects. It's vital I get a clear picture of what happened, right from the outset. So, please, leave nothing out. However trivial it might seem; it could be vital."

Nadia spoke first.

"My parents are Ukraine. I was brought up there. We lived close to Mariupol. My brother Andriy also lived there, with his wife Yulia and their two teenage children Olga and Ana. They were in danger. There was bombing every day. People were dying. People were starving. It was terrible. We spoke to them every day. We knew we had to get them out. They pleaded with us to help them. They managed to apply for asylum, queueing every day at the Embassy until they got their papers. But there were always delays. It was chaos. Yulia phoned me every day in tears. We had to help. We made arrangements for my parents to live with us and agreed to rent a flat on this street for my brother and his family. We had to wait. Delays. Paperwork. Everything. And all the time their lives were in danger."

She stopped to look at Tony, who squeezed her hand and nodded. She continued.

"One day, I saw a message on Facebook. Someone was taking food and supplies to Ukraine and were happy to offer transport back to England for refugees. I messaged them and they agreed to help. They were taking two vans and could bring back six people. It sounded too good to be true. And it was free! We jumped at the chance, and everything was organised. We were all so happy. We spoke to our family every day as they prepared and checked all their paperwork was in order. Everybody was so excited. But then it all went wrong...."

Nadia burst into tears as Tony comforted her. Brian waited patiently until Nadia composed herself.

"Could you show me the Facebook messages, please?"
"No. They've been erased. Everything has been erased."
"OK. Don't worry. We may be able to retrieve them. Do you remember the names of the people who were making the trip? Could you describe them?"
"They were both in their forties, I think. Dave and Stewart. Oh, and I took the registration of one of the vans they were posing next to when they had loaded it up for the trip. I sent it to my father so he would recognise the van. Here it is, on my phone. PU17 LBT. A white Transit van."

Brian noted the details.

"Thank you. I'll send this to HQ and see what they can unearth. So, what happened next?"
"Everything seemed to be going to plan. My father phoned me every day. They were all packed and ready, and then the vans arrived. It was a bit of a setback but nothing major."
"What do you mean?"
"They arrived in different vans. Black vans. They explained they had to swap them because the ones they had intended to use were needed elsewhere, so they had two smaller ones with no seats or windows in the back. They explained that my parents and my brother would go in one van and Yulia and the kids would travel in the other. They had no option but to agree, and the drivers assured them everything was OK. They had blankets in the back to keep them warm."
"Do you remember the date they set off?"

"The 7th. Five days ago."

"And did you hear from them during the trip?"

"Yes. Andriy and Yulia sent regular messages saying everything was OK. They passed through Customs and Immigration without any problems and were allowed out of the vans to use the toilet during the crossing. They called me when they docked. They all gave a huge cheer. Then soon they were driving again. After a while, the van with my parents and Andriy inside stopped at some services. The men explained the other van would be there shortly so they should use the facilities and wait for them. They agreed and went to use the toilets. Andriy phoned his wife. They were still on the road. Eventually, he went outside to ask their driver where the other van was. But his van had disappeared! He phoned Yulia. They were still driving. She didn't know where they were. They were all getting worried. Yulia banged on the van and shouted for the driver to stop but they just carried on. Then I got a message from Andriy. He couldn't get through to Yulia. Her phone was switched off. We got in the car and drove down the M1 to the services near Leicester where they were stranded. When we got there, the police were already there and took them into Leicester. We followed and were eventually allowed to take them home. All their belongings were in the van. They had nothing except their passports and visas and the other necessary paperwork. All their clothes and memorabilia were gone.

We ring the police every day, but there has been no progress in locating Yulia and the kids. We're at our wits end! Terry suggested you might be able to help."

"I'll do all I can, but there are no guarantees."

"Thank you. You're our last hope."


Brian walked back to his car. He could only think of one motive behind what had occurred. The passengers had been deliberately separated into two groups. They had no visibility from their transport. It had been planned that way, so that a young woman and her two teenage daughters could be abducted. He was certain he knew why. He called Teresa.


"Hi Teresa. I wonder if you could do a small job for me."

"Depends. What is it?"

"I need to trace a Facebook post that's been deleted."

"It's possible. You'll need to tell me who it was sent by and as much detail as you can give me. May I ask what it's about?"

"A woman and her two teenage girls have been kidnapped. A family of six were offered safe passage from Ukraine to England.

Three of them were dumped at a Services on the M1. The others have disappeared."

"Mmm. Sex trade, I'm guessing. Send me everything you've got, and I'll get on to it. One question. Why hasn't it been reported to the police already?"

"It has. And to Bradford, apparently. But nobody seems to have time to look into it."

"OK. Leave it with me."

"Thanks."

# CHAPTER 2

Brian was up early and having breakfast when he received the phone call.

"Morning, Brian. How are you this morning?"
"Sober, Teresa. How are you?"
"Busy. However, I have some news for you. The vehicle registration you sent me doesn't belong to a white Transit. It came from a Skoda saloon which was written off and scrapped in Skipton. I'll send you the address if you want to follow it up."
"Yes, please."
"OK. No joy regarding identifying the drivers yet. Have you thought about passing the photo to the T & A?"
"That's an idea I may try, Teresa. Thank you."
"I've requested CCTV footage from the M1 Services for that particular day. I'm afraid we don't have time to scan them here, but I can send them to you if you wish."
"Yes. Please do."

He waited patiently for the images to arrive, using the time to plan the rest of his day. But soon he was watching the computer screen intently as traffic came and went into the Services car park. He had the approximate arrival and departure time and concentrated, advancing a frame at a time until a black van appeared, parking close to the entrance. He watched as the driver alighted and walked to the rear, opening the door so the passengers could stretch their legs. He identified Andriy and his parents as they blinked in the daylight. The driver, though, had his back to the camera.

"Turn around, you prat. Let's have a proper look at you."

Brian gazed intently at the screen as the driver gestured, he guessed, that his passengers should stretch their legs and relax until the second van arrived. He watched as the trio walked off towards the toilets, and the moment they were out of sight, he saw the driver get back in the van and drive off. He watched again, forwarding frame by frame, but the best image he could capture of the driver was his profile. He sent it back to Teresa asking if she could run it through some databases. Meanwhile, he prepared to take a trip to Skipton.

********

He was just about to leave the apartment building when a neighbour stopped him.

"Excuse me. Are you Mr Peters? The policeman?"
"Yes. How can I help you?"
"A man stopped me in the car park and asked me if I knew which number you lived at. When I told him I wasn't sure, he asked me to give this to you."

He held out a sealed envelope and began to walk away as Brian tore it open. Inside was a photograph of his car with a message printed underneath. It read:

"You're being watched."

Brian was puzzled. Why would someone be watching him? He shouted to his neighbour.

"Can you describe the man?"
"About six feet tall, slim. Grey hair. 50-ish."
"Thanks."

He put the photograph in his pocket, got in his car and drove to Skipton.

Throughout the journey, he couldn't get the photograph out of his mind. Why would anybody photograph another person's car, then give it to a stranger to pass to the car's owner? It must have some significance. But what? He indicated and pulled into a layby on the bypass. He took the envelope out of his pocket, holding it carefully by one corner in case it bore fingerprints, and extracted the photograph, again holding it by a corner. He looked at it closely until he noticed there was something in the bushes behind the car. It was indistinct, partly obscured by foliage, but it was definitely a face, a man's face. Carefully, he replaced it in the envelope. He would let the lab have a look at it later.

The photograph preyed on his mind throughout the journey, and when he finally reached the scrapyard just outside Skipton, he again took the photograph out of its envelope and looked at it one more time. This time, he realised it wasn't taken at ground level.

"Idiot!" he thought. "You should have noticed that."

He made a mental note to park the car exactly as it was shown in the photograph. Then, with luck, he could work out which window of the apartments it was taken from.

********

His trip to Skipton turned out to be a total waste of time. The owner of the scrapyard wasn't even aware that the numberplates had been removed from the scrapped Skoda. Brian left, seething at the scrapyard owner's flippant comment that 'people will steal anything these days'. His thoughts returned to the photograph in the envelope and, on entering the car park, he took care to park his car exactly as the photograph showed. He got out and moved away until he was certain he'd lined up the car at the exact angle. He then turned to face the building and looked up. Sure enough, there were windows directly above him. Looking again at the photograph, he calculated the second floor would be the correct height, but he would only be certain once he'd viewed the car from the window. He entered the building and walked up the stairs trying his utmost to calculate his exact position in relation to his car. At the end of the corridor was a window. He looked out. He could see the car, but the sightline wasn't right. He judged the second flat along would most likely provide the most accurate view. He rang the doorbell and waited. Eventually it opened, but only a few inches and a face peered at him through the gap.

"What do you want?"
"I'd like to ask you why you've taken this photograph of my car."
"I thought you might like to know someone's watching you."
"Someone apart from you, you mean."
"There's been a man loitering since you moved in. I thought you should know, since you were a policeman."
"Why didn't you come and tell me?"
"I wasn't sure which was your flat. I don't get out much…."
"So, you asked a neighbour to pass it to me?"
"Yes."
"Do you mind if I just check the view from your window?"
"Come in. It's from the lounge. This way."

Brian checked. It matched perfectly.

"Do you make a habit of watching people from your window?"

The man looked nervous, then replied.

"I suppose I should tell you before one of the neighbours does. People call me Peeping Tom. I had to move from my last place because the neighbours thought I was too nosey. They verbally and physically abused me. I can't help it. It's an obsession."

"OK. So, you saw this man lurking in the bushes and so you took this photo."

"Yes."

"Any others? I mean, it's not very clear."

"I'm sorry. It's the best I could get. He was there over half an hour. He never moved. I thought you should know."

"OK. If you see him again, would you let me know?"

"You're not angry?"

"No. It's good that someone's keeping a watch on comings and goings. I'm in apartment 16. If he turns up again, let me know. Better still, here's my phone number. My name's Brian Peters. You are?"

"John Davidson."

"Well, thank you for your help, John."

"You're welcome."

Brian returned to his apartment, thinking. His mobile rang.

"Brian Peters."

"Brian, it's Teresa. I'm afraid we haven't found any match for the image you sent me, but I've been in touch with the Border Force at Dover. They've verified the date and time of arrival for the family and have kindly agreed to send me a copy of CCTV covering the area at around that time. I'll forward it as soon as it arrives."

"That's great, Teresa. Thanks."

"You're welcome. I'm sorry I can't help you with it. It's absolute chaos here at the moment. I'm afraid we're missing your calming influence."

"I'm sure you're all doing the best you can, Teresa."

"We are. It just doesn't feel like it's enough. I have to go. We'll talk later. 'Bye."

She ended the call. Brian made a cup of coffee while he waited for the CCTV footage to arrive in his Inbox. Then, he settled down for a long session requiring his full concentration.

********

When Teresa described there being chaos in the office, it was an understatement. The DCI had a meeting to attend in Manchester and was out for the day, and although Gary was ostensibly in control, the sheer volume of inquiries the officers were handling was overwhelming. Nobody could be accused of giving less than 100%, but they were stretched to the limit, even with the permanent addition of DC Joe (Scoffer) Schofield and DC Andy Thompson.

The list of active cases logged on the whiteboard grew longer daily, and it seemed that little progress was being made, so when another incident came through to Teresa, she took matters into her own hands and called Brian.

"Hi Brian. I'm sorry to have to do this to you, but I wonder if you could look into another case for me."
"I'm still suspended from active duty, Teresa. I shouldn't need to remind you of that."
"I know, Brian. I'm really sorry, but I don't think the team are actually capable of handling any more without you at the helm. I know I shouldn't say that, but I'm being honest. If things continue, I'm worried the department will start to lose the respect we've earned under your leadership."
"What is it?"
"A man has reported his wife missing, but he believes she's been kidnapped."
"Is he serious?"
"Absolutely. Can I send you some information so at least you can advise me on what to do?"
"OK. I'll have a look. But don't expect me to take the case on."
"Thanks. By the way, I've had no luck with the Facebook pages yet."

He really didn't want to take the case. He was supposed to be relaxing after the trauma he'd suffered, but the memory would never leave him. He thought back to the time when he'd made the decision to stay in CID, and then almost immediately regretted it. He couldn't shake off the past and began drinking more heavily to the point where his work suffered and his colleagues and bosses realised he was becoming a liability. The decision was taken to suspend him from active duty until such time as his mental health improved sufficiently to meet the demands of the job. He saw a counsellor regularly. She submitted her reports to his bosses who reluctantly agreed that unless his behaviour showed a marked and sustained improvement within six months, he would be pensioned off.

He was doing his best. With Teresa's encouragement he'd taken up running, lost a stone in weight and was generally in good health. But he was still prone to relapse. Something as simple as seeing kids laughing and playing in the park with their parents could suddenly plunge him into depression and he would go on a bender, once crashing his car into a wall on his way home from the pub. Fortunately, Teresa and his counsellor were gradually helping him back to normality.

When the email arrived from Teresa, he read it immediately. It described how a man was in despair that his wife had disappeared and how he believed she may have been abducted. He rang the phone number and arranged to meet the man at his home in Shipley later that morning.

As he pulled up outside the semi, the man, Mr Desmond Marshall, was waiting for him at the door. Brian introduced himself and was ushered into the kitchen. Brian could tell immediately that Mr Marshall was devastated and listened as he explained the situation.

He'd come home from work on the previous Tuesday and found a note his wife had left for him on the kitchen table. It explained she'd left him because she felt their relationship was floundering and she wanted a fresh start. Looking around the house, he realised she'd taken her coat, her handbag, a small suitcase and a small amount of money.

"I'm sorry, Mr Peters, but I just don't believe this. I admit we've been going through a bit of a rocky patch recently, but Diane wouldn't just leave me without explaining face-to-face. We always talked things through. And if she'd decided to leave, she would have taken more than a few quid. There's a couple of hundred in a box upstairs. She's contributed to that as much as I have. She has as much right to it as I have."
"Well, I agree it's unusual, but perhaps she wanted to soften the blow by making sure you had some money in the house."
"No. I don't believe that."
"Can you confirm your wife wrote this note?"
"Yes."
"Does it look normal?"
"What do you mean?"
"Does it look stressed? As if she wrote it under pressure."
"I don't know. She was always an untidy writer?"

"What about the words she used? Does she normally speak like this?"

"I'm not sure what you're getting at."

"I'm trying to find out if someone told her what to write. If she was put under duress."

"Well, what made me suspicious is she's put 'Desmond'. She always called me 'Des'. Has done all the time we've known each other. The last time she called me Desmond was when she spoke her wedding vows, and that's nearly twenty years ago."

"OK. It's possible someone told her what to write. It's worth following up. I'll see what I can do. Can I take the note?"

"If you want."

"Has anyone else handled it?"

"Only a constable when I went to the police."

"I'll see if forensics can get any prints from it. In the meantime, would you make a list for me of everybody you knew as a couple, and her workmates and anybody else she had more than occasional contact with?"

"Already done."

He slid a sheet of paper across the table.

"That's a list of her workmates. The one below is her personal friends and family. I've ticked the ones I've already contacted."

"Thank you. Could I also have a photograph of Diane?"

"OK. Can you tell me, though, why the police aren't handling this? I was led to understand you were freelance."

"I'm on leave at the moment. Just helping out because they're a little stretched. It's worth bearing in mind, though, that close to 100,000 adults are reported missing every week. And that's just the ones who are reported to the police. Only about 5% of that figure are missing for longer than a week. I'll be in touch."

Back at his apartment, he worked his way through the contacts list Des Marshall had provided, crossing off the names as he eliminated them as suspects while gleaning information about Diane's private life. Eventually, though, he did get one lead while talking to one of Diane's workmates, when he learnt that Diane had told her about a customer who chatted her up and asked her out. He arranged to speak to her face-to-face and drove straight up to Five Lane Ends where she worked at Morrisons. Unfortunately, Diane's workmate was unable to provide a description of the man. Further disappointment came when he discovered that the CCTV images for the day in question had already been overwritten.

Before he left, he spoke to the store manager, asking him to report immediately any similar instances in future to CID HQ. Lacking any further leads, he put the investigation on the back burner.

\*\*\*\*\*\*\*\*

Meanwhile, Lynn and Jo-Jo were interviewing Mary Sugden who was on remand, charged with the unlawful killing of PC Jack Carlyle. She expressed her motive clearly.

"I admit it. I killed him. But he deserved it."

She sat, arms crossed, a defiant look on her face.

"Would you like to explain to us why you think he deserved it?"
"It's over ten years ago now, but I'll never forget it. I'd been out in town with some girlfriends. It was a Bank Holiday, Easter, and three of us were going from pub to pub, getting smashed. Then at closing time, we went to a taxi rank and queued. My two friends got in the same taxi – they lived close together, but I waited for the next one. But then I realised I needed a pee, so I went into the nearest pub. Then, when I went back outside, I was at the back of a long queue so I decided to walk to the Interchange and try there. But I was a bit drunk and I must have lost my footing and fell on the pavement. The next thing I knew was a police car pulled up next to me and this officer got out and asked if I was OK. I can clearly remember him saying 'Been on the sauce, 'ave you?' He could tell I was drunk, and he offered me a lift home. I just thought it was a really nice thing to do. So, I got in the back and he got in next to me while his mate drove. Next thing I know, he's fondling my tits and he put his hand up my skirt. I screamed for him to stop. He put his hand over my mouth and called me a slut and I could see his mate in the front laughing. They drove out of town and stopped on a quiet back street somewhere. Then he raped me while the driver held me down. Then they swapped over and the other officer raped me. Then they threw me out of the car and drove away. I just sat at the roadside crying until a taxi stopped and took me to hospital. I just cried for hours. I reported it but nobody took me seriously. The police wouldn't believe me and I couldn't describe the coppers. I was just in shock."
"So, it never went to court?"
"No. There was nothing I could do. I've just learnt to live with it over the years. And then, last week I'd had a few drinks with some workmates and I was waiting at the taxi rank when a police car

pulled up, and the driver opened the window and asked 'Been on the sauce, 'ave you?' Well, that brought it all back. I could see him grinning. I knew it was him. I recognised his voice. And then he said 'Get in. I'll give you a lift.' I couldn't help myself. Since that first time I was raped, I've always carried a knife in my handbag. And I just reached in, grabbed it by the handle and stuck it into his neck. I could see the look of horror on his face. But I pulled it out and stabbed him again. There was blood everywhere, and people were screaming. But I didn't care. I just glared at him as he died. I was glad. He deserved it."

As they left the Interview Room, Lynn and Jo-Jo were of the same opinion. There was no doubt Mary Sugden had killed PC Carlyle. She'd admitted it, and it was up to the DPP as to how the charge should be presented. But there was another matter to be resolved. They needed the identity of the other officer who was with him at the time of the offence, and who also raped her.

"Let's talk to Teresa. She may be able to access the shift logs if records are kept that long."

********

Teresa was unable to take Lynn's call at the time. She was already on another line taking details of an incident.

"Just confirm for me, please. Chellow Dene Reservoir. Top lake. OK, an officer will be with you in just a few minutes, so just stay where you are. And don't touch the body. Thank you."

She closed the call and alerted Gary.

"A body's been discovered in a reservoir, Gary. Chellow Dene. I'm sending a squad car to secure the scene, and I'm alerting SOCO. The body was found by two anglers. I'm sending you the rest of the details as soon as I've typed them up."
"OK. Thanks, Teresa. I'll get someone up there as soon as I can."

Paula and Andy were the only officers in the office at the time. He allocated the incident to them.

By the time they arrived at the scene, a small crowd of dog-walkers and anglers had already gathered, phones in hand.

"Let's get some more Uniforms here to hold this lot back. The T & A will be here soon as well."

Soon, barriers and a tent were erected at the scene as Forensics officers got to work, taking photographs and evidence to examine back at the lab. Paula spotted Allen Greaves and approached him.

"Morning, Allen. What can you tell us?"
"Two anglers found the body snagged on some branches overhanging the water and phoned 999. We found the body of a woman, probably in her thirties. We're taking the body back for examination. At the moment, cause of death would seem to be drowning, but we'll confirm that in due course."
"Any identification on her?"
"None."
"Anything suspicious?"
"Yes. Her mode of dress. She was dressed like something out of a fairy tale. You've heard of the legend of King Arthur?"
"Yes."
"Well, meet the Lady of the Lake."
"Christ! I don't suppose she's got a sword? Excalibur?"
"If she has, we haven't found it yet. I'll let you know when we've finished our examination at the lab."
"Thanks, Allen. We'll get statements from the anglers, then get back to HQ and work out how we're going to identify this woman."

The anglers, who fished for carp at the same spot every week, both gave a statement before being allowed to leave. Their regular venue had been cordoned off and the area closed to fishing for the time being, until divers had searched the depths for evidence.

"That's it for now, Andy. Let's get back to HQ."
"OK. We'll put an APB out for King Arthur."
"Funny."

# CHAPTER 3

Louise and Scoffer both occasionally thought they were out of their depth with the investigation they'd been assigned, passed on to them by the NCA. Several cases were already under scrutiny nationwide and the NCA had asked all forces for their help locally. They had been obliged to sit in on a presentation given by Alex Sinclair in order to comprehend the sheer scale of the criminal activity involved. As Alex explained,

"As part of the Chancellor's program of aid to companies to help deal with the effects of the COVID pandemic, government loans up to £50,000, or a maximum of 25 per cent of annual turnover, were made available as part of a 'bounce back' scheme. Unfortunately, insufficient checks were carried out on the companies which applied, and 160,000 loans worth just under £5 billion were approved in the first three days. In all, about 1.5 million loans, worth around £47 billion, were issued, and about £4.3 billion was lost to fraud, as people were selling registered limited companies on social media, which were snapped up by criminals to qualify for the free loans. These criminals then abused the system to fund their illegal businesses, one of which involved the theft of high-value cars, many of them stolen to order for clients in the Middle East. Other loans were used by money launderers, drug dealers and sex traffickers. It would help us greatly if you could investigate the car thefts in your area."

Due to the massive amount of information forwarded to them by the NCA, Louise and Scoffer were given permission to use the Conference Room to lay out the evidence they compiled as it was the only space large enough for that purpose. It wasn't long before they had compiled a long list of stolen cars and worked out a schedule to talk to the owners.

Gary, meanwhile, did his best to co-ordinate the efforts of his team while himself investigating the doorstep thefts of parcels left by Amazon and other delivery companies.

After lunch, Louise and Scoffer drove off to interview some of the victims of car theft. Their first call was at a detached house in Clayton from whose garage the householder's Mercedes-Benz E-class had been stolen in the middle of the night. The noise disturbed the householder who went downstairs to see what was happening. When he opened the door, a masked man held a gun to his head, demanding the car keys while his accomplices broke open the garage door and drove the car out. The owner was then forced to lie face down on the drive until they drove the car away. The car has never been seen since. According to the NCA, it would either have been stolen to order, or else would be broken up for parts, to be shipped overseas, most likely to the Middle East.

The other victims interviewed during the afternoon told a similar story, but it was of little comfort to them to be told that the police were 'looking into it'.

********

The following morning, to add to Gary's problems, a call from Teresa added another incident to his list. The owner of a holiday rental had reported finding the body of a man in one of her properties. He had no option but to perform the initial investigation on his own and drove quickly up to Haworth to join Forensics at the property, a cottage just off Main Street. The constable at the door moved aside to let him enter, where Allen Greaves and his team were at work.

"Morning, Gary. The owner's in the kitchen. The rest of the property is out of bounds until we've concluded our work, so don't touch anything."
"I know the drill."
"Yes. Of course."

He walked into the small kitchen where a uniformed officer was comforting the owner, a woman in her late fifties. He nodded to the WPC and introduced himself.

"My name is Gary Ryan. I'm with Bradford CID. Could I have your name, please?"
"WPC Walters. This lady is the owner of the property, Mrs Duckett."
"I'm pleased to meet you. So, Mrs Duckett, would you please tell me what's happened here?"
"I had a couple staying here for a week. They were leaving today and were meant to wait here until I arrived to collect the keys and have a quick check that everything was OK. But when I arrived, the door was unlocked, and I found the man's body in the bedroom."
"What time was this?"
"10.30. That was the time they'd agreed."
"OK. Presumably, the body was one of the guests?"

"Yes. He introduced himself when he first arrived last week."

"And who was with him?"

"A woman, but I never really saw her. She stayed in the car. He said she was tired and travel sick."

"Can you tell me anything about her?"

"Short blonde hair. She was wearing sunglasses. I just got a quick glimpse of her really."

"Did you get their names, addresses?"

"It was booked in the name of Mr James Palmer, plus one guest. He said he was from Derbyshire."

"How did he pay?"

"Debit card."

"OK, if you give me the number, I can trace his account. Anything else you can tell me?"

"Not really. Once I've met them on arrival, I just leave them to it until they leave."

"Do you have a record of their car registration?"

"No."

"Can you give me any details about the car?"

"Not really. I don't know much about cars. It was dark blue. Quite modern. A Hatchback thing."

"OK. If you think of anything else, just let us know."

"OK."

He left the kitchen to check on Allen's progress as the body was being loaded for transportation to the mortuary for post-mortem investigation.

"Initial impressions, Allen?"

"Looks like poisoning. Cyanide, I believe. We'll confirm it soon enough in the lab."

"Where exactly did you find the body?"

"On the floor in the bedroom."

"Can you say how long he's been dead?"

"Since last night, I'd say."

"Anything else?"

"There's no ID. It looks like whoever killed him took everything which could identify him."

"Everything?"

"We've got prints. Trouble is, we've got too many. Different guests every week and the owner is unlikely ever to win the 'Cleaner of the Month' award. We'll eliminate them in time. I can give you a picture of his face if you want to show it around. It's not very pretty."

"OK. Let me know what you find. I'd better go canvassing the neighbours."

He made a quick call to Teresa.

"Can you see if you can find out something about a victim, please, Teresa?"
"Give me some details."
"We think his name is James Palmer, from Derbyshire. Probably in his late 40s, early 50s. Medium height, medium build. Short, grey hair. Sorry, that's all I've got for now. I'll send you a picture."
"Thanks. Don't expect miracles."

Gary went door-knocking and also visited the local shops, but few people could recognise the man from the post-mortem image, and nobody knew his identity. In addition, nobody was able to identify the make and model of his car, nor give any clues as to its numberplate. On a whim, Gary went back to the house and went through the rubbish in the dustbin. He found a receipt for a meal at a local pub, dated two days earlier. It was a start. It was lunchtime. Perhaps someone would remember the couple. He drove straight there and asked to speak to the manager.

He was allowed to speak to each member of staff in turn, until a waitress acknowledged she'd seen them and served them. Another staff member admitted she'd taken payment by card for the meal and drinks. She remembered watching the lady craning her neck behind the gentleman as he punched in his security number. Neither of them was able to give much of a description of the lady apart from the short (bleached) blonde hair and sunglasses.

As soon as he left the premises, he called Teresa, giving her the card number to track any further purchases. He had a strong suspicion this was not a one-off. His gut feeling told him the mystery woman made a living out of murdering and robbing innocent, gullible victims.

By the time he got back to HQ, a message was waiting for him. Allen Greaves had wasted no time.

"Gary,
Preliminary examination suggests cyanide poisoning. Will confirm when tests complete. There were also several scratches, bruises

to his body which would suggest rough sex. He ejaculated not long before he died. More details to follow.
Allen."

Gary considered texting back 'Did he have a smile on his face' but thought better of it. Instead, he tried to imagine how the crime had come about. His starting point would naturally need to focus on how the relationship between victim and killer had developed. As soon as Teresa uncovered details about the victim's background, he was sure the case would progress. In the meantime, he was waiting for information from the victim's bank, and Visa, regarding recent use of the debit card.

********

As soon as Gary logged into his PC the following morning, he found an email from Teresa. In it were details about the victim, including his home address in Long Eaton, Derbyshire. He phoned the number Teresa had provided. A hesitant voice replied.

"Hello?"
"Good morning. My name is DI Gary Ryan, from Bradford CID. I'm inquiring about James Palmer. Do you know him?"
"He's my son. What's happened?"
"Could I have your name, please?"
"Joan Palmer. Mrs."
"Well, Mrs Palmer, can you tell me when you last saw your son?"
"A week or so ago. He had to go to a conference or something for work."
"Have you heard from him since?"
"No. But I'm expecting him back any day. Why? What's wrong?"
"Could I possibly come to see you today? I really would like to discuss this face to face."
"If you think it's necessary."
"It would be better, Mrs Palmer."
"Very well. I'll be in all day."
"I'll be there before lunch."

He called the local police and asked for a uniformed female officer to accompany him. His request was granted. After leaving a message with Teresa, he was on his way, stopping only to pick up PCSO Travis from Long Eaton.

********

Mrs Palmer ushered them into the small living room and was clearly distressed.

"Can you please tell me what's going on? I've just tried to ring my son, but his phone just goes to voicemail."
"Do you have a recent photograph of James, Mrs Palmer?"
"Yes. Just a moment. I have some on my phone. Here."

Gary checked. It was undoubtedly the victim.

"I'm sorry to have to break this to you, Mrs Palmer, but we found a body yesterday. We believe it's your son, James."
"Oh, my God! What happened? Was it an accident?"
"We believe he may have been murdered."

Mrs Palmer burst into tears. Gary sat quietly while the PCSO tried to comfort her. Eventually, he continued.

"We believe James was poisoned, Mrs Palmer. We need your help to discover exactly how this came about and to catch whoever was responsible. So, did James tell you if anyone was going with him?"
"No. He just said it was something to do with work."
"And what did he do for a living?"
"He worked for an Insurance Broker."
"Do you have their address, please?"
"Yes. I'll get it for you."
"Thanks. One other thing – is he, *was* he in a relationship with anyone at the moment?"
"I don't think so. He and his wife divorced last year, and he moved back in with me."
"Do you have his ex-wife's name and address, please."
"Yes. I'll get them for you."
"Do you have anyone who can call on you to make sure you're OK? I know this must have come as a terrible shock to you."
"I'll call my sister. She lives near here."
"OK, PCSO Travis will stay with you in the meantime. I'm sorry to have to break such bad news to you, but rest assured, we'll do all we can to bring to justice whoever was responsible."

Gary was relieved to leave PCSO Travis to deal with all the grief, and drove straight into Long Eaton town centre, to James's place of employment. There, he learnt that James was actually on holiday and was expected back the next day. He'd told them he was going to visit an old friend in Yorkshire.

"Do you know if he was in a relationship at the moment?"

"He kept his private life very much to himself. I just know he was looking forward very much to his week off."

"Does he have a car?"

"Yes. A Ford Focus."

"Blue?"

"Yes."

"Do you have its registration, please?"

"Yes. It's insured through us. I'll just display the details."

"Thanks."

"Is he in any trouble? I mean, why are you here?"

"I'm afraid James Palmer is dead, sir. We believe he's been murdered."

"Oh, my God!"

"Thank you for your help, sir. If we need any more information, we'll be in touch."

Back in the car, he phoned the details to Teresa and set off back home. Before he was close to Bradford, he was informed the car had been found in a car park near Keighley train station.

********

Gary was back at his desk at HQ late in the afternoon while Teresa briefed him on the information she'd gleaned.

"First, fingerprints taken from the car were a match to Mr Palmer. Another set were a match to those found at the crime scene. We believe they belong to the mystery woman, however we have not yet been able to identify her. The Visa debit card used to book the cottage has been used at various locations and online, until it was blocked. We have access to CCTV showing the suspect using the card in cash machines. She has also used it in shops, explaining it belongs to her husband who allows her to use it. As she has the PIN number, it has not been questioned. The stuff she's bought online have all been 'click and collect' at various places. In the CCTV shots, she is shown wearing a variety of wigs to disguise her appearance.

Now to the interesting bit. I've circulated details of our case to all UK forces and details are starting to come in about crimes bearing similar characteristics throughout the North of England going back over a period of ten years as well as a recent one in North Wales. It's becoming apparent we have a serial killer at large."

"Let's check to make sure the other suspected cases have a match for fingerprints and DNA, otherwise we may have copycat killers."

She let out a gasp.

"Wow! That's a thought. Are we going to be able to handle this?"
"It wouldn't hurt to bring NCA on board. They have the infrastructure and manpower to devote to such a wide investigation. I guess that's the DCI's decision. I'll take it to him. It's up to him what the next move should be."

Before DCI Gardner had fully considered the case, calls began to come through, querying whether the DNA and fingerprint samples which had been sent out were correct. There were five cases along the east coast, from Teesside to the Humber, where DNA was a partial match to the Haworth case, but the fingerprint samples were totally different. As the reports trickled in, the lab checked all the samples before concluding there was, indeed, a copycat killer.

Allen Greaves was called to provide an explanation.

"It's clear we have two separate murderers, but the fact that they share most of their DNA would indicate they are related in some way. They are probably twins, possibly identical twins."
"Would they be identical in every respect?"
"Not necessarily. But they may have some matching characteristics, eye colour, for example."
"So, only their modus operandi is the same?"
"Correct. It seems highly likely that they've been in close contact with each other over the years, perhaps through school, university, work, etc."
"Or the same household. Maybe even foster kids or adopted kids?"
"Yes. That's possible. Adopted children often bond very closely."

Gary thought for a moment, before voicing his decision.

"OK. Let's focus on our own locality. By all means share information with the other areas, but let's give some thought to how she finds her victims. All the incidents we know of have occurred in neutral, temporary environments. Holiday homes, caravan parks, hotels, B & Bs. So, how do the victim and perpetrator get together?"
"Social media? Dating sites?"
"It's possible they have a shared interest. Maybe work together?"
"Social gatherings. Whist clubs, or the like?"

"Maybe they read the same newspaper or magazine. Maybe the killer places ads in Lonely Hearts columns."

"All these are good bets. Look into them. And work out which geographical area belongs to which killer. Liaise with other forces but concentrate on catching the killer who's working our own area."

********

Louise and Scoffer had completed their preliminary investigation and interviews with the victims of car theft. Gary looked at the figures. In the last three weeks, five high-value cars had been stolen in the area. He compared the data for other cities in Yorkshire. The pattern was similar. He wondered how they chose the targets. Did they just drive around until they saw a model which fit their needs, or did they get intelligence from some other source? A dealership, perhaps? A garage? He read the report the NCA had sent out. It was a national problem. Certain models of car were being targeted and the feeling was they were being sent abroad – to the Middle East, most likely – either to order, or for parts.

Teresa got straight to work examining social media for advertisements regarding high value cars. She was looking for anything which could hook a casual browser. Once someone showed interest in the ad, a conversation would begin, designed to ascertain whether the viewer had such a car. If not, the conversation would be curtailed. Otherwise, the viewer would be encouraged to post pictures and other information to help give away his address. She took her theory, with examples, to Gary, who immediately called the victims to discover whether they'd unwillingly taken part in the selection process. The results were mixed.

However, Teresa had a second theory. Someone may be paying for the information from a dealership. Or stealing it by hacking their computer system.

"How can we check that?"

"Easy. Leave it with me."

Over the next few hours, Teresa was able to hack the computers of three dealerships in Bradford. She took the results to Gary.

"Here, boss. Addresses of customers who've recently bought, or had serviced, their high value car. Mercs, Audis, Ferraris, Jags, and even some of the more luxury brands. And that's just from a few dealers in a couple of hours. I guess this is one of the ways they pick their targets."

"Well done, Teresa. I'll pay some of the customers a visit in the morning."

*******

His plans were disrupted the moment he walked into the office the following morning. He found a note from Teresa on his desk.

"Mr Wilkinson (on your list) had his car, a BMW 8 Series Convertible worth £84K, stolen last night when his house was burgled. Address attached."

He drove straight to the address in Rawdon, pulling up on the drive of a large detached house with a double garage at the side, to find Forensics had beaten him and were already dusting for possible prints. He took the owner, Gary Wilkinson, into the kitchen for a chat.

"We didn't know anything about it until this morning when my wife got up. The front door was open, and the car keys and the garage keys had gone."

"Where were the keys?"

"In a drawer of the table in the hall."

"How did they gain entry?"

"They removed a glass pane from the door and must have used a fishing rod or something to get the keys."

"The car keys?"

"No. Sorry. No, they got the door keys off a hook on the wall and let themselves in to get the car and garage keys. We never heard anything."

"Do you have an alarm system?"

"Well, yes. But we only set it when we go out."

"Did they take anything else?"

"No. I don't think so."

"Do you mind if I take a look at the garage?"

"Be my guest. It's open."

The first thing he noticed was the damage to the CCTV cameras mounted in the grounds. The garage doors were wide open, and though there were some costly items of gardening equipment inside, nothing had been touched apart from the car. He returned to the house to find Mr Wilkinson filling out an online insurance claim form.

33

"Excuse me again, Mr Wilkinson, but I've just noticed the CCTV cameras."

"Oh, yes. They were wrecked three nights ago. Nothing stolen. Vandals, I assumed."

"You didn't bother getting them fixed?"

"They were supposed to do it this weekend. It was all booked."

"Just unlucky, then, eh? I'll see myself out."

On his return to HQ, Teresa was able to confirm that Mr Wilkinson had purchased his car less than three months earlier from one of the dealerships whose computer systems she'd hacked the previous day.

"OK, Teresa. I think we need to inform these dealerships their computer security has been compromised and tell them to inform all their customers they are at risk of having their cars stolen. Make it their responsibility. We've got enough to do. However, I think we should ask the T & A to put out a general warning. Local radio as well."

"I'll sort that today."

"Thanks."

Regardless of the information about vehicle thefts which flooded the news, the thefts continued. In Yorkshire, 19 cars of high value had been stolen in recent weeks. None had yet been traced although all normal sales methods and practices had been closely monitored, including the sale of parts. CID and NCA were both in agreement. The cars were being exported illegally. This was organised crime. Fortunately, Teresa was adamant she could get to the bottom of it.

"If it's illegal, it's probably being organised and discussed on the Dark Web. Just give me time. I'll crack it."

"I don't doubt it, Teresa. Not for one minute."

"Any chance of some help to do the routine office stuff?"

"I doubt it, but I'll ask the DCI."

Gary thought he knew what the response would be but asked anyway. He was surprised at the reply from DCI Gardner.

"Leave it with me, Gary. I know you're all under pressure. I'll see what I can do. It will only be clerical assistance though."

"That would be fine, sir. It's just that only Teresa in this area has the skills to navigate the Dark Web."

"I'm well aware of that, Gary. That's why I always do everything I can to keep her happy. Just don't tell her that or she'll be asking for a rise again."

********

The DCI was true to his word and the following morning, two temporary clerical staff were being briefed by Teresa. Both Rachel and Ruth had worked previously at HQ while Teresa was on extended leave some years earlier and were familiar with their duties and the environment. They were also already known to some of the team and slotted easily into their role. Relieved of much of her day-to-day workload, Teresa threw herself into the new challenge. She created 'U Want It, We Get It', a site on the Dark Web, with the online persona Tee Ess, as the head of a small criminal enterprise who stole cars to order, recently moved to Yorkshire after hearing a rumour that the police were planning a massive crackdown in Essex where they previously operated. It wasn't long before her site was visited, and tentative chats commenced. There were also threats from established operators who resented anyone encroaching on their territory. Some were death threats. She passed these to Gary.

"Be careful, here, Teresa. These are not empty threats."
"Don't worry. The more conversations we have, the closer I get to identifying them. Anyway, some of the others seem happy to work with me."
"They may just be trying to establish who you are so they can eliminate you."
"I know. I'll shut the site down if they get too close."
"OK. Keep me informed."
"Will do."

Teresa wore a wide smile as soon as she was back at her terminal. She knew what she was doing and had no fear. It wouldn't be long before she could set a trap. She was dangling the bait to potential customers. Specify the make and model, the delivery address and the payment, and she would deliver. She had her first customer before the end of the day.

********

Throughout the evening, Teresa worked on her plan with Alex Sinclair of the NCA. The instructions from her 'employer' were to provide a late model Aston Martin V8 Coupé before the weekend.

Once she had it, she would send a secure message and be given a drop-off venue for delivery and cash payment of the agreed price.

"We'll have to substitute the car. There's no way we'll be able to borrow one before the weekend, even if the owner would allow it."
"So, we deliver in a transporter van, with the car under covers, and have an armed squad close by."
"We could send images of the model they asked for. I'm sure we can locate an owner who'll assist."
"I'm sure. It would be in his interest to remove the threat that his car may be on someone's wish list."
"OK. Let's plan the details."

Together they worked out how they would organise the 'sting'.

The following morning, Teresa presented her plan to Gary and DCI Gardner. Both gave their approval following a phone call to the NCA who would provide the armed support team. Gardner, however, made one stipulation; none of his staff would be present at the vehicle's handover.

"It's too dangerous. Let NCA look after the actual handover. It's likely there'll be an exchange of fire at some point."

********

They met at the agreed rendezvous point at 1.30am. It was secluded and surrounded by woodland, offering cover for the heavily-armed teams in attendance. After a quick check that everyone knew their role and the position they would take, Teresa was given approval to confirm the delivery to the buyer. She typed in the agreed message, giving the location. The buyer responded, stating that the exchange would take place within the hour. Teresa confirmed, before relaying the message to the waiting team. She sat back, safe in her office, and waited.

Five minutes before the hour was up, Teresa received a terse message.

"Vehicle approaching."

She typed the required command on her keyboard and was immediately rewarded with a view of the approaching vehicle's dimmed headlights, taken from one of the armed officers' shoulder-mounted cameras. She held her breath and watched as the lorry pulled to a halt and the passenger jumped out of the cab and approached the decoy vehicle, while the driver ran to the back of his lorry, opened the doors and started to let down the ramps. Suddenly the entire screen lit up as industrial searchlights illuminated the area and armed policemen broke cover, their weapons trained on the suspects who immediately put their hands up and allowed themselves to be pushed to the ground, face down so they could be searched for weapons. They were then handcuffed and thrown into the back of a police van which drove away at speed followed by an escort vehicle with armed police inside.

Teresa watched all this with tired glee. She yawned as her phone rang.

"Did you get it all, Teresa?"

She recognised the voice of the Task Force leader.

"Yes, sir. Thank you, and congratulations on a smooth and efficient assignment."
"Thanks to your accurate information. We'll get them down to HQ for a night's kip and take the lorry to the pound at Forensics, and that's our job done."
"Thanks again."
"A pleasure."

Teresa sent emails to all interested parties at HQ with information regarding the success of the 'sting'. She logged off her PC and went home.

# CHAPTER 4

Lynn and Jo-Jo finally got the information they'd been waiting for. Their investigation had been put on hold but now Teresa had provided the name of the officer who was paired with PC Carlyle on the night Mary Sugden was raped. They made an appointment to speak to her at home as she was currently out on remand. Lynn showed Mary the photograph Teresa had pulled from his personnel file. She was startled.

"Oh, my God! That's him! That's the bastard!"
"Are you 100% sure, Mrs Sugden?"
"Absolutely! I'll never forget that face. Are you going to arrest him?"
"We're going to talk to him, and yes, hopefully we'll be able to arrest him. The problem is, you were not able to describe him at the time, but I'm sure we can make a compelling case since we can prove he was present when the offence occurred. The other thing we never checked earlier is, did the hospital take a DNA sample?"
"I don't know. I was in such a state. I don't remember."
"Don't worry. We'll be able to check. Thanks for your time."

They drove back to HQ and spent the rest of the morning trying to ascertain if a DNA sample was taken, and if so, did it still exist. They drew a blank. No DNA sample had been requested at the time.

"Why don't we have a word with PC Hammond to get his version of what happened that night. We can pretend we got a sample."
"Worth a try."

When checking with Teresa for contact details for PC Hammond, they discovered he was no longer a serving officer. He'd left the force five years earlier and now worked as a security guard at a local supermarket. They arranged to speak to him in the manager's office. He agreed, reluctantly, to be interviewed without having a legal representative present.

"I've done nothing wrong. Ask what you want. If I don't want to answer, I won't answer."
"That's OK. It's just a chat. We really want to know what your partner was like. We have to appear in court at Mrs Sugden's trial."
"Whatever she said we did is a lie. She murdered my mate for no reason. She's mentally ill. She needs locking up."

"So, tell us exactly what you remember about that night."

"We were on patrol in the city centre. It was late. There were a lot of revellers, drunk, on the streets. We were keeping an eye on things, when this drunken woman lurched out in front of us. I slammed on the brakes. Jack got out and lifted her to her feet. She was well pissed. She was a danger to herself. She could hardly stand, so we decided it was best to take her home. It took a lot of doing to get her to tell us the address, but then we took her home and dropped her off. She thanked us and we left. The next thing we knew, we were being accused of rape. It was all lies. If someone *did* rape her after we left her, it wasn't us. She was a nutcase."

"OK. We'll leave it at that for now. Thanks for your time."

As they walked back to the car, both remained unconvinced of his innocence.

"We've no proof. That's as far as we can take it."

"I know, but I still think he's guilty. We'd better break the news to Mrs Sugden."

She didn't take the news well.

"I hope I never set eyes on him again. I know nobody believes me, but they both raped me, and if I ever see him, I'll kill him."

Lynn was genuinely upset and tried to console Mrs Sugden and asked Jo-Jo to go to the car and get the name and address of a recommended rape counsellor. When she returned with it, Mrs Sugden had calmed down and was almost smiling. They drove off back to HQ.

********

Two days later, Teresa was informed of an incident requiring police support. She passed the information to Lynn, who set off with Jo-Jo on their way towards Yeadon, without telling Jo-Jo where they were going and why. As they pulled into Morrison's car park, Jo-Jo had an awful feeling.

"Tell me I'm wrong. Something's happened to a security guard."

"It appears so."

They stopped close to where an ambulance was parked near the entrance. Lynn went immediately to the rear door and spoke briefly with the two paramedics before returning to Jo-Jo.

"Let's go inside and take statements."
"Not until you tell me what's happened."
"A member of staff has been attacked by a woman with a knife. He's in a stable condition."
"His name's not Hammond by any chance, is it?"
"Yes."

Inside, they went straight to the security office at the rear of the store where Mary Sugden sat calmly in a chair with another security guard watching her.

"OK, Mary. Tell me about it."
"Nothing to tell, really. I was just doing some shopping and I saw this man, recognised him, and stabbed him in the groin. As far as I'm concerned, he got what he deserved. At least, he won't rape anyone else."

Mary Sugden was handcuffed and taken to HQ, for a spell of reflection in the cells before an interview was organised. Meanwhile, Lynn wrote up the incident while Jo-Jo sat alongside. Eventually, Jo-Jo had to ask.

"So, how do you think Mary knew where Hammond worked?"
"No idea. I guess she was just out shopping and chanced on him."
"Why would she be out here doing her shopping? She lives in West Bowling for Christ's sake."
"Must have fancied a change of scenery."
"A likely story!"
"Stranger things have happened."
"Well, all I can say is, I wish *I'd* had the guts to tell her."

********

It was inevitable that, as soon as they sat down for a cup of tea, Lynn received a call from Gary.

"Sorry about this, Lynn, but when you and Jo-Jo have time, could you call at my desk? I have another job lined up for you."
"We'll be there in five minutes."
"Here we go again."

They duly presented themselves at Gary's desk.

"First of all, well done for closing the case regarding the police rapists. The DPP is preparing the case. His opinion is that Mary Sugden will get a non-custodial sentence. Now, I have a case I've been trying to look into for a while, but I can't find the time for it. I'd like you to pick it up for me."

"OK. What is it?"

"A number of people have complained to say that parcels are being stolen from their doorstep minutes, sometimes seconds, after delivery. It's not confined to one particular driver or one area, so we don't believe the drivers are running a scam. There's the folder. See what you can turn up, please."

"Surely, if the parcel is not received, the buyer shouldn't have to pay."

"It's not as straightforward as that. Some buyers can't guarantee they'll be in when the delivery arrives, so they designate a spot, say, behind the dustbin. The driver leaves it there and takes a photo on his phone to prove delivery. Then, it seems, someone nicks it. Judging by the scale of the problem, it's an organised gang."

"Do we have a list of stuff that's been nicked recently?"

"Yes. In the file."

"I'm thinking we might find some of the articles for sale on the internet's local goods-for-sale sites."

"Get to it."

"Hang on. Let's go to the depot first. There may be a pattern we can detect. They can't be just random thefts."

They made an immediate appointment to speak to a despatch manager at Knottingley and came away with a comprehensive list of addresses which had made 'missing parcel' claims in the last month. They also had a list of drivers who covered those areas on a regular basis and were able to speak to a few of them briefly before returning to HQ to work out a plan of action.

After comparing the statistics they'd accumulated from their visit to the depot, they identified three routes with a higher-than-average number of 'missing parcels' and decided to follow a delivery round unknown to the driver. They had a printed list of addresses on the round so that if they temporarily lost sight of the target vehicle, they could pick up the trail further on.

And so, they were waiting at the exit road from the depot as the target drove out, and pulled out behind it, following at a discreet distance. Whenever the van stopped, they did too and watched through binoculars as parcels were dropped off. Whenever a parcel was not handed over to the householder in person, they intended to stay in position for a few minutes before driving off to catch up with the delivery van. However, on only the third drop, as soon as the delivery van had left, another van drove up and stopped outside the house where the package had been left behind the dustbin.

"This could be it. Get your camera ready."

A man wearing a hoodie and mask jumped out of the van, picked up the parcel, ran back to his van and drove off. Lynn and Jo-Jo followed.

"He's following the route the van would be taking for its deliveries."
"Let's call in his vehicle plate in case we lose him. We'll follow him until he's got three or four parcels. Then we'll pull him over."
"Or catch him in the act rooting in someone's bin."
"There's another thing we should consider."
"What's that, Lynn?"
"This man who's pinching the parcels. How does he know where the delivery driver is going? He loses sight of him while he's stealing a delivery, but he picks him up again later. He *knows* the route. And he seems to know which packages will be available to nick. The driver's in on it."
"Let's drive straight to the next drop where the package is to be left outside. We'll find a good vantage spot where we can film, and we'll pick the thief up. We can catch up with the driver later."
"OK."

They were waiting a short distance down the street they'd identified for the next uncollected drop as the van pulled up. They ensured they had an unobstructed view of the parcel as the van drove off. In less than a minute, another van drew up – the same van they'd seen previously, with the same hooded driver. This time they were ready, filming as he picked up the parcel and intercepting him on his way back to his van. They phoned for backup to take the van back for examination and took the driver to HQ for interrogation.

********

The driver had given his name as David Golding and refused to say any more until they'd got him some legal representation. Now, with a lawyer present, he was prepared to answer questions. Lynn conducted the interview with Jo-Jo alongside her.

"So, Mr Golding. We caught you in the act of stealing a parcel meant for a customer who'd paid for it. We also saw you stealing from an address earlier on the round. And when we searched your van, we discovered a load more parcels from an earlier round. At the moment, your home is being searched and we'll no doubt find evidence of other offences. Have you anything to say?"
"No."
"Do you admit to stealing the parcels?"
"No."
"No?"
"You're making it all up. You must have planted the parcels."
"Let's show you the proof, then."

Lynn switched on the monitor and loaded the recording of the thefts. Still, he denied it.

"That's not me."
"It's *clearly* you. Even with the hoodie, it's definitely you. It's your van. They're the same clothes you're wearing now. How can you possibly deny it?"

There was a long pause before he answered.

"For years, someone's been impersonating me. I've been blamed for everything he's done."
"What? All these offences? Shoplifting? Burglary? Theft? You're trying to tell me it wasn't you? Some doppelgänger?"
"That's right. He's been doing it for years."
"So, your criminal record is all false?"
"Yes. I'd like to leave now, please."
"Sit tight. We'll be right back."

They left the room and stopped by the vending machine for a coffee.

"What do you make of that?
"He's obviously deluded. Let's have another look at his record. I want to know if he's used this excuse before."

He had indeed used the same excuse before and been nevertheless convicted of a number of petty crimes, even serving a short prison sentence on the last occasion. Lynn hadn't come across anything like this before but decided to charge him and leave it up to the court to make the decision. They relaxed until the result came back from the search of his home. It was as they suspected. Forensics took away a full vanload of stolen goods, matching up Amazon's records with what they found and presenting undisputable evidence. David Golding briefly appeared before a magistrate before being released on bail pending trial.

Following up, they checked the data Teresa had copied from his phone, finding a large number of texts to a person they discovered ran a second-hand shop in Shipley. There was also a record of items being placed for sale on websites such as Gumtree and Facebook. Again, these matched items stolen previously. Most of them had already sold; those remaining were still stored at his house. They decided to pay a visit to the second-hand shop.

The shop was empty of customers. Only a vastly overweight, scruffily-dressed man lounged in a chair in the corner, reading the T & A. He didn't even acknowledge the two customers, as they walked around, comparing items to their pre-printed list and ticking off ones which matched. Eventually, they caught his attention.

"Please don't manhandle the goods unless you intend to buy them."
"You're selling them, are you?"
"'Course. Why do you think they're on display?"
"Do you have a legal right to sell them?"
"I bought 'em. I can sell 'em."
"Not if we confiscate them, you can't. Most of these are stolen goods."
"Well, that's not my fault. I didn't nick 'em."
"Did you know they were stolen?"
"No."
"But you bought all these from the same person?"
"Probably. I can't be sure, but I have a man who sells me a lot of stock."
"Is this the man?"

Lynn showed him a photograph of Golding.

"I can't be sure. Looks like him, though."

"Shut the shop. I'm charging you with possessing stolen goods. You're coming with us to HQ."

"I want a lawyer."

"We'll get you one."

"I want a good one."

"You'll need a good one. Get your coat."

Further investigation unearthed the fact that David Golding's sister worked at the Knottingley depot and had access to delivery data, which she was passing to her brother. She was charged as an accessory to theft.

# CHAPTER 5

Lynn had argued the case for the temporary staff, Ruth and Rachel, to stay on for a while. She wanted to catch the next link in the car theft chain – the initial buyer who probably shipped them to their ultimate buyer. She still had contact details on the Dark Web for the man who wanted the Aston Martin.

She looked at the figures for the previous month: 2 Lotus, 2 Porsche, 1 Bentley, 2 Rolls Royce, 1 Tesla, 3 Aston Martin, 6 Audi, 3 Ferrari, 8 BMW, 1 Lambo, 3 Jaguar, 2 Range Rover, 1 Lexus.

These were astonishing figures, particularly as they had already captured a team who were to pick up a stolen car and move it further along the supply chain. None of them had talked yet, but obviously cars were still being stolen on demand and still delivered to another third party.

She decided to try a different tack. She would set up a scenario where the police, acting as car thieves, 'steal' a car as ordered but this time allow it to be transported away. It would be fitted with a tracking device and the recovery vehicle would be tracked by drone. She spoke to Teresa who was in favour, before seeking authorisation from DCI Gardner who was unable to give the go-ahead.

"It's the value, Lynn. I personally don't have the authority to authorise a set-up where an item of this value is put in the hands of thieves. What if something goes wrong? Our budget can't compensate the owner, in this case the dealership, if it goes missing. Sorry, no."

He could see the disappointment on Lynn's face, so offered a compromise.

"Let me speak to the NCA. Their budget may cover it."

The NCA were happy to help and quickly authorised the plan. Teresa then passed the message along the chain via the Dark Web that they had stolen an Aston Martin V8. Within minutes she'd received instructions where to take the car for it be collected. Immediately, she organised the loan of a drone, and had tracking devices hidden in the car, and installed the software on her PC. Throughout the afternoon and evening, there were frantic meetings and phone calls, checking and double-checking that everything was in place, everyone knew their role. And at midnight, the Aston Martin was loaded and driven to the rendezvous point, where the driver switched off the engine and the lights and waited.

Fifteen minutes later, a small black Ford pulled up alongside the cab and three masked men brandishing pistols motioned the driver to get out of the cab. He was frisked for weapons and knocked unconscious with a blow to the back of his head. The Aston Martin was unloaded as a large HGV pulled up and its ramp was lowered. Feverishly, the team transferred the Aston Martin to the transporter which immediately drove away, followed by the masked men in the Ford. It was all over in minutes.

As soon as the scene was clear, the injured man was treated and two unmarked police cars followed the transporter at a discreet distance while Teresa followed their progress on her monitor, while providing constant updates to all other parties involved.

To everybody's surprise, though, a second transporter turned up at the rendezvous site, evidently to pick up the Aston Martin. The police quickly moved in, arrested them and impounded their vehicle. Under questioning, they would only say they received a phone call to pick up a vehicle and take it to a warehouse in Doncaster. Eventually, it became apparent to everybody that information regarding the Aston Martin had been leaked to a rival gang of car thieves who had arrived first and stolen the 'stolen' car.

However, Teresa was still tracking the stolen car which was now pulling into an industrial estate on the outskirts of Castleford, with an armed police squad close on their heels. As soon as the target vehicle pulled to a halt in front of a warehouse, Teresa gave the order to move in. There followed a brief skirmish during which shots were fired, before the thieves were overpowered and forced to surrender. A cheer went up in HQ as the operation was successfully concluded with the bonus of the discovery that the warehouse was fully kitted out to dismantle vehicles and store and despatch individual parts. There were also nods of agreement when Teresa said,

"Brian would have loved this."

********

Brian was having a cup of strong coffee when his mobile buzzed. He checked the display. Teresa. Still a little hungover, he reluctantly took the call.

"Morning, Teresa."
"Good morning, Brian. I'm sorry to disturb you, but we have a case which might be of interest to you."
"I've enough to deal with at the moment, Teresa."
"I know. But we're really struggling down here. The DCI has already put out an appeal to borrow some officers from other regions, but we're getting overwhelmed. Please, can you help us?"
"What is it?"
"Two young women, 18 and 19, sisters, have gone missing. Apparently, they were having a night out in the city centre with some workmates. They had a lot to drink and left their friends at the end of the evening to get a taxi home. There was another girl from the same group in the queue behind them, who lived at the opposite end of town, otherwise she would have shared the taxi. She didn't think too much of it at the time, but she said she found it odd that the vehicle didn't have a taxi plate. Anyway, she tried to phone them this morning but couldn't get an answer. Both their phones went to voicemail. She left messages, but neither girl has responded. After she called us, we sent a car to their flat, but there was nobody there. None of the other tenants had seen them since yesterday. It appears the girls may have been abducted by the so-called taxi driver."

He sighed. He didn't really need another case to investigate.

"OK. I'll have a look. Send me the details."
"Thanks, Brian. Emailing them now."

It crossed his mind that Teresa had considered the fact that the case bore a similarity to one of the cases he was already working. Was there a connection? He would keep an open mind.

As soon as he had read the email, he tore off another length of wallpaper and pinned it up before noting the key facts in sequence. Then he looked at the two other makeshift 'whiteboards' alongside. All three related to missing persons. They were all female. Inexplicably missing, all apparently abducted. What the hell was going on?

He made arrangements to speak to the parents of the latest victims and called Traffic regarding the availability of CCTV footage of Market Street.

********

Paula had read the autopsy report concerning the body found at Chellow Dene. The condition of the body indicated it had been in the water for less than twenty-four hours, yet the organs indicated death had occurred earlier, and there were bruises around the neck and shoulders. The pathologist suggested the possibility that the victim may have drowned elsewhere before the body was dumped in the lake, and that the bruising indicated the victim's head had been forcibly held under water. They were now investigating a murder. Paula and Andy had still not uncovered the identity of the Lady of the Lake, and none of the current cases concerning missing persons corresponded with what they knew about this case. Now they decided to concentrate on the amateur dramatics scene and had been focusing on local societies, but so far had drawn a blank. Then Andy made a suggestion.

"What if it's nothing to do with a stage production. What if it's just someone's idea of fancy dress? Maybe we could try phoning costume hire shops."
"Good idea, Andy. Go to it."

Initially, Andy phoned the shops in alphabetical order, working from an online business directory. If any of them admitted to stocking the type of outfit he described, he would follow up by emailing a cleaned-up image of the dress they'd taken from the body. If he got a positive response to that, he would arrange to visit the shop and speak directly to the staff. By the end of the day, he had a list of four 'possibles' which he'd arranged to call on next morning.

The first shop they visited proved a chastening experience for Andy, for, while the dress was the same in design and material, it was the wrong size. The dress the shop had hired out was two sizes smaller! Andy apologised for wasting their time, but the owner took it well.

"Don't worry. If she doesn't return it by the weekend, we'll be asking you to trace it."

The next shop was the correct size but of different material. The third, however, was a match, but the shop owner was unable to recognise the customer from the image they showed her.

"I'm sorry. I'm really not sure this is the woman. It's difficult when it's been in the water for so long. It could be her. I mean, I just can't be certain."

"Do you have the name and address?"
"I should have. Let me have a look."

The owner was unable to locate it as a 'hire'. Then it dawned on her.

"She bought it. That's why I can't find it in the record of costumes on hire. Just a minute."

She looked through her 'Receipts' book before exclaiming.

"Nearly there. I've got the date of purchase. Now I can match it against the card payments for that day. Most of our transactions are 'hires', so it shouldn't be difficult. Ah, yes. Here it is. Paid by Visa. Here are the transaction details. What I don't have is an address, I'm afraid."
"Don't worry. We'll be able to trace it. Thanks for your help."

By early afternoon, with Teresa's help, they had the address and drove to Fagley, stopping outside a semi-detached house with a Range Rover on the drive. Paula smiled at Andy.

"OK, Andy. This is your big moment. You're running the show. Now, if I think you're going in the wrong direction, I'll interrupt you and you'll say nothing else. Is that OK?"
"Fine by me."
"Let's do it."

Andy knocked on the door, ID card in hand, ready to display it to whoever answered the door. Within seconds, a man's face appeared at the window, and the door opened.

"Can I help you?"
"We're here to speak to Vivien Raeburn."
"She's not in just now."
"And may I ask who you are, sir?"
"I'm her husband, Richard."

"Where is your wife, Mr Raeburn?"

"She's at her mother's. She's not well."

"I see. How long has she been there?"

"Since last week. Wednesday."

"Would you please be so kind as to phone her? We'd really like to speak to her."

"I don't know the number."

"You don't know your wife's phone number? I find that hard to believe."

"She lost her phone. She just got a new one. She must have forgotten to tell me the number."

"So, give me her mother's phone number."

"I don't know that, either."

"What about the address? Surely you know that."

"I'm not sure. I know it's in Knaresborough."

"You know what, Mr Raeburn? I think you should come down to HQ with us to see if we can help you get your memory back."

"Why? I haven't done anything."

"Precisely. You've given us no information at all. Perhaps an hour or so in the cells will help you get your memory back."

"You can't do this."

At that point, Paula interrupted.

"In that case, I think you'd better cooperate before we call Forensics to come and tear your house apart."

"OK. She's left me. I didn't want to tell you. I'm embarrassed."

"So, where's she gone?"

"I don't know."

"When did she leave?"

"Last Wednesday. I was out all day at work and when I got home, she'd left."

"No note?"

"No note."

"Why did she leave?"

"I don't know. Things haven't been great between us recently. I guess I should have seen it coming."

"Is anyone else involved?"

"I don't know. Maybe."

"Can you give us a name?"

"No. I just have this feeling that she might have been playing away."

"Has she taken anything with her?"

"Just personal stuff. Some clothes, make-up."

"Do you have a photo of Vivien?"
"Just a minute. Yes."

He held out his phone. It displayed a photo of Vivien in the gown her body was found in. It was clearly her. Paula nodded to Andy.

"OK, Mr Raeburn, I'm sorry to have to inform you we've found your wife, or, rather, we've found her body."
"Oh."
"You don't sound too upset. Or too surprised."
"Oh, I am. It's just a shock."
"I'd like you to come down to the mortuary to officially identify the body. Can you come with us now?"
"Yes. I suppose so."
"Are you not working today?"
"No. I've taken a few days off. Holiday."
"And where is it you work?"
"Sainsbury's. Greengates."
"And where did your wife work?"
"She didn't work. She had some kind of private income she never told me about."
"Don't you think that's odd?"
"She always said it was her business."
"Did you know about her financial situation when you met?"
"Oh, no. She used to work in a shop. Then, one day she came home and told me she'd packed it in. She said she didn't need to work any longer."
"Didn't you talk about it?"
"She said it was none of my business."

As Mr Raeburn went to get his coat, Andy and Paula were both equally puzzled by the nature of the Raeburn's relationship.

"What do you think? A lottery win?"
"Maybe. It's an odd sort of marital relationship."
"Mmm."

They drove to the mortuary. Andy and Richard got out, but Paula explained she had another call to attend and drove off.

She drove straight down to Sainsbury's and asked to speak to the manager. As she'd half expected, Richard Raeburn was not on holiday and, in fact, had been sacked two weeks previously for poor timekeeping and theft. Paula drove back to the mortuary having first called DCI Gardner to request a warrant to search Raeburn's house.

At the mortuary, Andy noted that Richard had confirmed the body was that of his wife.

"He took it quite calmly. Almost as if he expected it."
"He also lied about being on holiday. His boss at Sainsbury's told me he'd been sacked two weeks ago. We'll interview him while we have his house searched."

The search failed to deliver anything of much use, apart from the fact that there was very little trace of the fact that Vivien ever lived there. There were no personal belongings, no photographs. There was, though, a laptop hidden in the bottom of a drawer underneath a pile of bed linen which was taken away to the lab for examination.

Meanwhile in the Interview Room, Richard Raeburn was facing a grilling.

"We've just had news from the team who've been searching your house, Mr Raeburn. Could you please tell me what you've done with all your wife's belongings?"
"She must have taken them with her."
"Really? Everything?"
"I guess so."
"Her clothes? Her shoes? Her make-up and toiletries? Her jewellery?"
"She wasn't one for material possessions."

Andy sighed and paused for a while, shaking his head. He looked at Paula for confirmation. She nodded.

"Here's what I think, Mr Raeburn. You killed your wife in the bath. You held her head underwater until she drowned. Then you dressed her in her party dress and drove to Chellow Dene where you dumped the body. Am I right so far?"
"NO! That's not what happened!"
"So, would you like to tell me what did happen?"
"Like I told you. I came home and she'd gone. Packed her things and left. That's it."
"OK. You're going to sit in a cell while we look at your wife's laptop. Before we start, do you want to tell us what we're likely to find?"

"I've no idea. I didn't even know she had a laptop. Do what you have to do. It's nothing to do with me."

Raeburn was taken to a cell while Paula and Andy discussed the interview. Andy was convinced Richard Raeburn had murdered his wife and disposed of her body in the reservoir before clearing all her personal possessions from the house. Paula offered an alternative theory.

"What if he had an accomplice, or accomplices? Or, what if her lover killed her and made it look as if Raeburn was to blame?"
"Maybe there'll be something on the laptop."
"We'll see."

An hour later, they got the call from the Forensics lab. The information from the laptop was ready for examination. Allen Greaves handed both Paula and Andy a breakdown of the information on two A4 sheets.

"This contains the names of her contacts and their assumed relationship with Vivien Raeburn. The second sheet is a list of the websites she visited regularly. You may find the contents of some of the emails interesting."

They took the laptop back to the office and started to work their way through the email conversations while Teresa had the task of tracing the website activity. As they worked their way through, they compiled lists of the names and sites requiring follow-up, ranking them according to their perceived importance. They worked until mid-evening before deciding to call a halt, agreeing they would spend the next day making phone calls and visits.

********

The next morning, Paula and Andy left the office with a long list of names and addresses gleaned from Vivien's laptop. First, they went to her neighbourhood to do what they should have done much sooner: they needed to speak to her neighbours. However, it turned out to be a disappointment. None of her neighbours knew much about her. She rarely spoke to any of them, apart from the occasional greeting in passing. She didn't seem to have any friends in the area. She just kept to herself. One of her neighbours described her as 'aloof', and 'snooty' and 'full of her own self-importance'.

Vivien's former employer had a similar opinion of her.

"To be honest, I was glad when she gave her notice. She wasn't an asset to the business. She didn't engage with the customers. She was a bit stand-offish, if you know what I mean."
"Did she give a reason for leaving?"
"No. And I didn't bother to ask."

As they were driving to the next contact's address, Paula's phone rang. Teresa.

"Hi, Paula. Just letting you know you can cross Vivien Raeburn's mother off your list. She died six months ago."
"I wasn't expecting that. But, maybe, that was the source of Vivien's income. Can you find out?"
"I'll put it on my list."

By the end of the day, Paula and Andy had spoken in person to more than a dozen of the contacts on the list and had contacted many more by phone. They'd learnt little of any value. It seemed that Vivien Raeburn was rather an enigmatic character. They weren't too down-hearted, though. There was always the chance that Teresa would come up with the breakthrough they needed.

They didn't have long to wait. Both Paul and Andy had a cryptic message awaiting them when they arrived at HQ the following morning. They met in the Conference Room where Teresa had set up a whiteboard. She wasted no time.

"OK, this is what I've found. There's a communication on the Dark Web, on a site named 'Malory'. Does that mean anything to you?"

They both looked at each other, puzzled. Teresa enlightened them.

"Sir Thomas Malory was a fifteenth century English writer, most famous for his work 'Le Morte D'Arthur' – the Death of Arthur – which chronicled the Arthurian Legend. Are you at all familiar with it?"

Andy immediately piped up.

"There was a series on TV about Merlin. That was about King Arthur. I enjoyed that."

Paula nodded agreement.

"I watched some of it. But what's it to do with our case?"

Teresa smiled and began to print names on the whiteboard as she explained their significance.

"Let's start with Vivien. The name is used with slight variations for The Lady of The Lake in a number of works about the Arthurian Legend. She also raised Lancelot, who became a lover of Queen Guinevere, King Arthur's wife. So, we've got our corpse, Vivien Raeburn, whose forename is that of The Lady of the Lake, and who, not surprisingly ends up dead in a lake. You with me so far?"

They both nodded, though still a little puzzled until Teresa continued.

"In legend, Lancelot and Guinevere were lovers. Guinevere is a Welsh name, but nowadays it's often shortened to Gwen. Now, our dead victim's mother was named Gwen, and she died suddenly and unexpectedly at home. There was an inquest which eventually concluded death was due to natural causes following an epileptic fit. Therefore, her life insurance paid out a significant amount."

Teresa paused for breath before continuing, obviously enjoying the 'reveal'.

"So, what if Lancelot was also having an affair with Vivien? What if they conspired to kill Gwen for her insurance money, but Lancelot then killed Vivien and theatrically dumped her body in the lake?"

Her audience was silent until Paula asked the obvious question.

"Are you saying the inquest reached the wrong conclusion?"
"But what if it did? I've had a look at Gwen's medical history, and it shows she hadn't had an epileptic fit in the last ten years. If she was murdered, a lot of other incidental issues would make sense."
"What are the odds against this scenario? Do we have any proof?"
"I have proof that Vivien exchanged messages with a person called Lance on the Dark Web. I'm still trying to decode them, but it shouldn't take long. Then it's up to you to make a case."
"Sounds good, Teresa. It's a bit 'off the wall' but I'm happy to go with it as soon as you've identified this Lancelot guy."
"I'll let you know as soon as I do."

********

It took three more days before Teresa made an excited call to Paula.

"I've done it! I've found the proof! Conference Room?"
"We're on our way."

Teresa made a compelling case with undisputable evidence. She laid out printed sheets containing text of several brief conversations between Vivien and 'Lance' detailing where and when to meet to discuss 'the event', which was assumed to be Gwen's murder. It was evident from the tone of the exchanges that they were lovers.

"If you look at the time and date they agreed to meet in this particular communication at a café on Cheapside, I'll prove it. Just watch this."

She loaded a DVD, pressed 'Play' and fast-forwarded it to the required time.

"Watch carefully."

It was a video taken from a street camera on Manor Row and clearly showed Vivien walking up the street towards the café. Teresa forwarded the recording until it showed a smartly dressed man in his forties enter the same café. Thirty minutes later, they left together, and kissed before parting.

"Good work, Teresa. Now all we have to do is identify the man."
"Already done."

She pushed a sheet of paper across the desk.

"I ran it through facial recognition on our database. He's got a criminal record for embezzlement. He cons vulnerable women. And if you need further proof, look at his list of assumed identities."

At the bottom of the list was the name Michael Griffiths, which Teresa pointed out was his real name.

"So where does Lancelot come into it?"
"He has used 'Lance' as his forename on several occasions, apparently because one of his ex-lovers gave him the nickname 'The Lance' on account of the length of his penis, of which he was particularly proud. Is that enough evidence for you?"
"Let's go get him."

They drove to the address Teresa had provided, a cottage in Allerton, outside which was parked a pale blue Commer van. Teresa's notes confirmed it belonged to Michael Griffiths. Andy pressed the doorbell. From inside they could hear the sound of footsteps coming down the stairs before the door opened. Paula introduced herself and her colleague before explaining their presence.

"We'd like to talk to you about a lady you know."
"Oh, and who's that?"
"Vivien Raeburn."
"I don't know anybody of that name."

Andy pulled out a print of the photograph of them leaving the café together.

"Strange you should be kissing someone whose name you don't know, don't you think?"
"Oh, her. I'd just met her in a café. We got talking and seemed to get along OK. Before we parted, she let me kiss her. That's all. I never got to know her name. And I've never seen her since."
"We know that's not true. You had long conversations online with her. That's true, isn't it, Lance?"

There was silence for a few seconds as 'Lance' considered his options before answering.

"Why are you calling me Lance? My name's Michael."
"Officially, yes. But you seem to be quite proud when ladies refer to you as 'Lance'. We know Gwen called you Lance, and the name crops up regularly in your online conversations."
"I don't know anything about this. I think you should leave and quit harassing me with this nonsense."
"OK, we'll continue down at HQ. We'd like to discuss a murder we believe you committed."
"You've no evidence."
"We'll find it. Get your coat."

By the time they were ready to interview Michael Griffiths in the presence of his solicitor, a Forensics team was already searching his house, and a laptop and a detachable hard drive had been bagged up and taken back to the lab. Significant snippets of evidence were forwarded to Paula's mobile as the interview commenced. While Andy led the questioning, Paula was compiling further questions based on the new evidence being forwarded to her throughout.

After a number of non-committal responses from Griffiths, Paula took charge.

"You have already told us you only met Vivien Raeburn once, although you had online conversations. Is that correct?"
"Yes."

She turned her mobile towards him and played one of the video snips which Forensics had forwarded to her. It clearly showed a naked Vivien Raeburn fellating a naked Michael Griffiths.

"This would suggest otherwise. It's clearly not been taken in a busy café on Cheapside, has it?"

Andy chipped in.

"Now I understand why women call you 'Lance'.

His solicitor intervened.

"I'd like to have a private word with my client. Would you please suspend this interview for ten minutes?"

********

Upon resumption, Griffiths agreed he'd met Vivien on a number of occasions when they had consensual sex at his home. That was all. He knew nothing about her death. She just failed to turn up and didn't answer his online communications. That last comment was all Paula was waiting for.

"Can you prove this? There's no record of any communication with Viv after the time of her death."
"I must have deleted it."
"There's nothing on Viv's laptop either."
"She must have deleted it."
"After she died? That's unlikely, don't you think?"

She let the silence hang for a moment, then continued.

"So, how did you get hold of this image we found on your laptop?"

Again, she turned her phone towards him. The image displayed was of the dead Vivien on the bank of what appeared to be a large expanse of water. She was wearing the robe her body was later found in.

"You couldn't resist this last picture for your album, could you? And I bet you weren't even aware of the symbolism, were you?"
"I don't know what you're on about."
"Vivien. The Lady of the Lake in Arthurian legend."
"I don't know what you're on about. What Arthurian legend?"
"Interview suspended."

Outside the Interview Room, Paula was astounded that Griffiths genuinely seemed to be totally unaware of the legend.

"If it's just a coincidence, it's unbelievable."
"I agree. It's just incredible. There's Gwen, Vivien, Lance, or Lancelot, the Lady of the Lake. It's all there."
"Personally, I don't really care. I think we've got enough evidence to convict him for Vivien's murder. Let's see if we can pin Gwen's death on him as well."

Two days later, an excited Teresa called Paula.

"You won't believe what I've discovered! It could solve the case for us. I'm coming down."

Moments later, Teresa arrived at Paula's desk, clutching a handful of papers. Andy couldn't wait to hear her news.

"First of all, I found out that Gwen's late husband's name was Arthur. That, however, is not the reason I called you over. Guess what I discovered?"
"Stop playing games, Teresa. Let's hear it."
"OK. Sorry. I just got over-excited. The news is that Gwen had made provision in her Will that her brain was to be donated for medical research. And that's what actually happened! I made some enquiries and found it's been stored at the Cambridge brain bank at Addenbrooke's Hospital. I've put together all the background information for you to present to DCI Gardner asking if it's possible for it to be re-examined by an expert neuropathologist. Could you please check it over and pass it to the DCI for authorisation?"
"Wow! I certainly will. Good work, Teresa."

********

It took two weeks before DCI Gardner was able to organise the examination of Gwen's preserved brain. The work was to be performed by one of Britain's most experienced neuropathologists, Professor Stanley Withers, who regularly assisted the police. A copy of his report, written on conclusion of the examination, was hastily sent to Bradford CID, where DCI Gardner was the first to read it. He immediately called Teresa, Paula and Andy to his office. Once assembled, he read out the results of the examination.

"I'm sorry that there are some technical terms in the report, but here it is. The examination identified 'ischaemia in the hippocampus'. This happens when blood flow and oxygen to the brain are restricted. He was able to state with confidence that the damage was likely to have occurred up to an hour before death, meaning that it was not consistent with a fatal epileptic fit, where sudden death occurs quickly. Coupled with the fact that the victim had not suffered an attack for several years, he quickly deduced that the original verdict was incorrect. He also stated that the original report noted there were no signs of an epileptic fit, such as tongue biting or injuries from a sudden collapse. Finally, the conclusion was that Gwen's death was caused by 'prolonged restriction of her breathing from an outside source'. His belief is that she was put in a choke hold or had a plastic bag put over her head until she died."

He let the information sink in before continuing.

"First of all, I'd like to congratulate you all on bringing the investigation to this point. The means by which you reached the conclusion you did is immaterial to me, but the fact that you pursued the case so doggedly to unearth a murder that was previously never considered is a credit to you all. So, thank you."

Paula was quick to praise Teresa.

"It's all down to Teresa, sir. She should be given all the credit for this."
"While I agree it's largely down to Teresa, I wish to emphasise we're a team. We take the credit as well as the blame as a team, not as individuals. That's why you're all so good at your job and why our record during my tenure is outstanding. DI Peters evidently trained you very well."

"We all agree with that, sir. We're looking forward to having him back. Do you have any idea when it might be?"

"I'm afraid I'm unable to answer that. What I can say is that you've proved you can function without Brian's direction. I want to see that continue. OK?"

"Yes, sir. Thank you, sir."

"So, question the accused again concerning this new information, and pass it on to the DPP."

# CHAPTER 6

Gary was making little progress on the car thefts case. Those arrested had refused to speak when interviewed, and no further events had taken place. However, Teresa had identified those arrested by their fingerprints and matched them to images kept on their criminal records. Further research threw up another surprise. Two of those arrested had cottoned on to a novel way to set up their car thefts businesses. She explained the process to Gary and Lynn.

"I initially got this information from the NCA. You were out on a case when they gave the presentation. It falls neatly into the 'Law of Unintended Consequences'. During the pandemic, they'd bought limited companies on social media. The companies were worthless, but they just stuck money into them and then applied for 'bounce-back' loans to give them the capital to purchase storage warehouses and vehicles in which to transport the stolen cars. This is something I have spoken about before and it's evident that criminal gangs have taken full advantage of the easy money."

"So, the bounce-back loans were intended to help businesses stay afloat during the pandemic, but the unintended consequence is that they were authorised so quickly without sufficient checks that they've allowed the criminal fraternity to flourish."

"Yep. Maybe Mr Sunak will give us a loan to recruit some extra staff."

"Don't bank on it, Teresa. It's time we had another chat with those we arrested."

"If you can wait till the end of the day, I expect to be able to provide the names of the companies they run so you can check their storage facilities."

Teresa was true to her word. She found that one of those arrested, Shafique Khan, had paid amounts totalling £40,000 to a logistics company for transporting containers to Dubai. He also rented a warehouse in Oldham.

"My guess is that is where the stolen cars are stripped before being shipped. It's a 'chop shop'."

"Any idea where they ship from?"

"My guess would be Seaforth Docks on Merseyside. That's the route the logistics company normally uses for shipments to the Middle East."

"Well done, Teresa. We'll set up a raid on the shipping company, and on the Oldham warehouse if you'll send me the address."

He was quickly on the phone to the NCA.

"Alex, it's Gary at Bradford CID."
"Hi, Gary. How are you doing?"
"OK. I think I've got some work for you."

A videoconference was hastily arranged, and all the details thrashed out. A squad from Manchester and one from Merseyside would be used to supplement the manpower from the NCA. The two raids would take place at the same time – 11am on Friday. Bradford CID was excused due to their busy workload. Gary reported the agreed course of action to DCI Gardner, who, while annoyed at not being informed earlier, commended Gary on organising the operation.

********

Brian was still working the 'missing persons' cases when Teresa called.

"Any progress, Brian?"
"Not much. I interviewed the parents of the two sisters, and they couldn't help. They were just fun-loving young girls who loved to party and enjoyed a drink. There was no nasty side to them. Everybody loved them. So, have you got anything for me?"
"Not really. I just thought I should let you know I had a conversation with Chris Fox at the NCA this morning, and he mentioned they were seeing a rise in abductions recently. They're working on the theory that organised gangs are to blame, targeting vulnerable refugees, mainly from Ukraine."
"That makes sense."
"He also mentioned that his colleagues in Europe are facing the same problem and they have identified some Russian elements are at work."
"So, we're cutting off income to the oligarchs, but providing another source of income to the lower-level criminals."
"It seems so."
"Will you pass anything you get from the NCA to me, please?"
"Of course."
"Thank you."

He checked his notes. The names of those who abducted Terry Stanton's relatives were, apparently, English. Dave and Stewart. He had no information regarding the so-called taxi driver. Still, there was always the possibility that Russian criminals were running the show and paying others to carry out the actual abductions. He was certain he knew the reason for the abductions. They were all female, all under forty. It was most likely they were destined for a life of abuse and prostitution. He decided it was time he went for a walk.

He drove over to Manningham and was lucky enough to find a parking space off Darfield Street. He left his police permit on view in the windscreen in case any over-zealous parking wardens were in the area, before walking the full length of Lumb Lane to its junction with Marlborough Road. He stopped to talk to each female plying her trade on the way, inquiring if any new girls had appeared in recent weeks.

"There always are, love. They come and go. Some just need a bit of money to pay unexpected bills, and that. As soon as they've got the money you don't see them again for months."
"Any girls who you think may have been coerced into working?"
"There's always someone who makes a girl work the street. That will never stop. It's the nature of the game, love."
"Anybody who looks like they're being physically abused by their pimp?"
"They're more likely to be working indoors. Some punters like that sort of thing."

He pulled out the photos of the missing girls.

"Have you seen any of these?"
"No. Sorry."
"OK, love. Thanks for your time. Would you do me a favour? If you see or hear about any new workers, particularly two young girls, sisters, who are obviously not doing it for fun, will you give me a call? They were abducted after a night out, and I've got a strong feeling they've been forced into the game. Here's my number, and this is payment for your time."

He handed her his card and a twenty-pound note.

"I will, love. And I'll ask some of the other girls to keep a look out."
"Thanks. I appreciate your help."

He walked on and spoke to some other working girls before calling into a taxi office. He spoke to the staff, showed the photos, left his card, and walked back to his car. He was well aware that many of those he spoke to knew some of the answers he was seeking, but would not, or dare not, tell him. He needed another mode of access to the pimps. He wondered if there might be something on social media. He called Teresa and asked if she'd look into it. Then he drove to Leeds, to perform the same exercise in Chapeltown before moving on to Huddersfield. He drew a blank at both red-light districts.

He was beginning to wonder if the girls he was looking for were still actually in the area. It was even possible they had been taken abroad but he doubted that. Why would anybody go to the expense of sending girls abroad to work in the sex trade when there was already a large local market?

He took a call from Teresa.

"I've sent you a list of web sites and social media sites where prostitution and sex forums are open to browse. There are also loads of restricted sites I'm hacking. I'll send you access codes as I get them. I'm concentrating on the north of England. Good luck!"

He drove home, made a drink and a sandwich, and logged on, making copious notes and bookmarking everything which could be a potential lead. It was a lengthy process, but eventually one site in particular which Teresa had found on the Dark Web piqued his interest – a travelling brothel. He called her immediately, impatiently drumming his fingers on his desk waiting for her to answer.

"Teresa. I need access to one of the sites you sent. 'Pantechnicon Fun Club.' Urgent, please."
"Working on it."

The site advertised mobile brothels in customised commercial vehicles normally used for furniture removals and similar activities, but some enterprising group appeared to have converted some such vehicles to serve the sex trade. It was a promising lead he was eager to follow. Teresa's eventual response left him deflated.

"There's a problem, Brian. Invitations are by recommendation only. In other words, you need to be introduced by a current 'trusted member' of the club. What I can do, is give you a list of upcoming venues which you could stake out and maybe collar a customer and 'persuade' him to recommend you. What do you think?"

"That sounds like a good plan, Teresa. Send me the list, please."

"Will do. Good luck."

It was mid-afternoon before the list of venues for the next week came through. There were currently four pantechnicons each covering a different geographical area, and each using motorway Services areas as their operational bases. Brian selected the M62 as his starting point, working out a route and timetable. He reckoned he would need to visit each unit once only, and as quickly as possible. Then he would have to stake out the van and try to pick a customer whom he could 'persuade' to introduce him. He planned to take a picture of every customer leaving the van, note the make and numberplate of the vehicle they drove and pass the details to Teresa to see if she could identify anyone. It was all he could do. He prepared himself for long hours of lonely surveillance, making up a flask of coffee and some sandwiches and set off at 6pm, heading for the Birch Services, where Teresa had informed him that the pantechnicon was open for business from 8pm till midnight.

Arriving at the Services, he soon spotted the pantechnicon parked among the HGVs, and drove around for a while before he found a spot which afforded the best view of the rear entrance door to the vehicle. It was almost time. He called Teresa who was monitoring his progress from her home. By seven o'clock, a small group of men had gathered near the vehicle, impatiently waiting for the doors to open, and were admitted in turn; six initially, then one out, one in. Brian took a snap of each as he left and sent it to Teresa along with the details of his car. There was a steady stream of customers until the business closed at midnight. Brian left soon afterwards, following the last customer all the way to Bury. Teresa already had his home address, his name, marital status, and occupation. Brian smiled. His target would be embarrassed when confronted by the evidence he used prostitutes, and so should be easy to bargain with.

As the target vehicle pulled off the road into a wide, long drive and stopped by the double garage, Brian pulled in behind him, stepping quickly out of the car and approaching his target who was waiting for the remote-controlled garage door to open. He knocked on the driver's window, smiling as the man opened it.

"Sorry to bother you, sir. My name is Brian Peters. I'm a Detective Inspector with Bradford CID."

"And what the hell are you doing here? This is private property."

"I'd like to ask you about your visit to Birch Services earlier tonight, sir."

"That's nothing to do with you! It's not illegal."

"It is if the girls have been kidnapped and forced into prostitution. I just need some information, sir. I've no desire to implicate you."

"What do you want to know?"

He pulled out the photographs of the four missing persons.

"Did you see any of these girls in the brothel, sir?"

"No. I'm sorry. I have a 'favourite.' I'm just shown into her room. They're all private little rooms."

"How many, sir?"

"Six, I think. There's a small waiting area, then customers are called when their girl is free. You never get to see what's going on in the other rooms. It's very private."

"OK. Do you know any of the people who work there?"

"Only one. He's a bit of a bouncer, I think."

"Name?"

"He calls himself 'Ivan.' Sounds a bit east European."

"OK. Thank you, sir. I'm not charging you with any offence. All I will say is that not all these girls are willing participants. Some have been snatched off the street and forced to work. Some are missing their homes, their husbands, their children, their friends. I'd like to do something about it. Think about it before you book another session, eh?"

"I will. Thank you."

"Goodnight, sir."

He drove home. Hopefully, Teresa would have a list of clients for him to interview following their visit to the brothel. He would check when he arrived home and had a well-earned glass of malt.

********

Brian checked his watch.10.30am. He had work to do. He forced himself to get up, his head pounding from the volume of alcohol he'd consumed before dragging himself to bed. He made a cup of strong black coffee and switched on his laptop. As expected, an email from Teresa timed at 02.20. So, she had a late night too, although she no doubt stayed sober. He opened the email and read.

"Brian,
5 visitors identified from photos and car reg. Those without car reg. are going through criminal database image checks, so there may be more. Addresses included for those identified. Good luck."

He drank his coffee while he planned a route. Four of the five were in Lancashire; the other was in Cumbria. He'd do Lancashire today, all being well.

He was on his way before noon, driving carefully, aware that he was probably still over the limit. Nobody was at home at the first address, though his neighbour said the occupant was normally home at about 5.30. The neighbour didn't know where he worked so Brian decided to move on to the second address, near Liverpool. Here, he had more luck. The occupant was working from home and agreed to speak to Brian.

"My wife knows nothing about this. She thinks I was away on business."
"That's fine, sir. I've no desire to get you into any trouble. I'm just trying to trace some missing persons."
"So, how can I help you?"
"How long have you been using the mobile brothel service?"
"About six months. A client recommended it."
"And do you always use the same girl?"
"Whenever possible, yes."

He took out the photos.

"Do you recognise any of these?"
"Sorry, no. To be honest, they're too young for me. I prefer more mature women."
"I see. You mentioned that a client recommended the service. I take it, he uses them too."
"Correct, but he's based down south. They run an operation down there, too."
"Really? Well, thanks for your time."

He left and drove to the next address, in Southport. Again, nobody was at home. He continued to Preston where, again, he got the same story. The interviewee used the same girl each time and didn't recognise anyone from the photos.

Realising he'd had nothing to eat all day, he stopped at a café before setting off for home. He checked his phone for messages, finding good news from Teresa.

"NCA raid on chop shops and container warehouses successful. NCA pursuing prosecutions."

Brian smiled. It was a good outcome, which should lead to more raids and arrests as those in custody gave up information in return for leniency. He left the café to return to his car for the drive home. Then, on a whim, when he reached the junction for the M6, he took the road north towards the final destination on his address list, Arnside.

He pulled up outside a large, detached house overlooking the bay, and was walking up the path to the door when he heard a voice.

"Can I help you?"

He turned to see an old man in a wheelchair. He didn't look like the man he had photographed leaving the brothel.

"I'm looking for a Mr George Stead."
"I'm George Stead. And so is my son."
"Could I speak to your son, please, Mr Stead?"
"Who are you?"
"DI Brian Peters, sir. Here's my ID."
"Been in trouble again, has he?"
"Not at all, sir. I just think he may be able to help with an inquiry."
"He's in his office. In the rear garden. Just follow the path."
"Thank you, sir."
"Take him away with you. Bloody nuisance, he is."

Disregarding the remark, Brian walked round into the garden where a stylish wooden home office had been built. He could see someone inside taking a phone call. He waited outside, unseen, but listening to the call.

"Honestly, you wouldn't believe it! Two girls. Gorgeous teenage girls. Not very experienced but very willing. Half an hour of heaven. You coming with me next time? Yeah. Next Thursday. It's not cheap, but it's worth it. OK. Talk later. 'Bye."

Brian waited a minute or so before knocking on the door. George Stead Jr opened the door.

"Can I help you?"

"Mr Stead?"

"Yes."

"My name is Brian Peters. Detective Inspector Peters. I'd like to ask you a few questions."

"You'd better come in and take a seat."

"Thank you."

"So, how can I help you?"

"I was wondering if you had ever used a mobile brothel?"

"How dare you suggest such a thing! I'm a happily married man."

"Ever had sex with a teenager? Or two, maybe?"

"I'd like you to leave now. This is ridiculous. How could you think such a thing!"

"Let's get to the point, Mr Stead. I know you visited a mobile brothel at Birch Services on the M62 yesterday. I have a photo of you leaving. I have your car registration. I *saw* you! And on top of that, I've just listened to you bragging about it on the phone. So, look at this photograph and tell me if these were the two girls who gave you so much pleasure."

Stead looked at the photo and nodded.

"Yes. These were the girls. But they were willing and old enough. I haven't committed any crime."

"These girls were kidnapped. They were refugees from Ukraine, along with their parents and grandparents. Now, while you were at the brothel, did you see their mother? That's her in the photo behind her daughters."

"No, I didn't see her. Sorry."

"OK. Did the girls ask for help? Did they say they were prisoners?"

"No. They hardly spoke. They just did the business. They were, like, *detached* from it all."

"OK. Have you used this business before?"

"Occasionally. When they were in the area."

"Do you know where their next stop is?"

"The M1, tonight and tomorrow. I can't remember which stop, though."

"So, log on and ask."

"I can't do that."

"Why not?"

"I have to wait for a new password. It expires after every visit, and they send a new one."

"Here's my card. As soon as it arrives, find out their itinerary and call me. OK?"

"Yes."

"If I don't hear from you, I'll charge you with having sex with a minor."

"They were old enough. I was told they were both eighteen!"

"They lied. One of the girls was only fifteen."

Back in the car, he called Teresa to update her, and also confessed he'd told Mr Stead a lie about the girl's age. He felt no remorse; it was a necessary ploy.

The call came late that evening. M1 South, Trowell Services, between junction 25 and 26. He immediately contacted Teresa.

"Teresa, can you get a team together for a raid tomorrow evening? I'll send you all the details I have. NCA need to be in on this, I think."

At 9am the following morning, Teresa took a deep breath and knocked on DCI Gardner's door.

"Come in. Ah, good morning, Teresa. What can I do for you?"

"I need your authorisation for a raid, sir."

"How many people?"

"As many as you will permit, sir. The NCA will be leading it, sir."

"So, what is the purpose of this raid?"

"We have evidence that the working girls include some young women who were kidnapped when seeking asylum here from Ukraine, sir, and forced to work in a mobile brothel."

"Why haven't I heard of this case before now, Teresa?"

"It's been exposed by someone outside our team, sir."

There was a long pause before Gardner spoke again.

"Are you telling me that a major case has been investigated without my authority?"

"Yes, sir. Please let me explain."

"Go ahead."

"It's been clear for a while, sir, that the entire department has been under sustained pressure. We have had to put cases on the back burner because we haven't had the capacity to investigate fully. This is a case where two separate incidents of the abduction of a total of five females has, we believe, been orchestrated to staff mobile brothels where the abductees have been forced into being sex slaves. Initially, one of the incidents was reported by a man who had previously been involved in a case managed successfully by Brian Peters, and he came to HQ specifically to ask for his help. Eventually, there being no other option, I mentioned it to Brian, who felt he owed the man a favour. Then, when two young women were abducted by a bogus taxi driver, I naturally passed it to Brian as it seemed to overlap with the case he was already investigating."

"You should have asked me first, Teresa."

"I know, sir. I thought it would relieve the pressure on the team, sir. Particularly on Gary, sir, who, if I may say so, occasionally looks out of his depth, though I know he's doing his best. I did it for the good of the department, sir."

Gardner thought for a while.

"OK, Teresa. What you did, you did for the good of the department. I understand that. But I will not have you making this kind of decision behind my back. In future, you discuss it with me. Is that clear?"

"Yes, sir."

"Very well. Would you kindly ask DI Peters to come in for a chat with me?"

"Yes, sir. I'll arrange it."

"You have my permission to organise the raid, Teresa. Let the NCA know they will have to provide the bulk of the manpower. Liaise with them."

Teresa walked back to her desk unsure of whether she would face any disciplinary action. If so, she would accept it, and if necessary, give notice to quit. She knew the NCA would jump at the chance of employing her. And Brian Peters would also be on their payroll, were he to become available. She called Brian and made him aware of the situation, before calling Alex Sinclair at the NCA to iron out details of the forthcoming operation. Brian's response was that he would take part in the raid regardless of the DCI's feelings, and to hell with the consequences.

# CHAPTER 7

They met at 7pm in the car park of the Services, parking as far away from the pantechnicon as possible with only one sole car parked close by to monitor activity, photograph all clients, and relay instructions. They had all been briefed during the day regarding their roles and sat in small groups in the various eateries until they were called to action at 10.15pm, when the lookout reported something unexpected.

"I may be wrong, but I think a Member of Parliament has just entered the brothel."
"No problem, as long as he's not putting it down as expenses."

On the 'Go' command, the various small squads began to execute their rehearsed roles, beginning with two plain-clothed officers, one of whom was Brian Peters, knocking on the brothel door and demanding to be allowed in. An argument ensued when they were denied entry.

"Sorry, guys. It's by appointment only. You can't just turn up."
"Look, we've got a hundred quid each to spend. All we want is a half-hour each with a couple of pretty girls. How about it? There's an extra fifty quid for you if you let us in."

While the negotiation continued, the assault force was closing in, ready for the signal, which was to come from Brian. He continued to plead with the bouncers to let him in.

"Come on, how about it? Fifteen minutes, then. Just a quick shag. What harm can it do?"
"No chance. You're not on the list, you're not coming in."
"You've let the MP in. Why not us?"
"I told you. It's invitation only."
"Let me have a word with the boss. If he says 'no,' then we'll go. If not, we'll stay here and dissuade the rest of your 'guests' from coming in."
"Wait there."

He shut the door in their face and went to fetch his 'boss.' When he returned and opened the door, he was knocked to the ground by the assault team who forced their way in and rounded up all the staff and punters separately, guiding them at gunpoint into the fleet of secure vehicles which immediately transported them to

Nottingham Police HQ. The working girls were held in the pantechnicon and questioned briefly in turn, before being taken to a secure private clinic for examination and counselling. At that point, Brian sent a terse message to Teresa which read 'Mission Accomplished. More news later." Teresa immediately passed the message to the DCI, who replied 'Well done.' The MP was eventually allowed to leave.

As the teams completed their mission at the Services, Brian thanked everyone for their help, before driving to the clinic to check on the Ukrainian girls. Officers from the NCA were still interviewing the staff at the brothel to attempt to determine the whereabouts of other kidnapped girls. All information relating to girls from the Bradford area was being relayed back to Teresa.

After what seemed an age, Brian was allowed to see Olga and Ana, who had been reunited with their mother Yulia. He introduced himself as a friend of Terry Stanton and was pleased to tell them that their relatives had been informed and were on their way to see them and take them home. He left shortly after the Stantons arrived. The two girls abducted by a taxi driver in the city centre were still unaccounted for, but he would have to wait for the results of the NCA's interviews with those arrested. He needed sleep to prepare himself for his interview with DCI Gardner.

******** 

Brian hadn't slept well, but was up early, showered, shaved and dressed, and with time for a quick coffee before driving to HQ for his meeting with the DCI. He wasn't sure how it would go. He would play it by ear, and if it meant a longer suspension, a caution, or even dismissal, then so be it. He could always set up his own business as a PI. He had the connections.

He took a deep breath and knocked on the DCI's door.

"Come in."
"You wanted to see me, sir?"
"Yes, Brian. Please sit down."
"Thank you, sir."
"Now, Brian, first of all, congratulations on assisting, or playing a lead role, in fact, in the recent operation."
"Thank you, sir."
"However, I am disappointed you kept me out of the loop."
"Would you have authorised my role?"

"At least we could have discussed it. I'm disappointed you went behind my back."

"I understand that, sir. Let me explain why, if I may."

"Go on."

"Before you joined us, we had a case where a couple of kids were stealing cars and writing them off. One victim, Terry Stanton, lost his job as a result of losing his car. By chance, he came across the car thieves, who by now were in the drugs trade, and started to work for them. He put his life on the line to get revenge and in doing so, helped us uncover an international drugs business run by a detective here in Bradford HQ. I owed him a favour. So, when some of his wife's family, seeking sanctuary from Ukraine, went missing, he called on me to help, having been cold-shouldered by our people here. I owed him. Then, when two young women, sisters, were abducted by a bogus taxi driver, Teresa, recognising that the two cases may be linked, naturally passed it to me, knowing that staff here were already over-stretched. I'm still working it, by the way. I believe it may be the same gang who are recruiting unwilling girls for the sex trade."

"You should have kept me in the loop, Brian."

"You're right, sir. But would you have allowed me to investigate these cases? Or would you have kept me suspended?"

"I did that to help you get over your problems, Brian. I felt a break would do you good."

"And help preserve the image of your department."

"Yes. That's true. Look, Brian, the public needs to respect the work of the police force. We have an image to uphold. Your drunken behaviour was tarnishing that image. That was one reason you were suspended, but only one. The main reason was to give you time and space to come to terms with your problems and, with professional help, deal with them."

"I feel I've done that to some extent, sir. I think where I am now is as good as it will ever get. My passion, my focus, is on catching criminals. This is how I deal with my issues, by doing all I can to ensure others don't have to go through the same traumatic experience I suffered. However, it's your call, sir. If you sack me, I'll carry on chasing criminals privately."

Gardner leaned back in his chair and sighed.

"Brian, I don't want to sack you. However, I don't want a vigilante on my patch. So, here's the olive branch. Carry on investigating your current case. You can still call on Teresa to help, but you must keep me informed. Then, when it's concluded, we discuss how we can properly manage your return to full-time duties here. Nothing that's happened recently will go on your record, apart from the successful conclusion of your investigations. How does that sound?"

"Very generous, sir. Thank you."

"OK, and by the way, I'm fully aware that NCA have you on their radar, as well as Teresa. I'd rather you stayed here."

"Thank you, sir."

"OK, so tell me where you are regarding the abductions."

*******

Brian left the meeting with a satisfied smile on his face. It was the best outcome he could have wished for. He headed straight for Teresa's desk. She was overjoyed to see him looking so upbeat and threw her arms round him.

"Tell me it went well."

"It went well. I've been authorised to continue looking for the abductees, and then, after a period of rehabilitation, I'll be back at my desk. Provided I don't drink myself into a stupor in the meantime."

"You won't do that. You've got too much self-respect for that. And too many people who want to help you."

"Thank you. So, where are we with the other girls?"

"I'm getting regular feedback from interviews with those captured at the Services. Nothing useful as yet. I'll keep you posted. So, what are your plans for the day?"

"I'm going to call on Terry Stanton. See how they're doing."

"He rang me this morning. I put him through to the DCI. Apparently, he was singing your praises to the heavens."

"I'll thank him for that. He probably swung it for me, otherwise I'd be unemployed."

********

He parked up and walked up the drive. They'd moved house since their first encounter and welcomed him in, thanking him profusely.

"I should be thanking you, Terry. You just saved my career."

"Then we're even. You just saved our family."

"How are the ladies?"

"They'll be OK. They still attend counselling sessions, but they're settling. They're staying in a hotel for a while until their flats are ready. The decorators are just finishing off this week."

"So, they're all together? Grandparents as well?"

"They've got the flat next door. They need to be close now. Anyway, are you still looking for other abductees?"

"Yes."

"I've got something which might help."

He opened his laptop and brought up Facebook.

"Linda started up a page for people whose friends or family had disappeared without trace. There are stories from all over the country, from people who experienced what we did. All young women. It's heart-breaking."

"Let me take a note of the site's address. We'll have a look back at HQ. Glad to see you're handling it. If you need any help, give me a call."

"I will. Thanks, Brian."

Back at the office, he passed the Facebook address to Teresa. Between them, they identified seven girls who'd recently gone missing in the Bradford area. Brian arranged to interview the parents, starting immediately, while Teresa gathered background information on the others.

His first contact was with Irene Bradshaw, whose daughter had not been seen for more than a week. She had reported it but had no further contact from the police.

"I'm sorry to put you through this again, Mrs Bradshaw, but I've just been assigned to the case and I'm not up to speed on everything yet. Would you mind going through it with me?"

"Only if you promise me, you'll look into it and not just file it away."

"You have my word it will have my full attention."

"Very well. My daughter, Alice, went out on the Friday before last. She was meeting some friends in Bradford. They did that often. Girls from work. I always stay up until she gets home. Well, she texted me at about 11.30 to say she was just getting into a taxi, and she'd be home shortly. But she never arrived. I stayed up all night and then rang the police in the morning in case there'd been an accident. But there was nothing. No explanation. It was just filed as a missing person. A policeman phoned me up a couple of days ago and asked if she'd turned up yet. I just burst into tears. They don't seem to be doing anything! Anyway, someone told me there was a Facebook page, and it looks like I'm not the only one whose child has gone missing. So, they're my support group now. I look every day to see if anyone's child has turned up. But we live in hope."

"Do you have a photo of Alice, please, Mrs Bradshaw?"

"Yes, but there are loads on her Facebook page. Can't you use them? I don't want to be parted from my memories."

"I understand, Mrs Bradshaw. I'll use those on Facebook. I'll keep you informed of progress."

"Thank you. Please find her and bring her home."

"I'll do everything I can, Mrs Bradshaw."

He made two more house calls that afternoon. Both told a similar story. In both cases, a young woman in her twenties had failed to return home after a night out in the city centre. Both of them normally came home by taxi.

He made an appointment to visit the Council's Licencing Department to discuss their procedures for registration and was alarmed to discover that there had been cases where drivers had allowed their licence to be used by a friend or relative without the Council's knowledge. The Council's response -

"We don't have the manpower to police it."

He thought for a moment.

"Would you be able to let us have a copy of the paperwork and associated photo for each licenced driver?"

"Yes, I can do that. Why?"

"We'd like to do a spot check."

"Oh, OK. I'll just copy them for you."

He returned to HQ to be greeted with a round of applause from the team, which he acknowledged with a wave, before asking the question.

"Any of you ladies fancy a night out in Bradford at the weekend. Maybe even a couple of nights?"

As expected, Jo-Jo, Paula and Louise all volunteered.

"OK, let's cover Friday, Saturday and Sunday. Two ladies together each night but rotate it so you all do two nights each."

"What exactly is the assignment?"

"To find the man who's selling girls for the sex trade. What I'm thinking is, two of you ladies stand in a taxi rank pretending you've

79

had a few. You'll carry a copy of the legitimate paperwork for the drivers' licence. If you find one which doesn't match, be on your guard. You'll be wired and we'll follow you all the way in case you're handed over to a criminal enterprise. The girls we rescued told us they'd been drugged and beaten, so if you don't fancy it, just say so. This has to be voluntary. But it's the only way I can think of."

"I'm in."

"Me too."

"And me."

"Thank you. I promise we'll have someone tailing you all the way."

On his way home from work, it occurred to Brian that he had very little food in the house, and what there was would probably be past its 'best-by' date. He turned off at Thackley Corner, heading for the Aldi store in Idle.

Being unfamiliar with the layout, he meandered up and down each aisle, picking up items he thought might be handy and which would fill the cupboards as well as the fridge. He'd just reached the bottom of the first aisle and turned the corner when he noticed a man, probably in his early fifties, pressing himself against a store worker who was busy trying to fill a display shelf. She looked embarrassed and uncomfortable regarding the man's evident intentions. Brian stepped forward without hesitation.

"Excuse me. I'd like to get something from here."

The man jumped back, startled, as Brian stuck his ID card in his face.

"Whatever it is you're after is not for sale. I suggest you walk away. NOW!"

"I wasn't doing anything. Just trying to get hold of something nice for tea."

"I know exactly what you were doing."

He turned to the assistant.

"Are you OK, love?"

"Yes, thanks."

"I can see you're upset. Do you want to press charges?"

"I don't know. I'll have to ask the manager."

"It's your decision, love. Not the manager's."

"I don't know. I don't want to cause a problem. I haven't worked here long...."

"OK, love. I'll talk to the manager. I assume you've got CCTV."

"Yes."

"Leave it with me."

He turned back to the man.

"As for you, you're coming outside with me."

He gripped the man's arm tightly and took him to the exit.

"OK. Your name and address."

"Paul Hemingway."

"Address?"

"14 Stanley Street."

"Clear off."

"I haven't finished shopping."

"Try somewhere else."

Brian went back into the store to finish his shopping, finding his trolley where he'd left it. The assistant approached him.

"Thank you for your help. He was really creeping me out."

"Do you want to press charges?"

"No. I just hope I never see him again. I've spoken to the manager, and he's barred him."

"Good. Take my card. If you need any help, or just to talk to someone about what's happened, give me a call and I'll be happy to point you in the right direction."

"Thank you."

"Now you can do me a favour."

"Of course. What do you want?"

"Point me in the direction of the frozen pizzas."

# CHAPTER 8

At 10.30pm on Friday night, Jo-Jo and Louise, dressed provocatively in low tops and short skirts, came staggering along Market Street evidently the worse for drink, and stood in the short queue at the taxi rank. They were soon picked up, asking to be taken to Fagley. On the back seat, unnoticed, they compared the council documents with information on the dashboard. It seemed to be legitimate, and Louise sent 'OK. Genuine' on her phone to Brian. He acknowledged, following close behind, listening to the chatter on his earpiece. The driver kept up a conversation on his radio, in a language they couldn't understand. Jo-Jo sent a message to Brian.

"Next time, send a polyglot."

Louise nudged Jo-Jo as the taxi drove past the expected turning and continued towards Thornbury. Jo-Jo alerted Brian with a coded message. Brian in turn alerted the two other cars following closely behind. They all increased their speed, listening to Jo-Jo's prompts.

"We don't normally pass B & Q. Is this the scenic route?"

The driver remained silent, then suddenly turned left on Woodhall Road before pulling to a halt at the back of B & M's. A dark-coloured van was waiting as the taxi driver told them to get out.

Louise objected, stalling.

"We don't live here. Take us home before I piss myself in the back of this taxi."

Three men were running towards the taxi. As the first one reached the rear door, Louise pushed it open sharply, catching him off guard and winding him. At the same time, Jo-Jo had taken out her pepper spray and was liberally spraying it into the eyes of the man attempting to force open the door on her side, while the third man hung back, urging them to hurry. Seconds later, Brian's car pulled up sharply behind the taxi, followed closely by the other two pursuit vehicles carrying armed officers.

It was over in seconds. As soon as they saw the weapons pointed at them, the kidnappers, including the taxi driver, surrendered and were frisked and handcuffed until the van arrived to escort them to

HQ. The kidnappers' van and the taxi were both taken to the pound so Forensics could examine them. Brian drove Jo-Jo and Louise home, thanking them profusely, before driving back to Thackley. He went straight to bed forgoing his customary whisky. He wanted to be fully alert for the interviews in the morning.

For the first time in ages, he was first into the office in the morning. The fact that it was a Saturday meant fewer officers would be on duty unless they had urgent work to complete, but nevertheless almost everybody soon arrived. The work ethic was stronger now that Brian was back at the helm.

At the allotted time, Brian and Jo-Jo walked down to Interview Room 2 to find the taxi driver and his legal representative already waiting. As expected, he denied being an accomplice in a kidnapping. He'd only gone the way he did because he needed a pee and knew he could pull in behind B & M's. Teresa interrupted the interview with a text message indicating the driver's identification was a forgery. Brian smiled before continuing.

"What is your real name, Mr Choudhary?"
"Ali Choudhary *is* my real name."
"Then why are all your ID documents false?"
"That is a lie."
"Who printed them for you?"
"They are official documents, printed by the government."
"Government of what? Toytown? These are all rubbish. How much did you pay?"

His legal counsel interrupted.

"My client is telling the truth."
"I don't believe a word of it. So, he either cooperates or I'll have him deported."
"You can't do that!"
"Just watch me. Now, how long have you been working for these kidnappers?"
"Can I have a moment in private with my representative?"
"You've got five minutes."

Jo-Jo was smiling as they left the room.

"We've got him."
"This is the easy one. The kidnappers will put up more of a fight. They've more to lose."

When the interview resumed, the taxi driver admitted having false documents, claiming he was approached by a man who offered him well-paid work for delivering attractive young women into their clutches. He didn't ask why. He didn't need to know. He was just the delivery man.

A court hearing was rapidly arranged, and he was released on bail pending trial. Brian knew that was only the first hurdle.

"Now for the professionals."

The three men were interviewed simultaneously in different rooms, with the interviewers taking frequent short breaks to compare notes. It was soon evident that each interviewee had a different story to tell. Brian made a suggestion.

"Let the two older guys have some time alone in a cell. Concentrate on the younger bloke. Teresa's just sent me some background info. His girlfriend's about to give birth to their first child. Keep at him, then drop a hint that she's having a difficult birth and crying for him to be there. He'll crack if you put him under pressure. Tell him she's all alone. Make him feel guilty and remind him all he has to do is tell the truth and you'll take him to the hospital to be at her side. Rub it in a bit."

Louise and Jo-Jo continued with the interview, following Brian's suggestion. Their interviewee confessed after five minutes and told them all he knew. Brian immediately called the other two men back for interview, told them their companion had grassed on them and in time drew a confession out of each man. But none would identify anyone further up the hierarchy. He called his team for a meeting and laid out the situation.

"It seems we have an organisation whose bosses like to stay in the background while their ranks of workers carry out their orders and take the risks. It's no different from any other organisation except it's highly illegal. So far, we've got confessions from the people at the bottom of the chain, but we need to identify those at the top to bring an end to this enterprise. Any suggestions?"
"Have we discovered where they take the girls? Who they hand them over to?"
"They always seem to use motorway Services. They communicate via the Dark Web, and the final message is sent via text. Teresa's still working on it."

"So, we're always one step behind. But we can't let them kidnap someone else and hope to follow them. We can't put an innocent life at risk."

"Can we make a deal with the three we have in custody?"

"What do you have in mind, Andy?"

"Get them to inform their boss that the operation was successful. They have a girl and want instructions regarding her delivery. There was a delay, but it's sorted. I'm sure we can come up with some excuse between us. Then we set up a trap at the delivery point. It probably only takes us one more layer up the command structure, but at least it's progress."

"OK. Work on it between you. And quickly. They would have expected delivery either late on Friday or sometime on Saturday. The clock's ticking. Get to it."

They held separate interviews with the two older men they had in custody, offering them a deal for information as to how they communicated with the people above them.

"We understand the process. We just need access to the site you use and your passwords. In return, your help will be taken into account when you appear in court. It could make a world of difference to your sentence. And, if your information helps us crack the organisation, we'll get you a fresh start with a new identity."

Eventually they were able to strike a deal with one of the men, with the help of his solicitor. He identified the website and gave the access codes. He was given access to Teresa's PC while she sat alongside him, monitoring his interaction, and ensuring he did what he was told. She gave him a warning before they started.

"Don't ever forget I've been trained by the CIA on how to navigate the Dark Web. I have software here which will immediately recognise a trigger alert. If that happens, you'll be in prison for the rest of your life. My software is a hell of a lot smarter than you are, so be warned. If, for whatever reason, something goes wrong from this point until we catch your paymasters, you'll get the blame, and you'll get the punishment."

Whenever he hesitated, she prompted him how to explain why the abduction was two days later than expected, using the excuse that the captive girl informed them she had Covid and so they had to isolate her somewhere secure until they could get a negative test. They accepted the explanation and proceeded to give him instructions for transferring the captive. Teresa was satisfied with the information and passed it to Brian. M18, Junction 5, Doncaster North, 9pm. He made plans immediately, calling Alex Sinclair.

"We've got a break, Alex. A transfer is arranged for tonight at 9pm. Can you get a team to M18, Junction 5 to arrest the next level of the hierarchy?"

Alex jumped at the chance and arrangements were finalised.

********

They staggered their arrival so as not to raise any alarm and parked in different areas, communicating by phone and text. Brian was in the back of the van, along with an armed officer from the NCA, nervously ticking off the minutes until the message arrived.

"Target approaching car park. Be alert."

Brian warned the driver.

"Do exactly as you've been instructed. My friend in the back has a gun pointed at the back of your head."

The driver's phone rang. He listened to the message, and said 'OK', then told Brian.

"This is it. He's going to reverse up towards the back doors to make the transfer in a minute."

Brian passed the message to the other units, who watched as the van approached, reversing slowly to within a yard of the rear doors. The passenger got out and opened the rear doors of his vehicle then attempted to open the doors of the other van. At that moment they were surrounded by armed officers and surrendered without a struggle. They were bundled into a police vehicle and ordered to send a message to their boss to say they'd made the pickup and asking for a delivery address to be confirmed. The officers held a quick discussion before deciding their next move. Brian's solution was to take the pickup vehicle with armed officers in the rear to the delivery address, with armed officers in a following vehicle alighting prior to the delivery and approaching stealthily on foot. There was to be helicopter backup to illuminate the area at the point of delivery. The plan was accepted, and the convoy set off towards the delivery point, the car park of the

Travelodge, Doncaster off the A1(N), keeping at a varying distance, and constantly in touch. Two other vehicles were dispatched to the meeting point to keep an eye on proceedings from that point.

The tension was palpable as they approached the rendezvous. They had just received a message from the vehicles already at the site that the target had arrived and was under surveillance. Soon, the delivery van received a message detailing where to bring the captive. The message was passed to the rest of the team and the accompanying vehicles overtook the delivery van, arriving separately and parking in different sections of the car park, yet ensuring they had sight of the target vehicle. Now, they waited for what seemed an age until the delivery van entered the car park and approached the target, pulling to a halt a couple of yards away. The driver got out, waved to the target and motioned for the driver to come over to the van whose back door he was preparing to open. The driver walked slowly towards the van, only realising too late that a trap had been set. He pulled out a revolver but was too late. An M15 rifle was already digging into his spine. Its owner held it there while his partner disarmed him at the same time as the rest of the force stormed the target vehicle, ordering the two passengers in the rear to throw down their weapons and come out with hands on head. It was over in a matter of seconds. Arrangements were made to tow the target vehicle to the pound for forensic examination while the victors shook hands and congratulated each other before heading back to their respective base.

They were now one stage nearer to apprehending the head of the organisation – or so they thought. Their captives refused to talk, regardless of the incentives offered. Finally, though, they discovered the reason for their lack of cooperation. Each of them had at least one family member who was being held against their will by those at the head of the group, and those captives would be killed if their relatives were suspected of cooperating with the police.

Unable to think of any other way of breaking the impasse, Brian called Teresa.

"Teresa, pick one of the temps – whoever seems to have more knowledge of, or interest in, cyberwarfare – and between you, start hacking into any site which you know, or suspect, has some connection to this organisation. I don't care how you do it, just find something we can work with."

"Do I get a free rein?"

"Yes. Do whatever it takes. Identify these people."

\*\*\*\*\*\*\*\*

More than a week later, Teresa presented herself at Brian's desk with a beaming smile on her face. Brian, in the middle of a phone conversation, immediately ended it, realising Teresa had important news.

"What is it, Teresa?"

"The task you set me, Brian. I wanted to update you on progress."

"OK, go ahead."

"OK. First of all, I persuaded the DCI to let me borrow Ruth. She used to work as a computer programmer and jumped at the opportunity. Well, that first night, while Ruth was running data through our criminal database, I called a friend at the FBI. I told him basically what the problem was, and what I thought would help solve it. We talked for about an hour until he understood exactly what I thought I needed, then he rang me back the next day. The outcome was, I got access to some software they are testing over there, on the proviso that I feed them the results. They need to prove to the government that it works, or has sufficient promise, to justify further funding for its development. So, I loaded it and fed in every bit of information we have, then cross-referenced it to our criminal databases, plus all we have access to in the EU. And finally, it started churning out names, along with a score. The higher the score, the more likely the subject would be involved in the sort of criminal activities we're investigating. I got six names scoring more than 90% probability. Two are in jail, one has died. The other three look promising. Their files are here."

"Thanks, Teresa. And please thank Ruth for me. You've done a great job."

"Let's hope it's chosen the right profiles. I'd like to thank the FBI for allowing us take part in testing it for them."

As soon as Teresa had left, he opened the file. The first subject was Eamonn Murphy, a forty-year-old from County Cork, released from prison in 2021 after serving a ten-year sentence for pimping, living off immoral earnings and violence against women whom he'd procured. Attached to his profile were names of people who used to work with him. His last known address was in Cork.

The second subject was David Crowther (47), a Liverpudlian racketeer who also served a lengthy sentence for fraud and racketeering before being released in 2020. His last known address was Knowsley, Merseyside.

The third candidate seemed a bit of a wild card. A career criminal suspected of fraudulently claiming Government 'bounce back' loans during the pandemic, as part of a larger consortium of criminals. He was still under suspicion. Previously resident in Manchester, his current whereabouts was unknown. He was known by a number of aliases and was thought to be in his early fifties.

All three were currently 'off the radar'.

Brian looked at the photographs, pondering his next move. He decided to show the photographs to the men they'd arrested to see if they showed as much as a flicker of recognition. He had them brought one at a time to the Interview Room.

********

He had no luck with the first two he interviewed, who both totally denied knowing any of the three men whose profile he showed them. Brian was unsure whether they were frightened of identifying the criminals in case there were consequences. The third man, though, gave Brian the distinct impression he was lying when he said he didn't recognise any of the photos. He decided to push him further.

"I understand you're afraid of the consequences if you identify one of the bosses. But surely, you would prefer these three to be in jail so you can breathe more easily? They can't harm you if they're inside. And if you tell us what's stopping you from grassing, we can protect you and your loved ones. Putting these guys in jail is the only way you'll ever be free."

There was silence for a while as the man thought it over.

"What if I gave you the name of someone else who knows who they are? Can you make sure it's not traced back to me?"
"Absolutely. I guarantee it."

Brian could see he was weighing up the proposal, so attempted to tilt the balance in his favour.

"I guarantee you'll get a much lighter sentence if you help us catch the bastards who run this operation."

"Give me a pen and some paper."

Brian left the Interview Room with a smile on his face, and within ten minutes, he and Scoffer were on their way to the address in Leeds with a backup vehicle close behind. As they turned onto the road they were looking for, Scoffer could see a figure entering the house they sought. The two cars stopped outside. Brian indicated to the driver and passenger of the backup vehicle to go round to the back of the house and text when they were in position. They sat in the car until they received the message, then left the car and rang the doorbell. They could hear noises from inside until after a couple of minutes of repeatedly ringing the bell, their presence was acknowledged as a middle-aged woman opened the door.

"What do you want?"

"Police, luv. We'd like to speak to Gerry Watkins."

"Don't know any Gerry Watkins."

"That's funny, we were told he lives here."

"You were told wrong, then."

"That's odd, since we've just seen him a couple of minutes ago, going in through this door. Can we have a look inside?"

"Have you got a warrant?"

"No. We'd just like to look around. For sale, isn't it? I might want to buy it."

They pushed past the woman and walked into the kitchen. She protested, but Brian insisted.

"Look, we've travelled all the way from Bradford. Please let us look around, and if we don't find Gerry, we'll leave you in peace."

"I told you! I don't know any Gerry."

"Well, no harm in looking, is there?"

They went quickly from room to room, without finding their quarry. The harridan smiled smugly.

"I told you he wasn't here. Now, you'd better leave."

Scoffer piped up.

"So, there's no-one else here?"

"No. I told you."

"It's just that we thought we saw a man entering."

"You're wrong. I haven't had any male visitors all week."

"Really? Then why is the toilet seat up?"

"I... I don't know. I must have left it up."

"Right. Just like you left the folding step ladder on the upstairs landing, close to the access hatch to the loft space."

"I've been decorating."

"When? 1997? Certainly not since then. Step aside."

Scoffer placed the step ladder beneath the hatch, climbed up and pushed the hatch open, shouting.

"OK, Gerry, come on down, or else we'll nail this hatch shut, take this woman into custody and lock the house up. We'll be back in a few weeks to see if you've changed your mind."

They heard movement from within the loft.

"OK. I'm coming out. But I haven't done anything."

"We'll decide that when we've had a little chat."

********

In the Interview Room, they showed the photos to Gerry Watkins. Brian detected a momentary look of fear on his face before he composed himself.

"I don't recognise any of these."

"I think you do. We want to put them away for a very long time. By the time they get out, they'll be too old to come looking for you. Anyway, they won't know you've grassed. We'll keep your name out of it."

"Can you guarantee that?"

"As much as you can guarantee anything in life. But look at it another way. If you don't identify them, we'll tell them you did, and give them your address. How does that sound?"

"I want protection."

"You'll get it. If we can get them to trial, you'll get protection."

He thought about it before sighing and giving his response.

"OK. This is all I know. These guys got together a lot of years ago. I first met one of them at Aintree Racecourse. I was there with a group of mates. We'd had a few drinks and couldn't pick a winner in any of the races. Before the last race, this guy came up to me and asked if I wanted to make some easy money. All I had to do was get my mates to put money on a certain horse. He supplied the money – a hundred quid each – and promised us twenty-five each for the job, in cash, when we showed him the betting slips. Well, I don't know how he rigged it, but the horse won at good odds. I remember it was at sixteen to one when I placed the first bet, and eventually went down to four to one on the off. But they still made a packet, and we – all ten of us – shared two hundred and fifty quid. But there was something about him that frightened me. After we'd all got paid out, I asked him in jest what he would have done if we'd pocketed the money and done a runner. He said, cold as ice, he would have killed us."

He pointed at one of the photos.

"This is the guy. He said his name was Dave."
"Crowther?"
"I don't know. He just said 'Dave'."
"Were there any other guys with him?"
"Yes. Two, but they never spoke to us. These two."

He pointed at the photos of Murphy and the other man.

"And have you seen or heard of any of them since?"
"Only Dave."
"When?"
"About three months ago. He said he had a new enterprise and wondered if I'd like to join."
"What was it?"
"Prostitution."
"Any more details?"
"They were kidnapping girls and forcing them into prostitution."
"Would you be prepared to appear as a witness in court?"
"No way! Well, not unless you could guarantee my safety."
"We can give you a fresh start with a new identity. We'll look after you."
"I know they're already looking for me. That's why I've been hiding. I need protection."
"You'll get it. If you help us find Dave Crowther."
"I don't know where he is, but I can give you his mobile number and a website he uses."
"You've got a deal. Write them down."

He called Teresa and asked her to hack the website.

# CHAPTER 9

When he arrived at work in the morning, an email from Teresa was waiting for him.

"Got it! Enter this code to access the website: 947£%prosforU***
PS: Just browse it for now. Do *not* enter any text. It tracks all access!"

He logged in and was horrified at what he saw. There were pictures of girls, young girls, performing sex acts of the most degrading kind. He felt sick just looking at them, and more so when he read the accompanying text which promised, among other things, 'all your desires will be fulfilled, however perverted, as long as you are willing to pay. Members are able to see our schedule and book online.'

He was enraged as he texted back to Teresa.

"Book me a visit. Let's take these bastards down."

********

Brian was still seething when he took a phone call from Rachel.

"Sorry to disturb you, Brian, but I've just had a call regarding an explosion in Eccleshill. A witness said his neighbour had just got into his car when it blew up. SOCO's on their way."

"OK. Give me the address, please."

He took Louise with him and parked at the end of the street where a sizeable crowd of people were watching the action behind hastily erected barriers. The constable on duty recognised them and let them through. They headed straight for Allen Greaves, who was in conversation with a fireman.

"Morning, Allen. What's happened here?"
"According to a witness, a neighbour, the victim, David Sutcliffe, who was 35, had just left his house to go to work. He exchanged greetings with his neighbour and got in his car. And then it exploded, we think as soon as he turned the key in the ignition. We're just waiting for the Fire Brigade to give us the all-clear before we tow the car away for examination."
"I take it the driver was killed immediately?"

"Not quite. According to his neighbour, he could hear him screaming for about half a minute after the explosion. It's likely he died from burns, but we'll let you know more when we've got him on the slab."

"Thanks. We'd better start talking to his neighbours."

"His partner has been taken to BRI suffering from shock."

"OK, we'll talk to her later."

They went from door to door. The consensus of opinion among the neighbours was that the victim was a quiet man who kept himself to himself. Divorced a few years ago, he'd recently acquired a new partner, Anne, who'd now moved in with him. She was quite a few years younger than him. He worked for an insurance company in Bradford. There were no children from his first marriage, and he'd divorced his wife due to her infidelity. Brian left a message for Teresa to supply her address and as soon as he had it, drove to her house.

She didn't seem too distraught but explained anyway.

"Our relationship was over long ago, although we stayed together for a while after. We'd been married almost ten years. We'd both wanted children, but I found I couldn't have them. Then, he started seeing other women. We had rows about it, then, finally, we sat down and talked about it, and agreed we'd be better off divorcing. It was amicable in the end. And I've certainly been happier without him."

"According to his neighbours, he divorced you, due to your infidelity."

"That's the story he likes to tell. I can assure you; it was the other way round. I didn't start seeing anyone else until we'd split up and divorce proceedings had already started."

"How did he react to the divorce?"

"He was fine. He wanted to move on. I don't think either of us held a grudge against the other. Why all these questions? You don't think I've had him killed, do you?"

"We're just gathering background information, that's all. We don't yet know whether it was an accidental explosion due to the car's malfunction, or a bomb. We're not accusing you of anything. We're just investigating an incident where there's been a fatality. But, while we're at it, do you know any reason why anyone would want to kill him?"

"No. I can't think of anybody, really. I mean, not everybody loved him, but he was popular, he had a lot of friends. He didn't easily fall out with people. Why? Do you think someone's got a grudge against him?"

"We're just looking at all the possibilities, that's all. We'll know more after the car's been examined properly. If it turns out to have been caused by a problem with the car, then our job's finished. Thanks for your time."

They drove to the Infirmary, having been given permission to speak to Anne, who was no longer under sedation and was prepared to be interviewed by the police. They were shown to a side ward where three other patients were convalescing. They introduced themselves to the tearful woman.

"Anne, I'm sorry about your partner, but we have a job to do, which means we have to ask questions. Are you OK with this?"

"Yes."

"First, let me explain that as yet we don't know what caused the explosion. It could be down to a fault with the car. We won't know until Forensics have finished with it, but assuming it was no accident, can you think of anyone who might be responsible?"

There was a pause before she answered.

"No. He was liked by everyone, I think."

"You think? You mean, you're not sure?"

"Well. I don't know all his work colleagues, or other people he might mix with, through business. As far as I know, he's... he *was* a popular bloke."

"What about *your* friends? Did he get on with them?"

"Mostly, yes. Except my ex, maybe."

"Ex-boyfriend, or ex-husband?"

"Ex-husband."

"Go on."

"Well, he was upset when we broke up. And he went mad when he found out how old David was."

"How old is your ex-husband?"

"26."

"And may I ask, how old are you?"

"I'm 25. What's that got to do with it?"

"Just curious. Just wondering if your ex was jealous because you'd left him for a more mature man."

"No. I divorced Darren because he could be violent. He hit me more than once. He had mood swings."

"What did he do for a living?"

"Security."

"Before that?"

"He was in the army. He'd just been discharged when we met."

"Why was he discharged?"

"PTSD."

"Where was he serving?"

"Afghanistan."

"Do you know what happened to cause his PTSD?"

"He never said. He wouldn't talk about it."

"OK. One last question. Why did David divorce his first wife?"

"He told me she'd been unfaithful."

"That's odd. She told me that *he'd* been unfaithful."

"I don't think so. From what I've heard, she was a real slut."

Back in the car, Brian called Teresa.

"I need a favour, Teresa. I need the Army record for a man called Darren Mason. Aged 26. Served in Afghanistan. Discharged with PTSD. Soon as you can, please."

"OK. I'll get Ruth on it."

Ruth had the information ready by the time Brian returned to the office.

"He was discharged, all right, but not for having PTSD. He was court marshalled for brutally beating up an Afghan who was being questioned."

"OK, thanks, Ruth. By the way, just out of interest, which corps was he in."

"Royal Engineers."

"Thanks. That would make sense. It's quite likely that he learnt the skills regarding bomb disposal. I wonder if he learnt how to build a bomb as well. Can you dig a little deeper into his military training, please, Ruth?"

Brian walked over to the coffee machine, then changed his mind and went up to Teresa's desk.

"Any luck getting me an appointment at the mobile whorehouse yet?"

"Still waiting, Brian. I guess they're checking out the false ID I created for you."

"OK."

He returned to his desk to bring himself up to date with the work of the rest of the team. The case load was heavy. He decided to talk to Gardner about trying a different approach. He knocked on his office door.

******** 

He left Gardner's office with a smile on his face. He'd agreed to Brian's plan without hesitation. Gary would now take charge of all the cases except the abductions. Brian, along with Scoffer, and one of the female officers when required, would take the abductions. Re-allocating the cases made sense and the entire team were in favour as it allowed them to focus more on specific cases, with less multitasking. Scoffer was especially pleased; he enjoyed working with Brian and learnt a lot from working some complex cases.

The following morning, Teresa had the news Brian was waiting for.

"You've got your appointment, Brian. Saturday evening, 8.15 at Leeds Skelton Lake, M1 junction 45."
"That's handy. Just down the road. I'll talk to the NCA regarding backup."

He spent most of the morning in a Zoom meeting with Alex Sinclair and Chris Fox, planning for Saturday's operation. It was agreed that NCA would provide all the manpower and armed support, while Brian alone from CID would gain access and initiate the attack. He apologised to Scoffer.

"Sorry, but you're missing out on this one, Scoffer."
"Can't I just act as your driver? The experience will be good for me."
"My instructions are to come alone. But I suppose you could just happen to have called there in your own time, in your own car. As long as you don't show yourself until it's all over."
"It's a deal. I'll sit in a café in the Services. Call me when you're done."

Driving home at the end of the day, he called into the Ainsbury for a quick pint. He could happily have stayed for a few hours, but common sense prevailed for a change, and he took his leave after drinking only two pints. He knew how much was at stake on Saturday night and would not jeopardise its success for his love of alcohol. He called for a takeaway on the way home and intended to spend a quiet night in.

When he walked into his flat, however, there was an envelope on the mat. He picked it up and put it on the table until he'd finished his meal, and then opened it. Inside was a hand-written note and a printed copy of a photo. He read the note.

"He's been back today. First noticed him at 11.20. Still there at 2.30 but had gone next time I looked at 3.00. Took a couple of photos and printed the clearest for you. Hope it helps.
John Davidson."

He looked at the photo. It was much clearer than previous snaps. He scanned it on his desktop and sent it to Teresa along with a note.

"I need to know the identity of this man, ASAP."

********

He rose early, ate a light breakfast along with a mug of coffee and read his emails. After washing up, he checked the weather, put on a jacket and walked down to the canal towpath, crossing the swing bridge and turning right in the direction of Apperley Bridge. Walking briskly, he cleared his mind of all thoughts except the evening's task. It had to be successful. He would do everything in his power to make it so. And then perhaps he would celebrate.

Having reached the swing bridge at Apperley Road he crossed the canal and walked up to Leeds Road and from there, turned right towards Thackley. Thirty minutes later, he was back home for a second mug of coffee. His mind was clear. He knew exactly how he was expected to perform his role that evening. He would not fail.

He spent the afternoon in the flat relaxing, or at least trying to relax, but the prospect of the evening's action kept him on edge. He tried listening to some classical music on the radio, but the tranquillity he craved was shattered when Wagner's Ride of the Valkyries came on unannounced. He switched off the radio and checked his emails. There was a new one from Ruth. He didn't expect her to be working on a Saturday but approved of her dedication. The email title was 'Darren Mason: Military Training'. Eagerly, he opened it and read,

"Brian,

According to his army record, Mason never officially had any training in how to make a bomb during his time as a Sapper. That does not mean, of course, that he would not have been able to find do-it-yourself instructions on the Internet."

He replied with a brief 'thanks' and considered the prospect of yet another amateur bomber on the loose. He 'd already come across a few of them in his time. His deliberation was interrupted by another email which forced him to focus on the job in hand. Another young girl, fifteen years old, had gone missing and was believed to have been kidnapped at a bus stop on the Thorpe Edge estate. Lynn was on the case due to Brian's commitments.

At 6pm, Brian met officers from the NCA and Scoffer on a trading estate on the outskirts of Leeds. They gathered for a briefing to ensure everyone knew his own role and everyone else's. There was also a backup plan in case something unexpected happened. Before they set off for the eventual destination, each person in turn had to step forward and recite his role in the operation. Then, at 7.15pm, they began to move off, leaving a few minutes' gap between each vehicle so as not to raise unwanted attention. They kept in touch during the journey.

********

Since 6.30pm, a car containing two officers had been stationed at the Services, awaiting the arrival of the mobile brothel so that they could direct the assault force where to park so as not to attract undue attention. At 7.30pm they were getting worried that the target vehicle had not yet made an appearance. They informed the assault force.

"No sign of mobile yet, sir. They're cutting it fine."
"OK. Keep us informed."

There was still no sign of the mobile brothel at 7.50pm. Again, the assault force was informed, and slowed down their approach, arriving at the Services at 8.05pm, although they had been repeatedly informed there was still no sight of the mobile brothel. They parked up in their allocated areas and waited, then convened at 8.30pm for a quick meeting at which it was finally accepted the target vehicle would not be arriving.

"Either we've been rumbled, or they've had a breakdown. We have patrols on the motorway looking for them, and helicopter units scanning the area, but no joy. We'll give it another thirty minutes."

Brian cursed, then called Teresa who was monitoring the situation from Bradford HQ.

"Teresa, has there been any communication about tonight's session being cancelled?"
"No, Brian. Nothing. Do you want me to contact them to ask why? I could say you're livid having travelled all that way for nothing."
"Please. It can't do any harm."

She called back at nine.

"Sorry, Brian. Nobody's responded to my message."
"OK."

Brian informed Alex, the operation leader, who organised a check of all the CCTV images at the Services. There was no sign that any vehicle matching the description had ever arrived within the previous twelve hours. Alex then extended the search to include all motorway cameras until finally the vehicle was spotted on camera leaving the M62 at Junction 22, heading towards Saddleworth two hours earlier. Helicopters were despatched to the area immediately.

Eventually a vehicle was found abandoned and on fire at a wooded picnic site close to a reservoir and a patrol was despatched to the site. Shortly after their arrival, the vehicle was confirmed as the one they were seeking. The area was cordoned off as the emergency services were summoned to attend. Once the fire was extinguished, Forensics took over and found the charred remains of a body inside. Brian and Scoffer arrived just as the vehicle was being towed away for close inspection by Forensics. He approached the leader, showing his ID.

"What can you tell us at the moment?"
"It seems the fire was started deliberately, probably to destroy evidence of a murder. We found a body inside. The victim was shot in the back of the head at point blank range. That's all I can tell you for now."
"OK, thanks."

The night's operation ended there, with Brian and Scoffer driving back to Bradford in silence.

********

On Monday morning, the atmosphere in HQ was one of anger and disappointment. On arrival, Brian went straight to Teresa's desk.

"Any theories about what happened?"
"Same as you're thinking, probably. They were tipped off about the operation. Probably thought the person they shot was responsible for passing information to the police and destroyed all the evidence."
"Any luck getting in touch with them yet?"
"I've asked why you weren't informed your appointment had been cancelled but they're not answering. Their website's been removed."
"So, where do we go from here?"
"It's odds on they've got more than one mobile brothel in operation. We'll just have to find another."
"OK. I'm sure you'll do your best. Where's Ruth this morning?"
"She's covering admin. Rachel hasn't come to work. A friend rang in sick for her."
"I hope she's back soon. Ruth's been doing excellent work with you."
"She's very knowledgeable."

However, Rachel was not at work the next day. There was no answer when Teresa rang her mobile. She left a message for her to call to give an indication when she might return, but no message ever came. Teresa looked up her address; she had a flat in Little Germany, so Teresa and Ruth walked over at lunchtime and rang the doorbell but got no response. She reported back to Brian that afternoon.

"It's odd, Brian. No answer at her flat, and there's mail behind the door. I peeped through the letterbox."
"She must be really ill, or something's happened to her."
"She never indicated she was feeling ill before she got her friend to ring in for her."

Alarm bells were ringing for Brian.

"Did you get the name of her friend?"
"No. But it was a male. I've never heard her talk about a boyfriend."

"Brother?"

"Her personnel record says she's an only child. Parents live in Plymouth."

"Let's go over and get entry. I'll borrow a Ram in case nobody answers."

They walked to the flat, accompanied by Scoffer, who insisted on using the Ram, because he'd never had the opportunity to use one before. One blow was enough to snap the bolt. They stepped in, gingerly, looking around quietly. There was nobody there, but there were signs of a struggle, and some bloodstains on the kitchen floor. On the worktop was Rachel's mobile. Teresa switched it on and listened to her unanswered voicemail.

"There are two more voice messages on this, Brian, and a few text messages."

"Bring it with us. We'll see if anything is any use to us, then pass it to Forensics. I'll report her as missing."

Back at HQ, while Teresa wrote the reports, Brian asked Ruth how well she knew Rachel.

"Not that well, really. I mean we never saw each other socially outside work. We were just workmates. We got on OK."

"Did she know about the case you were working?"

"Well, yes. She asked how it was going. I think she was jealous that I was involved in it while she was just filing, and that."

"Did you tell her anything specific about it?"

"Well, no, not really. Just that we were trying to trap some mobile brothel-keepers."

"Did she ask how we planned to do it?"

"I might have mentioned we were planning a raid. I can't remember."

"Concentrate, please, Ruth. It's important. It might explain what's happened to her."

"Well, yes, I think I might have told her something big was planned for last Saturday."

"That's all I needed to know."

He sent Scoffer to interview Rachel's neighbours while he called Alex at the NCA and explained what he'd discovered.

"It seems she's done a runner, either that or she's joined the list of abductees."

"Let me know if you get anything from her neighbours. For now, I'll put her on the list of potential abductees."

Scoffer soon returned with unwelcome news.

"One of her neighbours heard raised voices from her flat on Saturday morning. He described it as a fight rather than an argument. Unfortunately, he's disabled. He says he tried to ring 999 but the phone line was dead. By the time he'd written an email to BT, everything was quiet. Apparently, BT came later in the afternoon and repaired some damage to the box. Sounds like someone had ripped the phone lines out."
"So, you think she's been abducted?"
"Yes. I think there's a high probability."

Brian went to pass the shocking news to his DCI, who was not at all pleased.

"Get her back, Brian. I don't care how you do it, just get her back."
"Yes, sir."

He called Teresa.

"Teresa, I want footage from every CCTV in the area of Little Germany for Saturday. All staff are to stop what they're working on and focus on this. And get Forensics to dust the flat for prints."

Back at his desk, he noticed an email from Forensics, with the word 'Fingerprints!' in the subject line. He opened it and read,

"Brian,
We found nothing of any use inside the shell of the burnt-out pantechnicon. However, outside, on the fuel filler cap, we managed to lift some fingerprints. They're being processed now. I'll let you know as soon as we identify the owner.
Allen."

# CHAPTER 10

Lynn was furious. She'd spent the best part of her week trying to find a girl whose mother had reported having been kidnapped. She'd interviewed all the neighbours; nobody had noticed anything unusual that afternoon. One even insisted she'd seen the girl get on the 645 bus towards Bradford centre, yet the girl's mother was adamant she'd been forced into a car which drove off at speed. Lynn decided to talk to the girl's father who lived with his new partner on the Ravenscliffe estate. To her surprise, when she knocked on the door, it was answered by the girl herself. She recovered her composure and asked the girl if she could come in and ask her a few questions.

"What about?"
"You've been reported missing."
"I bet I know who by."
"Who?"
"My mam."
"What makes you think that?"
"She doesn't like me coming to see my dad."
"Why not?"
"'Cos he was shagging Ellie while he still lived with us."
"Are you telling me she reported to the police that you'd been kidnapped, knowing that you were here?"
"Yes."
"Is your dad here? Can I talk to him?"

"Daaadddd," she screamed at the top of her voice. Soon, loud footprints could be heard coming down the stairs. Her dad entered the room, angry.

"I told you not to call me when I was busy!"

He noticed Lynn and turned to her.

"Who the hell are you?"
"DS Whitehead, from Bradford CID."
"What the hell do you want?"
"I'm investigating a report that your daughter was kidnapped."
"That's rubbish. She just came to see me."
"Did her mother know?"
"No idea. I don't care."
"Well, thanks for your time. I won't waste any more of mine."

Exasperated, she got in her car and drove across to Thorpe Edge, parking outside the girl's mother's house. She could hear loud music coming from inside, so hammered on the door. The girl's mother opened it, a can of beer in her hand.

"Mrs Revell, I've found your daughter."
"Well, where is she?"
"At her father's."
"I told her not to see him. She's always going to see him."
"So, you knew she was there?"
"I expected she would be."
"Did you think about ringing to ask if she was there?"
"I don't speak to him."
"So, you thought you'd waste police time when a phone call would have confirmed where she was."
"Well, it's your job."
"My job is to catch people who break the law and charge them accordingly. So, I'm going to do my job and charge you with wasting police time. Turn around, please, while I put the handcuffs on."

Lynn bundled her into the car and drove back to HQ, where Mrs Revell was duly charged before being allowed to go home. She was angry.

"Aren't you giving me a lift home?"
"That would be a waste of my time."
"But I haven't got any money."
"Ring your daughter. She might lend you some."

Returning to her desk, Lynn wondered how Bradford had ever managed to be selected as City of Culture when families like this existed on its estates. Shaking her head, she said to herself, 'there's more culture in a Greek Yogurt.'

********

Late on Wednesday afternoon, Brian received another email from the Forensics lab regarding the prints on the fuel filler cap.

"We've got a match, Brian. Tommy Denton. Career criminal. Small time stuff, mainly. Burglaries, theft, receiving, etc. Been out of prison for three months. Sending you the full record in attached file. Last known address included."

Brian opened the attachment and printed it, before calling Scoffer.

"Get your coat on, Scoffer. We're going to Queensbury."

There was no response at Tommy Denton's home. His neighbour told Brian she hadn't seen him in the last week or so, but that he'd had a female visitor the last time she saw him. Brian asked if she could describe her.

"She was young, tall, brunette. Long, straight hair. Very attractive."

Something clicked in Brian's mind. He took out his phone and searched the images stored on it.

"Is this the woman?"
"Yes. I'm sure it's her."
"Did they leave together?"
"Yes."
"Did she seem anxious? Worried?"
"Not at all. She was laughing."
"Thanks for your time."

As they walked away, Scoffer asked,

"Whose picture did you show her, boss?"
"Rachel's."
"What's going on? Is she undercover?"
"Not to my knowledge, Scoffer, but it's a possibility. Either that, or she's just an innocent girl caught up in it."
"Or she's part of it."
"Well, yes, it's a possibility. We'll look at all the angles."

********

Back at HQ, the first thing Brian did was call Alex at the NCA.

"I want a straight answer, Alex. Was Rachel Wells working undercover for you?"
"Absolutely not, Brian. What makes you think that?"
"She's been seeing Tommy Denton, whose prints we found on the burnt-out vehicle. And now she's gone missing."
"This has nothing to do with our investigation, Brian. However, if Denton was involved in the mobile brothel business, maybe she's got caught up in that."

"That's my thinking. It seems there was a struggle at her flat before she disappeared. Yet a week earlier a witness said she'd seen her laughing in Denton's company."
"We'll keep our eyes and ears open, Brian. I'll let you know if anything turns up."

He called a team meeting in the Conference Room.

"I've called you all together because Rachel has gone missing. She was last seen last Saturday morning. There are signs of a struggle at her flat and a neighbour says he heard a commotion at the time in question. More importantly, it appears she'd been seeing Tommy Denton, an ex-con, whose prints we found on the burnt-out mobile brothel. My feeling is that she's got innocently caught up in criminal activity. I think she's been abducted and could be forced into prostitution. We need to find her."

After the meeting adjourned, Teresa reported that CCTV had images of Rachel being forced into a van in the car park near her flat. Her abductor could not be recognised. The car's plates were not visible. Worse news followed shortly afterwards, when a call from Forensics confirmed the corpse found in the burnt-out mobile brothel was that of Tommy Denton.

However, the mood lightened later in the day when Teresa announced she'd created a new identity on the Dark Website used to advertise the mobile brothels, it had been authorised, and she'd booked an appointment for Brian and his 'son-in-law' for a night of pleasure at the M6 Services at Burton-in-Kendal. They started planning immediately.

********

There was further good news when Brian took a phone call from the NCA the next morning.

"Brian, it's Chris Fox. We may have made a breakthrough, thanks to forensic investigation."
"Tell me more."
"The burnt-out vehicle had had its number plates removed prior to being set alight, so that we couldn't trace its owner. But what they didn't do, and I'll never know why, is remove the VIN – the Vehicle Identification Number – from the chassis."
"They left the VIN? What a load of numpties!"

"Precisely. We checked the DVLA database and got the name and address of the registered owner."

"I take it you're mounting an operation to arrest him."

"Yes. Just asking out of courtesy if you'd like to join us."

"Have we got the manpower to do it at the same time as the raid we're planning on the mobile brothel?"

"Yes. We'll draft people in from other areas. The only problem is it's a long way from home for you."

"Where?"

"Belgrave Square, London. He's a Russian oil millionaire, and a part owner of a football club. Andrei Kuznetsov."

"I'd better sit that one out. I'll be busy raiding one of his businesses up north."

"OK. We'll keep you informed of our operational plans. I'll send it through to Teresa."

Brian passed the news on to DCI Gardner, who authorised the planned raid and helped recruit the manpower from other areas. It was late in the evening before any of the team left the building.

Brian felt exhausted but resisted the temptations of the pubs he drove past, instead calling for a takeaway to eat at home, washed down with a couple of glasses of malt.

The week passed quickly. Brian made sure that every member of the team put together for Saturday's operation knew his role before they made their way up the M6 towards the services, arriving and parking as arranged, and waiting for the operation to commence. A message reached Brian and Scoffer, who were still on the M6, to inform them that the target vehicle had opened for business, and everything was going as planned. They were only minutes away.

"Ready for this, Scoffer?"

"Yes, sir. And don't forget to call me Joe. I'm your son-in-law, remember?"

"I remember."

They pulled into the Services, parking out of sight of the mobile brothel. Brian checked all the personnel were ready before he and Scoffer got out of the car and walked quickly towards the brothel, laughing and seemingly in high spirits as Brian knocked on the rear door. It was opened by a huge shaven-headed man. With a smile on his face, Brian introduced himself and Scoffer while the man checked his bookings, before allowing them entry into a small anteroom.

"Wait here."

They sat silently; aware they were probably being watched. They had both noticed the covert cameras trained on them. A few minutes later they were greeted by another man.

"Come, your pleasure awaits."

They followed him down a corridor on one side of which were numbered doors. They could hear noises from within the rooms but chose to ignore them. They stopped outside Room 6, where the man said,

"This is yours. Enjoy. You have half an hour."

He unlocked the door and let them in, closing it behind them. A young girl sat on a bed in the corner, a frightened look on her face. Brian guessed her age at about sixteen, maybe seventeen. He looked round the room, noting the cameras suspended from the ceiling, before turning his attention to the girl, and whispering in her ear.

"Do you speak English?"

She nodded.

"Then please stay calm. We're here to help you. Just act as you would with other visitors. We won't hurt you. I'm going to ask you some questions. I'm going to whisper them in your ear so they can't be picked up outside the room. I know they're watching and listening. OK?"

She nodded.

"How many girls are here tonight?"
"Six. One for each room."
"How many guards are there?"
"Two. One on the door. One watching the monitor."
"OK. We're going to bring the troops in. Just be calm and stay here while we start the action. OK?"

Again, she nodded as Brian opened the door and shouted down the corridor whilst Scoffer texted furiously.

"Hey! We need some help here."

The shaven-headed man appeared at the end of the corridor.

"What's the problem?"
"Your girl won't cooperate. She wants more money."
"I'll give her a slap. Then she'll do whatever you want."

The second he walked into the room, Scoffer, waiting behind the door, got him in a chokehold, having already activated the 'Go' signal, causing the back-up team to race towards the vehicle. As the man struggled, Brian punched him twice in the stomach, taking away his energy long enough for Scoffer to slap the handcuffs on his wrists. At the same time, the rear door was smashed in, and the support team flooded the corridor, some of them running to the front, forcing open the door to the control room and overpowering the other member of staff. The rest of the assault team forced open the doors of the other five bedrooms, rounding up the customers, and escorting the working girls to nearby ambulances where they were quickly checked before being whisked away to safety.

The assault team went en masse into the Travelodge bar for a quick impromptu celebration before getting back into their vehicles and returning to base. Brian and Scoffer followed the ambulances to Lancaster Hospital where the girls were accommodated until cleared to go home. Most of them were traumatised from their ordeal, having been snatched off the streets and forced into the sex trade; they were sedated and allowed rest in guarded rooms while Brian and Scoffer interviewed those who were considered able and willing to talk. Each had a similar story of being forcibly abducted, sometimes with a friend, but separated immediately and forced to work. None of the girls had ever seen Rachel.

Brian and Scoffer crashed out in the Staff Room, grabbing a few hours of sleep before driving home. They had a list of the names of all the girls they'd rescued, and another list of their friends from whom they'd been parted, and who were still missing. There were still fifteen girls unaccounted for. As they slept, armed police smashed their way into the home of Andrei Kuznetsov, arrested him and searched the house, removing piles of documents, along with his laptop and mobile phone.

After a quick breakfast, Brian drove back with Scoffer to HQ to be greeted by a round of applause for their part in the successful operation. DCI Gardner invited them into his office.

"First of all, I'd like to congratulate you both for your part in this operation. Chris from the NCA told me this morning that they have already begun raiding the homes of other members of the criminal enterprise, in conjunction with CID officers from different areas. So far, forty-seven girls, including most of those from the Bradford area, have been released from their imprisonment and forced labour, as it were. Alex at the NCA has sent his thanks to you and the rest of the team, and you can rest assured that this operation will soon feature on our Hall of Fame."

"Thank you, sir. But it wasn't a total success. We didn't find Rachel Wells."

"Would you please leave us, DC Schofield. I'd like a word with DI Peters."

Five minutes later, Brian left the DCI's office with a huge smile on his face. He was now officially back full-time leading the team and all his recent 'aberrations' had been removed from his record. He was back! However, he still wanted desperately to find Rachel.

Rachel's absence apart, Brian's spirits were still high when he drove home at the end of the day. He didn't feel the need to stop anywhere for a drink; he just wanted to go home, make a meal and relax. For the first time in ages, he felt positive. He would be OK.

He parked in his allocated space and got out of the car, locking the door before turning towards the entrance to the flats. As he did, he suddenly heard an angry roar and the sound of footsteps fast approaching. He turned just in time to see someone charging at him with a machete in his raised hand. Quickly, he shifted his weight and moved sideways and back, raising his arm to attempt to deflect the blow. The searing pain in his upper arm told him his action had been only a partial success. The blow had missed his head and caught him just below the left shoulder. The rush of adrenalin helped him deal with the pain and he swung a punch with his right fist, catching his assailant on the left cheek and knocking him backwards, allowing Brian precious seconds to think. He looked quickly around. Running away was not an option. His upper arm was painful, and blood was seeping through his coat, dripping off his fingers. One of the residents had left a gardening spade at the side of the door. He grabbed it and raised it in both hands, just in time to ward off another blow from the machete. As it struck the shaft of the spade, he turned his body quickly to the right, so his assailant was caught temporarily off-balance. Brian reacted quickly, freeing the spade, and swinging it hard into his assailant's face, knocking him to the ground, the machete falling from his hand. But he wasn't finished. He rose slowly, picking up the machete and preparing to attack again. Brian was beginning to feel his strength draining as he fought against the pain from his wound. He was almost spent, raising the spade once more in a desperate attempt to ward off the next imminent blow.

He never saw the officers running towards them. All he was aware of was his assailant screaming and falling to the ground as the Taser was applied to the back of his neck. At that point, Brian lost consciousness.

********

He woke to find a familiar face at his bedside. He turned to look at his surroundings and felt the wave of pain from his left upper arm. He gasped.

"Lie still, Brian. You'll be OK."
"I don't feel it, Teresa."
"Do you remember what happened?"
"I'd just got home and got out of the car when someone attacked me. With a machete, I think."
"That's right. Luckily, one of your neighbours saw your attacker hiding in the bushes with the machete and called the police. An armed unit was on its way before he actually attacked you. You owe him your life, Brian."
"I think I know who it might have been. I'll thank him as soon as they let me out."
"Expect to stay for a couple more days. Your arm's not broken but it's a nasty wound. Give it time and it'll heal."
"What about the attacker?"
"My fault, Brian, I'm sorry to say. He's the man you asked me to try to identify from a photo. He's been watching you for a while, but I hadn't been able to match the photo with any records. The image just wasn't clear enough."
"Do we know who he is now?"
"Yes. He has a criminal record, and, it seems, a grudge against you. We don't know why at the moment, but it shouldn't take long. He's in a secure hospital for now. You broke his jaw."
"Good. He deserved it."
"Get some rest, Brian. There'll be someone coming to interview you this afternoon."

\*\*\*\*\*\*\*\*

He was surprised when he saw her walking down the ward. Helen Moore, a reporter with the Telegraph and Argus, had been given permission to interview him.

"Good afternoon, DI Peters. How are you?"
"I'm fine, Helen, apart from having a slight wound to my arm where some lunatic tried to saw it off. And you don't need to address me as DI at the moment. As you can see, I'm not in uniform, or on duty."
"OK, Brian. What can you tell me about the attack?"
"Not a great deal. It happened so fast. It was a matter of survival."
"Did you know your attacker?"
"He'd been seen skulking in the bushes near where I live a few times recently. A neighbour said he'd been watching me. The neighbour actually took a photo of him, but it wasn't very clear, and we were still trying to identify him when he attacked me. I'd like to make a point of thanking my neighbour. He saved my life by calling the police when he realised I was in danger."
"Can I have his name, please?"
"John Davidson. Please don't bother him without asking me first. He likes to keep himself to himself. In fact, please don't print his name without his express permission."
"OK. If my editor asks for details, I'll come and ask you first."
"Thank you."
"So, you've no idea what grudge your attacker had against you?"
"All I know at the moment, is that he had a criminal record, so it's possible our paths have crossed in the past. I should find out soon enough, and you'll be the first to know."
"Well, thank you. Is it OK if we run the story with the information we have, and follow it later when all the facts are available?"
"That's fine."
"So, what about the future? How long before you expect to be back at work?"
"I've no idea. I've got plenty time to consider my options while I'm lying here."
"You might take early retirement?"
"It's worth considering, before any other body parts get hacked at."
"Well, I personally would like to see you back at work. You don't always accommodate the press, but you never bullshit us."
"I'll take that as a compliment. Anyway, if you'd like to hold the story, I'm sure we'll get to know the full facts in the next couple of days."

"I'll see what my editor says."

"OK. In the meantime, I promise not to speak to anyone else from the press."

"Thank you. I appreciate the scoop."

"You deserve it. As soon as I have some more information, I'll call you."

"Thanks, Brian. I'd better go. You take care."

"I will."

# CHAPTER 11

A call came from Teresa later that afternoon.

"Brian, we've identified your attacker."
"Go on."
"Remember when you first joined us in CID, you had a case where a couple of kids were nicking cars and writing them off before quickly graduating to become major drug dealers?"
"Yes. I remember the case. I can't remember their names. Remind me."
"Darren and Andy Fisher."
"Ah, yes. Funny thing is, it was one of their victims of car theft who came to see me a while ago. He had relatives in Ukraine who sought refuge over here. Two teenage girls and their mother disappeared in transit, which started the whole investigation into the abduction of young females for prostitution. So, what about the Fishers?"
"It was their father, Stuart Fisher, who attacked you. Apparently, he held you responsible for their deaths."
"Well, let's not disappoint him. He's going away for a very long time. I wouldn't want him released to start stalking the person who was really responsible."
"You know who it is?"
"Yes. But, officially, no. Officially, they died when a car they'd stolen hit a tree and burst into flames."
"I understand. I won't say anything."

After Teresa had left, he called Helen Moore.

"Helen, I've some more details for your story."
"Great! Fire away!"
"I was attacked by a man called Stuart Fisher. He was released a while ago from Hewell Prison after serving a long sentence for armed robbery. However, that was before my time. I had nothing to do with that. Where I *did* become involved was a few years ago when his kids, Darren and Andy, were prolific car thieves, joyriders and drug dealers. The net was tightening on them when they nicked a car and drove it into a tree. They were both under the influence of drugs, and were not being chased at the time, so I had no real involvement, nor any direct responsibility for their deaths, other than the fact I was investigating the crimes they committed. Somewhere along the line, with his warped logic, Stuart Fisher had come to the conclusion that I caused their deaths. End of story."

"Oh, That's all a bit anti-climactic. I'd imagined a tale of revenge."
"In his mind, that's what it was. But it wasn't my fault. I had nothing to do with their deaths. I have to say, though, off the record, I wasn't sorry to hear they'd met such a violent end."
"Of course. Well, thank you, Brian. I'll report it so there's no blame attached to you or any of your colleagues. Just the product of a warped criminal mind."
"Thank you, Helen. 'Bye."

Left alone, with only the regular visits of doctors and nurses checking his vital signs, he began to think about his future. Did he really want to continue in this line of work with all the dangers it brought? If not, what would he do instead? He had plenty to think about and plenty time to think about it.

********

A week later, having been released from hospital but not yet cleared to drive or return to active duty, he patiently awaited his grocery delivery. When it arrived, he removed the item he'd ordered specially and walked along the corridor to Mr Davidson's flat. When Mr Davidson opened the door, Brian handed him a bottle of Speyside Malt whisky.

"What's this for?"
"To say thank you for calling the police when you did. You saved my life."
"Anyone would have done it."
"Maybe so, but I'd like to give you this for acting when you did. I asked a neighbour. She said you like the odd glass of malt."
"Well, thank you, Mr Peters. I do appreciate it."
"You're welcome."

The following day, he was on an early train to Birmingham New Street Station from where he had booked a ticket to Redditch. He was able to relax for a few hours and think about his appointment. He took out his notes and read through them for the umpteenth time. He wanted to make his point very clearly.

From Redditch, he took a taxi to his ultimate destination, HM Prison Hewell, where he had an appointment with Stuart Fisher who was back there on remand. He signed in and was shown to a small room containing a table and two chairs on opposite sides and a large mirror on the long wall. On the other side of the 'mirror', were two prison officers, watching and listening to the conversation about to take place. Five minutes later, the prisoner was brought in and seated. Arms folded, he glared silently at Brian.

"Good morning, Mr Fisher. How are they treating you?"
"Like shit. Get to the point. What do you want?"
"How's your jaw?"
"Healed. How's your arm?"
"Healed."

They stared at each other in silence until Brian spoke.

"I wanted to set the record straight, Mr Fisher. I want to tell you what really happened to your sons."
"Let's hear it then."
"Since your steadying influence was not available to them as they grew up, since you were in prison most of the time, they were wild kids. They took to stealing cars and joyriding before wrecking the cars and dumping them. They were responsible for many incidents of this type. As they grew older, and more ambitious, they started dealing drugs and carrying guns. They mixed with some nasty types, eventually employing a driver so they could distribute drugs more efficiently. Unfortunately, the driver turned out to be one of their previous victims. They'd stolen and written off his car some months earlier. On their final night on earth, the three of them were celebrating a large deal, when, discovering their driver was a previous victim of their car thefts, they tried to kill him. He managed to get out of the car before your son Andy, who was now driving, lost control and drove it into a tree. The car exploded and killed both your sons. They killed themselves, Mr Fisher. Nobody killed them. They were totally responsible for their own deaths. Is that clear?"
"I don't believe you! You, and people like you, hounded them to their death."
"They were high on drugs when they died. They have to take responsibility for what happened. Andy was in no fit state to be driving. He didn't even have a licence! Like their father, they were criminals, and nobody but them can be held responsible for their deaths. Now, tell me why you've been hounding me."
"I was told you were in charge of the case against them. You had it in for them."
"You're right. I was in charge of the case. But I never wanted them to die. I would have preferred that they were locked away in a cell for years, so they couldn't make anyone else's life a misery. Make no mistake, I'm not sorry they died, but I didn't kill them, or hound

them to their deaths as you seem to believe. Anyway, you're due to appear in court soon. And you'll find yourself serving another long sentence. You deserve it. And when you eventually get out, I hope you'll find some useful way of spending the rest of your life rather than trying to pin the blame on someone else for the death of your children, which was actually caused by their intake of drugs, coupled with their innate stupidity. Think about it. This discussion is over."

"It isn't. When I get out, I'll come looking for you again."

"I'll be ready. But take my advice and watch your back while you're here. There are a few inmates here who owe me a favour."

"I can look after myself."

"Pity that's a trait that didn't rub off on your kids."

Brian rose from his chair and knocked on the door to be let out. Back at Reception, he signed out and got into a waiting taxi. He knew that his discussion with Mr Fisher would not influence the man's opinion on the death of his sons in any way, but he was happy to shoulder the blame if it meant he kept Terry Stanton's name out of it.

He spent the return train journey thinking carefully about his future. He had no doubt Stuart Fisher would come looking for him again after his eventual release, but he didn't care. He would deal with it when it happened.

His taxi from Apperley Bridge Station dropped him off at Thackley Corner. It was early evening and he'd eaten nothing apart from a sandwich at lunchtime. No matter. He would order a takeaway after first nipping into the Black Rat for a quick pint. Two hours later he was still there, sitting quietly, drinking his fifth pint while occasionally chatting with Alyson behind the bar.

His phone buzzed. A message from Teresa.

"How did it go? Are you OK? Shall I come over?"

He replied, tersely.

"I'm fine. Speak to you tomorrow."

He was in no mood for company. He finished his drink and left as rain started to fall.

********

118

A week later he returned to work, speaking to his staff one at a time to get their views on the progress of the current cases before leaving them to continue their work while he attempted to catch up with his backlog of reports. He despised paperwork and couldn't wait to be back out in the field, doing what he enjoyed, what he was good at. But for now, he was still confined to the office, like it or not. His shoulder injury was slow to heal and prevented him from driving and therefore a minimum of field work. Administrative tasks bored him. The fact that Rachel was still missing preyed on his mind. He decided to talk to Teresa about her.

"Is there any way of finding her on the Dark Web?"
"I can try. If you believe she's been abducted and caught up in the prostitution racket, she might possibly have an online presence. She's a very attractive woman."
"You mean she might be in some business's shop window?"
"Possibly. Let me have a look."
"Thanks. Why haven't we done this weeks ago, Teresa?"
"Nobody mentioned it, Brian. Things don't work the same here without you."

He returned to his desk and looked back through the report on Rachel's disappearance. He couldn't understand why it hadn't been followed up. Finding her would now take priority over all other cases. He called his team together.

"I want to know why nobody has been following up on Rachel's disappearance. She's one of ours, for Christ's sake."
"It's never been assigned to us, boss. We understood abductions were your case. And we've had our hands full with other business."
"Well, from now, it's top of everybody's list. I want her found!"

It took two days of trawling through the Dark Web, but eventually Teresa found a mention of Rachel in an obscure chatroom. She called Brian immediately.

"Here it is. Just a thread of the conversation where these perverts are bidding for a half-hour with Rachel."

He looked at the screen, noting the price list on the left-hand side, and the rising bids being entered and rapidly updated on the right.

"Get me into the bidding, Teresa."
"OK. I'll call you when it's done."

The thought of what Rachel must be going through made him feel sick, but he returned to his desk to attempt to concentrate on other duties. However, he couldn't get Rachel's plight out of his head. She *was* his responsibility. He went back upstairs.

"Teresa, is there anything I can do to help?"
"Not really, Brian. The bidding had closed by the time I got on. Unless you want to look though some online, real-time porn."
"Not really."
"OK. What if I run it though some facial recognition software? All you have to do, is start the video, and wait for a hit. If you get one, you'll hear a 'ping', so stop the video and watch it. If not, just load the next one."
"OK."
"The software's loaded on the PC over there. Just press start."

He did as she'd instructed, loading video after video. Then, suddenly, he heard a 'ping'. He reached over and stopped the video, then restarted it from the beginning and watched, closely. After a few minutes, a tall, willowy figure appeared on screen and began to undress. As she turned to face the camera, Brian recognised her. It was Rachel, without a doubt. He stopped the video.

"She's here, Teresa. It's her. It's definitely her."
"OK. I'll take over. I need to isolate it and find out where it's been uploaded from."
"You can do that?"
"It depends. But I'll give it a go. Get yourself a coffee while I load some software."

He stood next to the vending machine in the corridor, looking at the selection on offer. In the end, he bought nothing. He just stood there, killing time, waiting for Teresa to call him back. Eventually, his phone buzzed. He raced back to her desk.

"Any luck?"
"Yep. There's a marker on any software, indicating its digital origin. It's just a matter of finding it, and then converting it into a physical location. I'm running a program that should do that for us. Just take a few more minutes."

Brian was impatient, but eventually, some code began to appear on the screen.

"Here we go. Just change it into legible English."

She typed in a command and soon an IP address appeared.

"We're in luck. That's a real IP address, not disguised by VPN. Here we go. Just let me look it up."

Again, she typed a string of characters and pressed 'enter', then sat back, waiting.

"There we are. Just let me phone the Internet provider to confirm and get the user's real name. Then you can go and arrest him."

He waited anxiously while Teresa made the call. After some hesitation from the Call Centre operator, she was put through to the manager, who sought permission from *his* manager before providing the user's name and address. Brian immediately snatched up the piece of paper she'd written it on and ran down the stairs to the office. Scoffer and Ruth were the only ones currently at their desks. He called them.

"Come on, you two. We're going to look for Rachel."

He filled them in with the background details while Scoffer drove. He called for armed backup but when informed there would be a delay carried on regardless. They pulled up in the car park of a unit on an industrial estate in Cleckheaton. Ruth was nervous.

"Shouldn't we wait for backup, boss"
"If you prefer, Ruth, stay by the car. If you hear any noise from inside the building, like gunshots, call for urgent backup. OK?"
"Yes."
"What about you, Scoffer? Do you want to wait for backup?"
"I'm with you, boss. Where you go, I'm at your side."
"Come on then."

They walked through the front door into a small Reception where a young woman sat behind a desk reading a magazine. Brian decided to brazen it out.

"Hi, we've just been talking to your boss about a girl. He told us to come here, and you'd let us straight in. Just through here, is it?"

The receptionist was caught off-guard and merely nodded her assent. Smiling, Brian and Scoffer walked through the door into a short corridor at the end of which was another door with a glass

121

pane. They looked through. On the other side was a warehouse, with a film set built in. They could see two men talking, by the side of a video camera on a stand.

"Ready, Scoffer? This could get rough."
"Let's do it."

They walked in, smiling as they approached the pair.

"Which one of you is the boss?"
"I am. What are you doing in here? Who gave you permission?"
"Your boss. He said you had a woman we might be interested in if the price was right. Well, we're here to negotiate. We'll pay top price, if she's anything like she appears on film."
"Which one is she?"
"Tall, sexy. Classy. Called Rachel."
"Yeah, she's here."
"Well, bring her in. I want to see her in real life. Then we'll agree a price."

The two men conferred, whispering, before one left the room, returning shortly with Rachel, her hands bound behind her back. Brian walked towards her and gave the impression he was sizing her up, while Scoffer, out of their direct line of sight, was busy texting Ruth.

"Get armed backup. Immediate. She's here."

Rachel showed no visible sign of recognising her co-workers. She was drugged. In a stupor.

Scoffer stepped forward to pronounce the coded words which would tell Brian that assistance was on its way.

"Do you want me to get the money from the car, boss?"
"Not until we agree a price, Harry."

The word 'Harry' indicated that Brian wanted to play for time until backup arrived.

"Have you any other girls we might be interested in?"
"A few, but they're not here. We only bring 'em here for filming."
"Pity. If they're as sexy as this one, we'll pay whatever you ask. So, what's the price?"
"I'll have to ring the boss."

"OK. Go ahead. Get him down here if he wants to negotiate face to face."

"He won't do that."

"Why not?

"He's in Italy."

"Can we talk on Zoom?"

"If he agrees."

"Ask."

Brian was simply stalling until backup arrived. He had no idea how many others there were at this facility. He was counting every second. Scoffer too was visibly nervous.

Seconds later they heard a rumpus in Reception and the door opened as a squad of armed and armoured police swarmed through, surrounding the two men. Brian immediately put his hand gently on Rachel's arm.

"Rachel, do you remember me? Brian. Brian Peters, from Bradford CID. Do you remember working there?"

She looked at him, puzzled, and shook her head slowly.

"I don't think so. I don't know."

"Do you remember your friend, Ruth? You worked together."

"I... I don't know."

"OK, Rachel. Don't worry. We're taking you somewhere safe where they can make you well again. We'll look after you, Rachel. I promise. Everything will be OK."

The ambulance soon arrived, and Ruth got in alongside Rachel, who showed a glimmer of recognition as Ruth gave her a hug before it raced away. Brian called Allen Greaves.

"Allen. Get your team over to Cleckheaton quickly. I'll send you directions to a unit on the industrial estate where some serious criminal activity has been taking place."

While they waited, Brian, Scoffer and two armed officers inspected the rest of the premises. They found three more scantily dressed young women locked in a room, along with a large quantity of obscene DVDs among other extremely pornographic media. The women were taken to hospital for examination. Brian and Scoffer remained until the forensic staff had gathered all the evidence available before returning to HQ. Teresa, not surprisingly, was still on duty. Brian went directly to her desk, updated her on what had taken place and thanked her profusely for enabling Rachel's rescue. Before leaving, he ensured the two men arrested at the warehouse were booked in for interviews in the morning. Unusually, he went straight home, without calling at a single pub. He was exhausted, physically and mentally, and slept like a baby.

# CHAPTER 12

Brian was at work early even though he'd arrived by taxi. He'd slept well and was prepared for a couple of gruelling sessions in the Interview Room.

Along with Scoffer, he waited for the first interviewee, who was obviously of low rank in the hierarchy, to be brought in with his legal representative. They arrived on time. Brian couldn't wait, briefly introducing himself and Scoffer before commencing the interrogation.

"Please confirm your full name."

"Anthony McAuley."

"In what capacity were you in the warehouse when we turned up yesterday."

"I was there to shoot some promotional videos."

"What sort of 'promotional' videos?"

"Porn, as you well know."

"Who was the star of the video?"

"A woman called Rachel."

"Was she a willing subject?"

"I don't know. I just do as I'm asked."

"In your opinion, was she a willing subject?"

"I suppose not."

"Because she'd been drugged?"

"Probably. I had nothing to do with that. I just operated the recording equipment."

"So, you willingly filmed a half-naked doped woman?"

"That's what I was getting paid for."

"And how many of these videos have you made?"

"I don't know. Probably dozens."

"All the women were doped?"

"They acted as if they were doped. I can't say for certain. I didn't dope them."

"Who did?"

"Philip Carter."

"The man we arrested with you?"

"Yes."

"He was your boss?"

"Yes."

"And who was *his* boss?"

"I don't know. You'll have to ask him."

"Do you do any other work, either for Carter, or anyone else?"

"Some freelance photography."
"Porn?"
"Occasionally. It's not illegal."
"Drugging girls and filming them being abused is."

He let the silence hang in the air for a full minute before continuing. He opened his file and took out some photos.

"I'm going to show you some photos. I want you to tell me if you've ever seen any of them before. OK?"
"Go on."

He showed them one at a time without provoking a response from McAuley, until he came to one of the girls who'd disappeared after getting into a taxi with her sister. At that point he spoke.

"I've seen this one."
"At the warehouse?"
"Yes. She was there to do a promotional video."
"Drugged?"
"Yes."
"What about this one?"

Brian showed him the photo of the girl's sister.

"Yes. She was here too. They were co-stars in a video."
"Do you know what happened to them after they left there?"
"No."
"Who took them away?"
"Their boss."
"What's his name?"
"I don't know."

Brian turned to another section of his folder and rotated it so that the three photos on it were fully visible to McAuley.

"Do you recognise any of these?"
"Yes. This one. He took the two girls away with him."
"You sure?"
"Absolutely."

Brian was elated and spoke clearly and calmly.

"For the benefit of all who watch or listen to this recording, let it be clear that Mr McAuley has identified a career criminal who has used a number of aliases over the years, the most recent being Lenny Berkeley. His whereabouts are currently unknown. He is now our prime suspect."

He turned back to McAuley.

"Any idea where we might find him?"
"He mentioned he had a brothel in Edinburgh."
"Interview concluded. For now."

Brian raced up the stairs to Teresa's desk.

"Top priority, Teresa. I need this man identifying and I want to know his whereabouts. Last known as Lenny Berkeley and had a brothel in Edinburgh."
"I'm on it."
"Where's Ruth today?"
"At hospital, visiting Rachel."
"OK."

Ruth returned after lunch and went straight to Brian's desk.

"Just thought I'd let you know, boss. Rachel's responding well to treatment. She's quite lucid most of the time now, but she still can't clearly remember what happened. At least she knows who she is and what she did for a living. The doctors reckon her memory will improve along with her general health as soon as the drugs are out of her system."
"Thanks Ruth. Anything happening with the car-bomber?"
"I'm chasing up some of his colleagues who served in the army with him. I'm hoping they'll give me the answer as to whether he learnt any bomb-making skills there."
"OK. Stay on it and keep me posted."
"Will do."

Ruth spent a fruitless afternoon on the telephone to a few of Darren Mason's ex-army colleagues. The consensus of opinion was that he was well-liked, but none of them had stayed in touch with him after his discharge. As one ex-colleague explained,

"He changed in Afghanistan. He had mood swings. He threatened violence sometimes, especially when he'd had a drink. He could be silent and unreachable. He was discharged with a diagnosis of PTSD and just withdrew. He didn't answer any calls. He didn't want anything which reminded him of his time in Afghanistan."

"Did he ever commit violence against anybody to your knowledge?"

"He *threatened*, but I don't believe he ever committed any violence against anybody. He was all talk."

"My information is that he was court-marshalled for beating up an Afghan being questioned."

"That was a trumped-up charge. They needed a scapegoat. The prisoner's wounds were inflicted by another prisoner."

"Was he a heavy drinker?

"We all were. It was the environment we were in."

"Did he make any enemies in particular?"

"No. I don't think so. We were all in it together. We watched each other's back."

Ruth looked through her notes concerning Darren Mason. He had PTSD, was a heavy drinker, and had mood swings. Wrongly court-marshalled? She wondered if he'd taken his temper out on someone by bombing his car. His army experience had changed him, but somehow, she didn't believe he was responsible for Sutcliffe's death. She decided to speak to Sutcliffe's boss and his co-workers and made an appointment for the following morning with the manager who spoke of Sutcliffe in glowing terms.

"I have nothing bad to say about David. He has worked here for years. He was well-liked and respected by all the staff, and all his clients. We were devastated to hear he'd been killed."

"Are you saying he had no enemies? It seems that everyone regards him as some sort of angel. He must have crossed swords with someone, sometime."

"All I'm saying is he was universally liked and respected here. In all his time here, I can honestly say I don't think anybody would have a bad word to say about him."

"Do you mind if I talk to the rest of the staff?"

"Go ahead."

The feedback she got from members of staff were as she'd expected. Well-liked, respected, easy to get on with. It all seemed too good to be true. She doubted anybody could be such an angel, and eventually her doubts were justified when she spoke to a woman, Julie, a part-time receptionist, who had a different point of view.

"I had a brief affair with him quite a few years ago. Please don't make this public. None of the staff here knows anything about it.

And I don't want to speak ill of the dead, but he was no angel. Yes, he was well-liked and respected, but he kept a dark secret. He was a heavy gambler. That's why I broke up with him. I had to lend him money once, to pay off a debt."

"How much was it for?"

"£1000. I got it back straightaway as soon as our monthly salary was paid, but he asked me again the month after and I refused. He wasn't happy and we stopped going out together after that."

"Did he get the money somewhere else?"

"He must have done. He was really on edge for a day or two and then he suddenly calmed down."

"Did he learn his lesson and stop gambling after that?"

"No. But he must have had a long winning streak, because he seemed to be perpetually in a good mood. Then occasionally, he must have had a losing streak."

"Did he tell you that?"

"No. I could tell by his demeanour. He would bite his nails. He never did that when he was winning."

"Do you know where he did his gambling?"

"He used the internet, but once I saw him coming out of the betting shop down by the traffic lights. He didn't see me, but he had a big smile on his face so I guess he must have won."

"Thanks for your time."

After checking with the hospital and finding that Anne had been discharged, she drove directly to Sutcliffe's home for a quick chat.

"How are you feeling, Anne?"

"A little better, thank you."

"Are you up to answering a few more questions?"

"If it helps you find out who is responsible for David's death, then, yes."

"I've been informed that David was a gambler. Do you know anything about that?"

"Oh, I wouldn't call him a gambler. He played the stock market. Bought and sold shares. He seemed to do quite well, normally."

"What do you mean by *normally*?"

There was a pause while Anne thought about her answer. Eventually, she conceded.

"Well, occasionally he'd make a small loss. I don't think it was a huge problem, though. I mean it only happened a couple of times."

"What happened?"

"He came home once. He was agitated. Eventually, he told me his shares had dropped and he needed money quickly. I don't understand all this, but he insisted it was just a blip. He could pay it off and everything would be OK."

"So, what happened?"

"He pawned some jewellery to pay it off, then everything was back to normal."

"You said it happened a couple of times."

"Well, yes. A few months later. Apparently, the stock market had bombed. He said everything was fine, he just needed a quick loan to get things back to normal."

"So, did you give him money?"

"Some, yes. But he said he needed more. I didn't have any more. I'd emptied my Building Society account. My savings."

"So, what happened?"

"The next day, he was all happy again. He said he'd got a loan from his bank and fixed it and the market was back to normal and to prove it, he'd bought me a beautiful necklace. It must have cost at least a thousand pounds."

"How lovely! Could I see it, please?"

"He had to take it back to the jewellers the day before he died. He told me he'd been admiring it and dropped it and the clasp broke. He took it back to have it fixed."

"Do you know which jewellers?"

"Samuels, in the Broadway Centre, I think. That's where he said he'd got it from. Gold and diamond, it was."

"Thanks for your time. By the way, who does he bank with?"

"Barclays."

"Thank you. I'll see myself out."

She drove back to town, parked up and called at Barclays. The manager, after being convinced his cooperation was essential in a murder trial, confirmed that Mr Sutcliffe had not been granted a loan, and had in fact been turned down for one. Satisfied, she confirmed her theory by calling across the road at Samuels, where she was informed that the necklace had indeed been bought by Mr Sutcliffe on his Barclaycard but had not been returned for repair.

Ruth was learning more about the real David Sutcliffe. She decided to talk to Brian about it.

"So, Sutcliffe had a gambling problem. You're thinking he's got deeply into debt and been bailed out by a loan shark who's put pressure on him to repay. He's got behind with his payments, probably been warned about the consequences of non-payments, and tried to gamble his way out of it. And the debt's just spiralled to the point where the consequences have been enforced."

"That's how I see it."

"So, prove it."

"Any chance of some physical backup? I'm a bit wary about taking on a murderous loan shark on my own."

"Andy?"

"Andy would be fine. Thanks."

"You know, Ruth, since you came here to assist in a clerical position, you're proving to be a very capable investigator. Well done."

"Thanks, boss."

"OK, so you need to find this loan-shark. How do you plan to go about it?"

"I'm not sure yet, boss."

"Well, how do you think they'll communicate? Face to face?"

"Probably. Wait a minute, why didn't I think of that? By phone! I need to check his phone."

"That's right, Ruth. Get on to Forensics and ask if they still have his phone. If so, ask if any of its memory survived the blast. And if so, what then?"

"Check the numbers in the memory, eliminate those I can identify, and call the rest under some pretext about needing cash, and arrange to meet."

"Correct. Well done, Ruth."

"I should have thought about that in the first place."

"You got there. That's the main thing. Now, you and Andy can go and find the loan shark."

Soon Ruth and Andy were on their way to Forensics after having been assured the phone's memory had survived the blast, although the casing was burnt and melted. It had been saved from total meltdown due to being inside a briefcase which delayed its complete destruction. They were able to read the contents of the memory and check the numbers. Of those not listed in the database, Andy called them in turn, stating he was in financial trouble, and someone recommended he should call a particular number. Most answered politely that he'd got the wrong number, but he persevered until they eventually hit the jackpot when the call was answered by someone sympathetic to his problem.

"I may be able to help you. Who gave you this number?"

"A bloke in a bookies. He said you'd helped him once."

"What was his name?"

"He didn't give his name."

"OK. Tell me exactly what the problem is, and I'll ask you some questions and we'll see if we can help you."

Andy took a deep breath and started his rehearsed spiel.

"I've had some really bad luck on the horses recently. It's never been a real problem for me before. I've just bet what I could afford to lose. But it's got out of control and now, apart from a credit card bill I have to keep paying, I've got household bills I can't meet. The wife doesn't know anything about it. She'll go apeshit if she finds out. I just need a short-term loan, just to get me over this bad batch. I know my luck will change. I just need help. Can you help me?"

"It depends. Are you working?"

"Yeah, full-time for the council."

"What do you do?"

"Bin man."

"How much is your immediate debt?"

"Just over five grand. Can you help me?"

"Maybe. We'll meet. Do you know the Hockney in Shipley?"

"I think so. I can find it."

"I'll see you there tomorrow. 2pm. Stand at the bar. Carry a copy of the Racing Post. I'll ask you if your name's Marty. You say 'yes, Marty McFarty'. OK?"

"OK. Thanks, I'll be there."

Andy put the phone down with a smile.

"Marty McFarty. What do you think?"

"Suits you."

"Let's decide how we want to play this, then discuss it with the boss."

"OK. I think we need more than the two of us. We don't know if he'll have backup. He may even be armed."

"What if we get maybe four of five of our lot in plain clothes in the pub just in case anything gets awkward?"

"I doubt we can get so many without raising attention. It's probably a 'regulars' pub where everybody knows everybody else. So many strangers might raise eyebrows."

"OK. What if we're wired and our people can listen in from outside?"

"Yeah, I'm happy with that. Let's take it to the boss."

Brian listened carefully as Ruth outlined their plan, nodding occasionally, before broadly agreeing the idea.

"No offence, but I want two male officers outside. Apart from them being more physically suited to handling armed violence, they're less likely to stand out, chatting outside a pub, maybe having a fag."
"So, who can we have?"
"Scoffer will fancy it. Ask Teresa to arrange the loan of a couple of uniformed officers from the local division, in plain clothes, of course. Let Scoffer be indoors, sat at a table, and the 'guest' officers outside with you. Scoffer will wear an earpiece and will hear Andy's conversation and communicate with you."
"OK, boss."
"One more thing. It may be that the person you're meeting has backup. If you sense any problems, you either get reinforcements fast, or you abort the whole operation. Don't put yourselves or anyone else in danger. And finally, work on your story. Make sure you have the answer to any questions regarding collateral, because nobody will lend you money without it."

********

The backup officers were quickly recruited and informed what their roles would be, before the team set off for Shipley, parking in the Asda car park and walking singly down to the square before taking up their agreed positions at 1.55pm. Andy walked into the bar, Racing Post under his arm, and ordered a pint, standing at the bar, waiting patiently. His earpiece clicked as a voice whispered.

"Nod if you can hear me OK. Then cough, so I know if I can hear you."

He nodded, and then coughed, receiving an 'OK' in return.

At a little after 2pm, a tall man in his late forties walked through the door, looked around and approached Andy, standing alone at the end of the bar, Racing Post in hand.

"Are you Marty?"
"Yes. Marty McFarty, that's me."
"Let's go to my car so we can discuss things in private."
"Can't we do it here?"
"I prefer more privacy."

Andy's brain was racing. He needed backup close to him. He sensed possible danger if he were alone with this man.

"But I've just bought a pint. I'm not wasting it. Can I buy you one, so we can sit down and talk?"

The man looked around at the rest of the customers and deemed it safe, so agreed.

"Get me a pint of bitter, and we'll sit at the table in the corner."
"OK. I'll bring it over."

Andy ordered the pint and heard the voice in his earpiece.

"Well done, Andy. He doesn't suspect anything. Just get him talking. We'll decide when to interrupt if need be."

Andy took the drinks over to the table and sat down opposite his potential loan shark.

"So, can you help me?"
"Yes. How much do you need?"
"It's six grand, now. I borrowed some money from my brother-in-law after we'd spoken on the phone. It was a cert. But it lost!"
"What was the name of the horse?"

Andy had done his homework and was prepared.

"Firecracker. 2.35 yesterday. Kempton."

His target looked it up on his phone. It was correct.

"OK. Before I offer to help you out, I need to know you can pay me back."
"I've got regular money coming in. I've got a full-time job."
"Any other income? Property?"
"We rent, but my mother left me something in her Will. It's just taken a long time to be sorted out."
"Tell me about it. How much?"
"She died a couple of months ago. She lived in Australia. Dad died a couple of years back and left everything to her. So, now everything is to be split between me and my brother."
"How much?"
"A couple of hundred thousand, approximately. There's a house to sell, but they were comfortably off. It's just taking longer than I thought."

"OK. I'll check out what you've told me when you provide me with names, addresses and that. If it checks out, we can do business."
"Great. I'll give you the solicitor's name and address, if that's OK."
"That'll do for a start. Providing it checks out, I'll be in touch."

They shook hands and parted. Andy phoned Teresa immediately to check that she'd been able to fulfil her promise to create a number of false stories on the Internet which would back up his claim regarding his financial position. Her response was as he expected.

"All in place, Andy. Enough info to fool all but the most inquisitive."

********

Teresa's work obviously paid dividends as Andy received a call within a few hours. A second meeting was scheduled for the following day. Same time, same place. It went as expected.

"OK, your information checked out. We can do business. We'll take on the full £6000 loan as soon as you sign the paperwork. It's straightforward stuff. Here's a leaflet explaining it all. Read it if you like."
"I'll trust you."
"OK. We've taken on the full debt of £6000. Added to that is 10% interest, so you now owe us £6600. Understood?"
"Yes."
"So, before the end of every month, you need to pay back at least £600, and that's just to pay off the interest. Obviously, the more you pay, the less you owe. If you pay less than £600 on two consecutive months, the interest rate goes up to 15%. Do you understand that?"
"Yes. The more I pay, the less I owe. I know what it's all about."
"Right. Now, if you fail to pay less than £600 on three consecutive months, the interest rate goes up to 20%."
"OK."
"And if you miss three consecutive payments, your arms get broken."
"You're joking!"
"Yeah. Only kidding."
"I won't miss three times."
"Right. Here's details of the bank account to pay into. The first payment is due next week. Just make sure it goes in on time or suffer the consequences."

"It's a deal."
"Thanks. Let's drink to it."

They both took a long swallow of their drink before Andy spoke again.

"So, do you do this full time?"
"Yeah."
"Sorry, I don't know your name."
"Gordon."
"Who do you work for, Gordon?"
"You don't need to know that."
"Just curious. Just wondering if he needs any more staff. I'm fed up with working on the bins."
"He's got enough staff, thank you for asking."
"So, how long have you been working for the boss? What's his name?"
"You're asking too many questions. I'm off. See you next week."
"OK. See you."
"And don't think for one minute you can walk away from this. I know where you live."
"Really. Wow, that's impressive. You've done your homework."
"And I know where you work too."
"Where?"
"Council. You already told me. But I knew anyway. I know everything about you."
"How?"
"Your Facebook page."
"Oh. Of course."

"Good old Teresa!", he thought. "She thinks of everything."

They shook hands and parted.

# CHAPTER 13

The following Saturday they were once again in Shipley, except this time they had rotated the placement of the officers involved to lessen any hint of a set-up. Andy was at the bar when Gordon walked in. Andy immediately bought him a pint and wasted no time.

"Gordon, I'm sorry, I don't have your money."
"Why not?"
"Well, I had it last night. I'd had a good week. I was on a roll. £800 to the good. Then last night I thought I'd have a quick bet on the dogs. I lost £50 on the first race."
"So, how much have you got for me?"
"Nothing."
"Nothing?"
"Zilch. After that first bet, it just got worse. I was desperate to win it back. But it all went bad."
"You're in real trouble. Your debt's just gone up to £7200. You need to start reducing it, or you're in big trouble."
"How big?"
"Let's just say your expected lifespan will be drastically shortened. To a matter of days."
"Look, there's no need for this. I just need a couple of weeks, and with a bit of luck I'll pay it all off."
"You'll need more than a bit of luck. I hope you'll have enough money left to pay for your funeral."
"What exactly are you saying?"
"You'll be eliminated."
"I'll be murdered?"
"You got it in one."
"Let me talk to your boss. We can sort this out."
"How?"
"I'll think of something. Let me talk to the boss. I've got a proposition for him."
"Wait a minute. Stay there while I call him."

He took out his phone and called.

"Boss. He's got no money. He says he's got a proposition. He wants to talk to you."
"Put him on."

Andy took the phone.

"Look. I can get the money. Dead easy. I just need to borrow some manpower."

"What have you got in mind?"

"A petrol station. Only one old man on duty. Gets a lot of trade. Till's always overflowing when he cashes up at 10pm. Just disable the CCTV and the panic button and it's done. I *know*. I put the system in."

"Where is it?"

"Oh, no! I'm not saying. You'll do it without me and leave me with nothing. Give me a break. You get the takings. That's easily enough to make a dent in my debt. Then I can point you at some other easy targets."

"Go on, I'm interested."

"Oh, no. Give me your agreement on the petrol station, first."

"OK, you've got it. Put Gordon back on."

He handed the phone back.

"Yes, boss."

"Bring him to see me."

"OK."

He turned to Andy.

"Come on, the boss wants to meet you."

"Oh, no. Not a chance. I've fallen for that one before. I go with you and it's a trap. I get a good hiding and you get the info you need to do the job. Not a chance, mate. I'll meet the boss on neutral ground. Out in the open, or nothing."

"I'll talk to him."

He rang the boss again.

"Boss, he'll only meet you in the open. He thinks you'll beat the information out of him."

"OK. We'll meet in the pub next week. But tell him I want to see him put some money on the table this time or no deal."

"OK, boss."

"You've got your deal, Marty. But you need to pay off some of your debt as a gesture."

"I will. I've got a feeling my luck's about to change."

"Same time, same place next week."

"OK."

They shook hands and parted. Once out of sight, he called Scoffer.

"Did you get all that, Scoffer."
"Yep. Good work, mate. The boss is going to love it. Let's get back to HQ."

Brian did, indeed, love it, and started planning immediately. But, because the meeting was due to take place in a public house, he was obliged to make it known to the manager, who would in turn inform his staff. It was fraught with problems. All it would take would be for someone to leak the information without considering the consequences. Brian met the manager in private before he considered discussing the operation. He wanted to weigh him up first.

********

The meeting did not go well. The pub's manager was honest with him.

"A few years ago, I would have said it's no problem. I trusted my staff. But since the pandemic struck, I had to lay off a lot of staff and most of them found other jobs. Then, when restrictions were finally lifted, I couldn't get the quality of staff I needed. Some of them might be a bit dodgy. Even I don't trust them fully. There's often a shortage in the till when I cash up at the end of the night."
"Can we run the operation without informing the staff?"
"Fine by me."
"OK. Here's what we plan to do…."

They were fully prepared for the operation. Plain-clothed officers were placed strategically around the Market Square and in the pub. Fortunately for Andy, it was a cold afternoon which meant he could wear a stab vest under his heavy outer coat without it being noticeable. Full of confidence, he walked through the pub door, approached the counter and ordered a pint of bitter, looking around as he waited. All his team were in place and ready. Within a few minutes, the message text arrived on his phone.

"Target approaching with TWO men. Extra men not yet ID'd."

"Probably extra security. Our man's wary of being out in the open", Andy thought. "Maybe he's right."

The three men entered, Gordon first. He looked around, saw Andy and motioned the others to follow him. He introduced them.

"This is The Boss, and his pal Carl. This is Marty McFarty."

They all shook hands. Andy spoke.

"As you requested, I've brought some money. £600. It's all I have. Take it and we're even when I tell you about the filling station. Is that OK?"
"As long as the information is genuine and it's as straightforward as you said it would be."
"So, provided I give you all the info you need, you'll rob the filling station?"
"Yes."
"What about guns? Will you be armed?"
"Yes. Just in case."
"He won't give you any trouble. He'll just hand over the cash. He's no hero. He just works there. He's an old man. Promise you won't shoot him."
"Unless he tries to play the hero."
"You'd shoot an old man?"
"If need be. It wouldn't be the first time."
"You've shot people before?"
"Yes, but it's none of your business. So, let's have the address."
"I've changed my mind. You won't need it."
"Don't screw with me! I'll kill you. Now, what's the address?"
"City Hall, Bradford. I've some friends I want you to meet. OK, lads! All yours."

The Boss saw the group approaching them from all directions and heard the word 'Police!" He pulled a knife from his pocket and plunged it into Andy's stomach, causing him to double up with pain. The vest did its job, preventing the blade from penetrating his flesh, although Andy was left winded and bruised. In minutes, the trio were handcuffed and bundled through the door where a van was waiting to take them away.

The bemused customers returned to their drinks as if it was an everyday occurrence, while, outside, those involved in the operation shook hands and went about their normal duties.

As soon as the prisoners were booked in at HQ, a team including Forensics officers was sent to the business address of The Boss, a first floor flat in a nondescript building in Holme Wood, where they found a safe loaded with banknotes, and, in a storage room, all the material required to make a remote-controlled bomb.

After extensive questioning continuing deep into the night, confessions were extracted from the trio admitting to their roles in the murder of David Sutcliffe who was killed by a car bomb as punishment for failing to pay off a debt.

The following morning, Brian congratulated the team for a successful conclusion of the case and arranged for a small party to be held early doors upstairs at the Ainsbury where he thanked all those involved in the case. Later in the evening, he took Ruth to one side.

"Ruth, I just wanted to say how impressed I've been with the way you've dealt with this case."
"But that's only because when I wasn't sure what to do, you quickly pointed me in the right direction."
"I was only doing *my* job, just as you were doing yours. You'll soon have enough experience to make these decisions automatically, but, if not, I'm always here to help. You've blended nicely into the team, and you've quickly become an asset. I'm very pleased with you. Keep up the good work."
"Thanks, boss. I will."

Ruth had a big smile on her face for the rest of the evening.

********

The following morning, Brian had the unenviable task of informing David Sutcliffe's current partner, Anne, of the outcome of the inquiry into his death.

"Anne, I'm sorry to have to tell you that your partner, David, was killed because of his gambling debts."
"Oh."
"You don't sound too surprised."
"I suppose I've known for quite a while, but always believed him when he said it was just temporary. He said it was due to stock market fluctuations, but I found it hard to confront him. I guess if I could have made him understand what it was doing to our relationship, he might have changed. I guess I'm partly to blame."
"No, Anne, you can't think that way. He was a compulsive gambler. He couldn't stop. Like them all, he believed the big win was just around the corner, but as happens so often, he ended up in the

hands of a loan shark, who, when he didn't keep his promises and pay back his loans, warned him of the consequences of non-payment. David chose to ignore those too."

"Thank you for telling me."

"Well, the only consolation I can give you is that we've caught the people responsible for his death and they're going to trial."

"I'm glad. Now I have to wait to see if David's life insurance policy pays out. If it does, I'll get that necklace back out of pawn. I found all his pawnshop receipts, by the way. I was a bit shocked. But at least it's over. I can move on."

"I'm so sorry, Anne. I hope things work out for you. Goodbye."

"Thank you. Goodbye."

He walked down the path to his car and started the engine, wondering how David Sutcliffe must have felt when he did the same thing that morning when his car exploded. A horrible death, due to compulsive behaviour. Like his own compulsive behaviour regarding alcohol. Still, who cared if he lived or died. His family – his wife, Sarah, and kids, Daniel and Samantha – had died. What did they do to deserve to be killed? If it had anything to do with his drinking, he would abstain immediately. If not, he would console himself the only way he knew. Who would care?

Brian was at home cradling a glass of malt went the phone rang.

"Hi, Brian, it's your dad.

"Hi, dad."

"We were just wondering if we could come over and see you."

"I'm really busy just now, dad."

"How about the weekend?"

"I'm working. You've no need to come over. I'm fine."

"You sure?"

"Honest, dad."

"OK, son. Let us know if you need anything."

"Will do. 'Bye."

He put down his glass, picked up the framed photo of his smiling and happy family, and wept.

********

It didn't take long before Teresa located Berkeley. She went straight to Brian.

"Ever see a 1968 horror film called Witchfinder General, Brian?"

142

"No. I've heard of it, though."

"So has Berkeley, apparently. The online pseudonym he uses is Whorefinder General. He's a procurer."

"Did you manage to get an address?"

"I got a business address in Stockbridge, in Edinburgh, on Danube Street. Here."

"Thanks. I'll have to go by train as soon as possible. I can't drive that distance yet."

"Leave it with me. I'll get you booked for tomorrow. It may be wise to stay over for one night at least."

"OK. I'll leave it with you."

He rushed to DCI Gardner's office to clear it with him.

"That's fine, Brian. Do you need to take another officer with you?"

"If you can spare one, sir."

"Your choice. I'll authorise it."

"Thank you, sir."

Brian went straight to Scoffer's desk.

"Fancy a day out tomorrow, Scoffer?"

"Business or pleasure?"

"We'll be visiting a brothel, but it's strictly business."

"That's a let-down, but you can count me in."

"We'll be staying overnight."

"No problem."

"OK. I'll ask Teresa to book us both."

********

They met in Leeds station next morning, each carrying an overnight bag, and boarded the train to Edinburgh. During the journey, Brian explained the purpose of the trip.

"Two girls, sisters, caught a taxi in Bradford City centre and haven't been seen since. McAuley, one of the guys we arrested in Cleckheaton, identified them when we interviewed him."

"Yes, I remember."

"He also identified a man called Lenny Berkeley, who has a brothel in Edinburgh. We believe that's where the girls are working. Teresa has booked appointments for us tonight with two girls who look suspiciously like them, although they are working under different names. We need to get them out and back with their family."

"Any leisure time built into the schedule?"

"Yes, but not at the brothel."

"Pity."

"Well, you'll still be able to claim legitimate expenses."

"We'll do the tourist attractions, then."

"You mean the pubs?"

"Aye."

The train stopped at Waverley Station just after 3pm. They left the station and got in a taxi in the rank outside. Ten minutes later they were checking into their hotel in the New Town before walking to a nearby restaurant off Leith Walk. During their meal, Scoffer confided to Brian.

"Do you know, this is the first time I've ever visited a brothel."

"Me too, Scoffer. Apart from on business, that is. Anyway, don't forget this is a business visit."

"I know. I've no intention of paying for it anyway."

"Never taken your girlfriend out for a meal? Never bought her something nice?"

"That's different."

"Is it?"

"Well, I think so. Sex isn't necessarily part of the transaction. It's just a welcome bonus."

"Well, don't forget. We're not seeing these girls tonight for pleasure. This is business only. Understood?"

"Of course. Can't abuse company expenses."

"When I found we were coming up here to a brothel, I googled the area. Did you know there's been a brothel at 17 Danube Street since the end of the Second World War?"

"Really?"

"Yes. The business ran until the late 1970s. The property was put up for sale recently for £1.45 million. However, the place we're visiting is not number 17."

"Pity. We might have been served a glass of champagne. Now, we'll probably be offered a pint of heavy."

"Don't forget. It's strictly business. If these girls have become sex slaves, we need to offer them a way out."

"I've memorised the drill, boss. I'll be OK."

"I don't doubt it, Scoffer. I wouldn't have brought you if I didn't have complete faith in you."

They had each booked one of the girls, in separate rooms. Brian had chosen Tina; Scoffer had her sister Mandy. They were shown to their respective rooms.

Brian was greeted by a smiling, beautiful and relaxed young woman, with whom he felt immediately at ease. She asked him to use the sanitizer as soon as he entered the room and initially sat two metres away from him while she asked him what he wanted from his visit. He came straight to the point.

"I'm not here for sex, Tina. I'm a Detective Inspector with Bradford CID. I'm here because you are listed as a missing person, as is your sister Mandy. My colleague, Joe, and I are here to get you out and back home safely."

Tina laughed.

"Before you say anything else, Brian, you should know that our conversation is being monitored. I have a special phrase, which will bring a couple of heavies bursting in, so, please, be careful what you do. Now, you need to understand that neither Mandy nor I are being kept against our will...."

Brian interrupted.

"But you were abducted, by a bogus taxi driver in Bradford."
"That's correct, but ever since, we have been treated like princesses. We don't have to do anything we disagree with. We're free to leave whenever we want, but we love being here."
"I don't believe it."
"It's *true!* We're not prisoners. *We* decide which clients we accept. *We* decide what we charge. All we pay is rent for use of the premises, and that's very reasonable, and negotiable. We work the hours *we* choose. Honestly, we have full control of our lives. And Mandy will be telling your colleague exactly the same. I'm afraid we're staying, regardless of what you or our parents decide. We have some very rich and generous clients. We're adults. We're free to make our own decisions. And we love our life here."
"You're telling me you're not sex slaves?"
"Look. We enjoy what we're doing. We work the hours we decide, normally about 25 hours a week, five days, and we make good money. Our clients are respectful, gentle and generous. We've discussed this over and over and we both feel the same. This is the life we choose to live, and we wouldn't go back to our old life for anything. So, I'm afraid you've wasted your journey. Now, I won't charge you for this appointment, but I'd rather not waste any more time. I need to prepare for my next client."
"You're sure this is what you want to do?"

"Absolutely! And Mandy will be saying exactly the same to your colleague. Life couldn't be better. There's no way I'm going back to the old one."

"I'm sorry we've wasted your time, Tina. What do you suggest I tell your parents?"

"Just say, we're fine. We're safe, we're happy and they don't need to worry about us. You don't have to tell them what we do for a living. We'll be able to retire early and live a relaxed life up here. I'll see you out."

"OK. One last thing. You were abducted by a bogus taxi driver. We still need to investigate that offence. Is there anything you can remember about that?"

"No. Sorry, not a thing."

"I'll see myself out."

He waited in Reception until Scoffer joined him. The look on his face told Brian he'd had a similar experience.

"I couldn't believe it. You'd have thought she'd won the pools. She was unbelievably happy. She said there was no way she would return to her old life."

"Well, Scoffer, there's nothing we can do. They're not prisoners, they're not being coerced. It's the lifestyle they've chosen to accept and enjoy. We can't make a case here. Let's go for a pint."

"Might as well."

They called in a few of the pubs on Edinburgh's famous Rose Street, before retiring to the hotel. It had been a long day, but over a nightcap, Brian still wrestled with the problem of what exactly he would say to the girls' parents.

********

During the train journey home, both Brian and Scoffer were largely silent, each wrapped up in their own personal dilemmas. Eventually, though, Scoffer aired his concerns.

"Do you think there's any future for me in CID, boss? An honest opinion, please."

"One thing you'll always get from me, Scoffer, is the truth. As for your question, it's difficult to answer. You have a number of things in your favour; you learn quickly, you show good judgment, and you act according to orders if any are specified. The problem is, there are other officers in the team who are equally good at the job, and opportunities for advancement depend largely on others

146

leaving, or the expansion of the group's responsibilities. All I can say is, you have as good a chance as anyone else in the team. But you may have to move to a different area or take on a different role to advance. Is that an option for you?"

"Well, yes. I mean, I like working in Bradford, but, if necessary, I'll relocate if there are opportunities."

"Keep an open mind, Scoffer. Keep performing as you are. Keep learning, and you'll do for me."

"Thanks, boss."

There was silence for a while as both men were deep in thought. Then Scoffer asked the question to which he already knew the answer.

"So, what is it that keeps *you* going, boss?"

"Taking criminals off the street. Getting revenge for the innocent victims. That's what we're all in it for. Sometimes it's the best job in the world. Sometimes it's the worst. But the moment you think it's no longer worth the effort, then it's the time to quit."

Brian didn't mention to Scoffer that he thought he might have reached that point himself, and it constantly preyed on his mind. But the decision would have to wait. He still had work to do. There were still missing persons he needed to trace, and other open cases to be resolved. He would have time to think about his future when the whiteboards were wiped clean. Then he would make the decision, and once made, there would be no going back.

# CHAPTER 14

Brian walked into the empty Conference Room and stopped in front of the whiteboard, looking at the outstanding cases. It obviously needed to be updated. He called a meeting to discuss the situation. He pointed first to the item 'MPs' on the whiteboard.

"OK, we need to pick up some of this work. It's been a while since Des Marshall reported his wife, Diane, missing. Although she left a note to say she was leaving him, he believes she was coerced into writing it and left him a clue. Apparently, she called him 'Desmond', something she hasn't called him since she spoke her wedding vows. We need to follow this up. Paula, Jo-Jo, will you take this?"
"OK."
"Next, we have a possible serial killer, or maybe two copycat killers. Gary, you were on that. Any progress?"
"No, boss. I discovered the latest victim's ex-wife was no longer in contact with him. As soon as the divorce was finalised, she cut him off. She said he was a serial adulterer. Then, I had to drop it to concentrate on the car thefts."
"And what's the progress on that?"
"Still ongoing. NCA were looking at it as well, but I don't know how far they've got."
"OK, let's just reallocate to try to give it some impetus. Lynn, Andy, will you take the killers case? Liaise with NCA?"

They nodded their agreement.

"Next, more missing persons. Alice Bradshaw?"
"We'd interviewed the bogus taxi driver, Choudhary. He didn't recognise Alice."
"OK. Gary, will you pick this one up? With Louise?"
"OK."
"And the Amazon parcels. Anywhere with this?"
"I think that's cleared, boss. We charged a man, David Golding, with the thefts. He's out on bail. And another man has been charged with receiving stolen goods. They're just awaiting trial."
"Well, that's good news. Let's get the other cases closed."

Mr Choudhary was hauled in again for interview but was unable to recognise the ladies in the photographs he was shown.

"You're absolutely sure?"
"Absolutely. I'm telling the truth."

"We can make you take a lie detector test."
"Go ahead. It will make no difference. I assure you I've never seen either of these girls before."

By the end of the interview, they were convinced he had, indeed, told the truth. They turned their attention to the men they'd arrested making porno videos – Anthony McAuley and Philip Carter. They were interviewed separately, and their comments compared. Gary let them go after reporting to Brian.

"I can't find anything to suggest they are involved in the disappearance of either Alice Bradshaw or Diane Marshall or the others featured on the Facebook page set up when Alice went missing."
"Let's try a different approach. Concentrate on Diane Marshall, since there's no link between her and a taxi driver. I'll get Scoffer to look into Alice's disappearance along with the other two."

Scoffer read up on the case so far and looked at the Facebook page. He was surprised to find there were several different pages set up by different people, usually covering different geographical areas. Some of the pages had been set up by private investigators to publicise their expertise and availability. Tracing missing persons seemed to be a booming business. However, Scoffer concentrated on the Bradford site, looking for similarities, patterns, links between victims, and bookmarked several pages for comparison. He was the last one to leave HQ that evening and returned early the following morning to pick up the work again.

It wasn't long before he spotted an anomaly. He picked up the phone.

"Teresa, could I ask you to take a look at something I've found regarding the missing persons cases?"
"Are you using the FBI or Europol database?"
"Neither. It's on Facebook."
"Facebook? Oh, very well. Do you want me to come down or I can do it up here if you give me the addresses?"
"I'll come up."

He raced up the stairs and took a seat next to Teresa.

"OK, direct me to the page."
"OK. Start by looking for 'Alice Bradshaw'. We can follow the threads from there."

After a while, Scoffer asked Teresa to stop.

"OK, time to change perspective. Open the page of one of her 'friends.' Just pick one at random."

"Is this going to get us somewhere? I'd rather go straight to the result."

"OK. Open the page of this woman, Ira Wentworth. She's a 'friend' to everybody who posts an MP."

Teresa duly did as Scoffer requested.

"Now, open her profile."

Her profile gave her address as Aberdeen.

"Don't you think it's odd that there are images on her page showing her attending protests, fundraisers and other events in West Yorkshire. And look at this; a photo taken supposedly in her back garden with Listers Mill in the background."

"A lot of people give a false address on Facebook. It proves nothing."

"OK. Look at the pictures of her supposedly missing child. They're not all of the same person. Convinced?"

"Not really. There's always been the odd nutter on Facebook."

"OK. Try this woman's page."

"OK. Oh, it's the same missing child! It's a different person's name, different personal details, address, etc, but the pictures of the child are the same as the last one we looked at. It can't be just coincidence. Let me set up a page for myself as a victim, and see if I can get private messages, because I have a feeling this woman, if it is a woman, uses a private messaging service either to gloat over victims or to pick new ones. Leave it with me, or we could speed up the process by each setting up a page."

"That would be a good idea, as long as you can give me some tips how to post so I don't sound like a man."

"Dead easy. Just drop the macho posturing."

"You're joking, aren't you?"

By early afternoon they were producing results. Five different women in different parts of the country were posting pictures of the same 'missing' child. Posts arrived thick and fast on both Teresa's and Scoffer's site. They were followed by private messages which started innocently enough but soon started asking highly personal questions, and questions irrelevant to the missing girl. Finally, one of the messengers asked to meet in person. Before giving an answer, they consulted Brian, who authorised it with the proviso that backup would be close at hand awaiting a signal, and that the meeting would be secretly videotaped. It was set for the following afternoon, at one of the NCA's safe houses. Technicians spent the morning setting up and testing the recording equipment; Scoffer and Teresa rehearsed their parts as distraught parents of a missing child.

They were ready when the call came from the recording van parked just down the road.

"Your caller has just got out of a car and is coming down the road. We're all switched on and ready."

Seconds later the doorbell rang. Scoffer opened it to a worried-looking middle-aged woman who introduced herself as Beth. Teresa was confused.

"You called yourself Annette on Facebook. Why's that?"
"People are trying to catch me. They have my child."

Scoffer chipped in.

"And which exactly is your child? There are three different girls on your page."
"Jean, the one in the first picture is mine. The other two belong to women I've met who are frightened to use social media because of all the weirdos. So, I'm just helping them out, really."
"OK. Tell me about Jean. What happened?"
"She went out with some friends one night for a few drinks. She was eighteen a couple of days earlier, and she was celebrating in town. I got a text at about 11.30 to say she was just getting into a taxi. And that was the last I heard from her."
"Didn't the police do anything?"
"Yes, but they didn't find her."
"How long ago was this?"
"Just over eight years ago…."
"And the women you're helping out?"
"Same story. Night out. Called to say they were about to get in a taxi, and never heard from again."
"I don't remember any of this being in the newspapers."
"It was in our local paper. In Lincoln."
"This happened in Lincoln?"
"Yes."
"So, why are you here?"

"Because the more people who are on the internet pleading for help, the more chance we have of connecting with others in the same boat. Working together, we've more resources to pool, and more chance of getting to see our children again."

"OK. Give me the exact date, time and place your daughter went missing. Also, her full name."

"Jean Walker. Here, I can show you the text she sent as she was getting into a taxi outside the Castle Hotel in Lincoln at 11.17pm June 18th, 2014."

"Just give me a couple of minutes."

Scoffer walked into the kitchen, waiting for confirmation on his phone, but despite a thorough search, there was no record of the incident. He returned to the lounge to confront Mrs Walker."

"You reported this incident to the police. Correct?"

"Yes."

"So, why is there no record of the report?"

"I don't know."

"Perhaps it never happened."

"Perhaps the records got lost."

"Perhaps you're lying. Why are you lying?"

Mrs Walker broke down in tears. Scoffer decided it was time to end the charade.

"Mrs Walker, we're police officers. We're looking for some young ladies who've recently gone missing. So, would you please come clean and explain what this is all really about."

"OK. One of the ladies lost her daughter who disappeared after a night out. She was waiting for her to return home when she got a phone call to tell her that her daughter had been abducted, and was safe, but she would be killed if her mother went to the police. So, she said nothing, hoping they'd release her. Eventually, she realised she had to do something, so she put it on Facebook and received messages from other people who'd had the same experience."

"Why the false photos?"

"Some of the parents were frightened their daughters would be harmed if their faces appeared all over, so they decided to use and re-use the same photos over and over again, to help the site grow and pool information and resources. Yes, there are a few nutters who've got on the site, but most of the members are genuine. We just don't know what to do for the best. All we want is to get our children back or at least know they're safe."

"So, you're telling us that all the members of the site have genuinely had a daughter abducted?"

"I guess there may be one or two who just post for the sake of it, but most are genuine. That's why I visit potential members."

"So, how many of the girls have been found?"

"None. No, sorry, one. But she was found dead. A drugs overdose, they said."

"So, your Facebook appeal isn't really working, is it?"

"No. I guess not."

"So, isn't it time you took the risk and passed it to the police?"

"Well, I think so, but I can't speak for the others."

"You're not getting any results with your Facebook scheme. It's your choice. If you don't report it, we won't investigate."

"I'll put the word around."

Once Mrs Walker had left, they considered their next move.

"This is a dead end, Teresa."

"Maybe not. Let me have a look at the file on the dead girl. The overdose. It may lead somewhere."

"OK."

"And there's another thing. She gave the time precisely as 23.17."

"What's odd about that?"

"Initially, she just said she got a text at about 23.30."

"Well, it's close enough."

"What if the number's exact, but it wasn't the time?"

"You've lost me."

"She said she'd got a text message from her daughter as she was getting into a taxi at about 23.30. She showed it to us. It read, 'castle hotel taxi here now 2317.' The time of the text was 23.30. So, what's the relevance of 2317? If one number is the time, 23.30, as per the text time, 2317 is perhaps the taxi's local authority registration number?"

"Let's check."

They fed the numbers one at a time into Lincoln's Taxi Register website. They found that 2330 had been issued to four different drivers from 2013 onwards. 2317, though, had belonged to only one driver in all that time. Seeing the name on the registration, Scoffer decided to pay him a visit first, after informing Brian and getting permission to take Ruth with him. First, though, he wanted to do some research on the named driver, Abdul Choudhary.

********

Ruth was waiting at the roadside when the taxi she'd ordered pulled up. She checked the licence number before climbing in and giving her destination – a multi-storey car park a couple of miles away, directing the driver to the top floor, where Scoffer was waiting by his car. The taxi stopped next to it, and Scoffer got into the front passenger seat.

"Where to, sir?"
"Just switch off the engine while we have a chat, Mr Choudhary."
"What's this about? I have to drive. I have to make a living."
"We won't keep you long, sir. We just want some answers. I want you to cast your mind back to 2014. You picked up a young lady outside the Castle Hotel and she hasn't been seen since. What happened to her?"
"I don't know what you're talking about. I have hundreds of passengers a year. I can't remember every particular one."
"How many of them do you put in the hands of pimps?"
"I don't know what you're talking about."
"I think you do. I think you get paid for being an accomplice in kidnapping young women for prostitution."
"If that's what you think, prove it."
"We will. When we've spoken to your relative in Bradford, who coincidentally also drives a taxi for a living."
"I don't have any relatives in Bradford."
"We'll see. We'll be in touch. You're free to go – for now."

They drove back to Bradford, discussing their next move.

"Back to Alice Bradshaw? And this Ira Wentworth.?"
"I think so. Perhaps we should check first how Gary's doing with Diane Marshall."
"I'll call him."

Gary had made no progress at all and was too busy to focus on it. Basically, he was waiting for a break in the case.

********

Back at HQ, both Scoffer and Ruth were looking through social media sites for any mention of Abdul and Ali Choudhary. They immediately established that they were related – uncle and nephew. Abdul's parents came to the UK in 1948, following Pakistan's independence, they married in 1958 and Abdul was born in 1960. Abdul's brother was born in 1964, he married in 1984 and had a child, Ali, in 1988. Both families lived in Thornbury, until Abdul and his wife moved to Lincoln where the bus drivers were better paid. Unfortunately, after three years he was made redundant and became a self-employed taxi driver. Twice, since then, he was accused of sexual assault by female passengers, but charges were later dropped.

By the age of sixteen, his nephew had become a drug dealer in Bradford. He served time, but continued his criminal pursuits after his release, becoming a taxi driver in 2017 while still dealing drugs. He was arrested in 2019 after being accused of sexual assault by a passenger and released due to lack of evidence. A year later, he was stopped by police for a traffic violation and drugs were found in his car. He maintained they were left by a passenger and was eventually released. His taxi licence was revoked.

"They've both got form, Ruth."
"Yes, but can we connect them to any recent abductions, since Jean Walker?"
"Back to Facebook."

An hour later, Ruth had made a potential breakthrough.

"I've found a picture of Ali Choudhary with Philip Carter. Even more interesting is another with Alice Bradshaw. And she looks very happy indeed with his arm around her waist."
"How come we missed this earlier?"
"It's on Abdul's page. At a birthday party he attended. Both pictures were taken at the same do."
"Let's have another chat with Ali. But first we'll review the file on Alice."

They brought Ali Choudhary back in for questioning.

"The last time you were interviewed, you stated you didn't know Alice Bradshaw. Is that correct?"
"Yes."
"Perhaps you'd like to look at the photo on Facebook and tell me who is the girl you're talking to, with your arm around her waist?"
"I don't know. I was just chatting her up. She seemed friendly."
"The last time you were interviewed, we showed you some photos. One was of Alice. Yet you stated you didn't recognise anyone in any of the photos. Why did you lie, Mr Choudhary?"

"I didn't. I didn't remember her. I only saw her for a minute, and I'd had a lot to drink. I've never seen her since."

"Where is she now?"

"How should I know?"

"Because you get paid for supplying these girls."

"You can't prove that!"

"Maybe not. But we will, given time. You see, there's a pattern here. Girls get into taxis, and then disappear. The next time we see them, they are working as prostitutes. Is that a coincidence?"

"Must be."

"OK. You're going to stay in custody for now while we execute a warrant to search your house. Is there anything you'd like to tell us, before we go?"

"Good luck."

They searched the house thoroughly, taking fingerprint samples in every room. They also found blood stains in the bathroom along with items of women's underwear in a laundry basket, which they took back to the lab for analysis. Scoffer took the expected call from Allen Greaves the next day.

"Some good news, Scoffer. We have fingerprints matching Alice Bradshaw's, and we also found her DNA on the items of laundry we took. I don't suppose it will come as a surprise to you that we also found fingerprints belonging to another missing person, Diane Marshall."

"Well, that wasn't expected. Thanks, Allen."

Scoffer informed Brian of the discovery of Diane Marshall's prints.

"I'll join you for the next interview if that's alright with you, Scoffer."

"Of course, boss. It might be a good idea for you to lead the interview. I'm not getting far with him."

"OK, let me have a go at him. Let me read what you've got so far and then bring him down to the room."

After going through the ritual of introductions for the sake of the recording of the conversation, Brian wasted no further time.

"What was Diane Marshall doing in your house?"

"Who?"

"Oh, sorry. You don't go through the courtesy of introducing yourself to your captives, do you? Names don't mean anything to you. Bodies are all that count. Bodies to sell for sex."

156

Choudhary remained silent, but Brian persevered.

"We found her DNA in your house. We found Alice Bradshaw's too, as well as her underwear. You seem to have a knack of getting females into your home without knowing who they are. And then, they disappear. Don't you think that's a bit odd?"
"No comment."
"Well, I'll tell you what we're going to do. We're bringing Philip Carter and Anthony McAuley back in for a chat. If I were you, I'd grass them up before they put all the blame on you. I know they paid you to bring women to them. I know they used them to make sex films. So, we'll be charging you as an accomplice. You'll go down for a long time."

He could see that Choudhary was close to breaking point so decided to push his luck.

"You know how they treat these girls, don't you? They load them with drugs so they're not really conscious of what's happening. They can't object. They can't say 'no'. They just become sex dolls. They get raped several times a day. And you're to blame!"
"I don't do any of this. I just deliver girls who've drunk too much. It's not my fault what happens to them."
"Yes, it is your fault! You know what happens to them. You're complicit in all this. And I bet you supply the drugs to keep the girls semi-conscious. Boy, you're in big trouble."
"I want to speak to my lawyer."

Brian and Scoffer left them to it. Both men were clearly agitated, especially Choudhary. It was less than five minutes before they were called back into the room.

"My client wishes to make it clear that he had no idea that the girls were being used in this way. As far as he was aware, they were being recruited to do fashion shoots, underwear mainly, for a reality TV program."
"Do you really expect us to believe this?"
"If you accept this, he can name people who organise and profit from this enterprise, in return for protection."
"We'll see what we can do. But the level of protection will depend on the quality of the evidence he provides. So, let's hear it."

They were impressed with the amount of information he provided. Names, places, times. After the interview was completed, Choudhary was informed he would remain in custody until they had checked the evidence he had provided. If it led to arrests and prosecutions, they would come to an arrangement regarding his protection.

********

The meeting was held in the Conference Room. Brian outlined his plan.

"We have five venues to hit; all at the same time, so we need outside help. I'll be discussing it with the NCA, but I think it may be better if we can handle it in house, with the assistance of uniformed officers. I've already outlined what we need regarding forensic support and Allen will get his staff organised. So, I propose we carry out the operation this Friday evening, 8pm. Is everyone OK with that?"

There were no objections, except from Scoffer who asked in jest if they would be finished before the pubs closed.

"If you're buying, Scoffer, I'll make certain we're finished before closing time."

Scoffer, having had recent experience of working in uniform, knew many constables who would jump at the chance of gaining experience of joining CID in an operation. He recommended sixteen officers who, he guaranteed, would perform to Brian's high standards. Brian was happy to accept them. He also acquired the service of ten armed officers for the operation. They quickly agreed how to configure the teams which would be led by Brian, Gary, Lynn, Paula and Jo-Jo. Two armed officers would accompany each team, along with three uniformed constables. The rest of the officers were randomly allocated to make up the squads so that each team had seven members. The Forensics teams were similarly allocated so that three members would attend each site, and medical teams had been alerted and were on stand-by.

At 19.55 all units were in place close to the venues which were all in different trading estates in the Bradford area. As soon as they received the 'Go' signal, they stormed the venues and made arrests without any opposition. Transport was organised to take those in charge of the venues to HQ, while the victims were taken to a clinic for initial examination. The customers were interrogated on site, before being allowed to leave in the knowledge they may face criminal charges later. All those involved in the operation were thanked and allowed to leave if they wished, but otherwise were invited to join in a short, impromptu celebration at the White Bear in Idle after Brian phoned the landlord for permission. It was time to relax, before the arduous process of interviews would commence the next morning. However, before the party broke up, Brian reminded the team leaders that their completed reports were required to be on his desk by 09.30 on Monday morning. Brian went home and, by his recent standard, had an early night.

********

On Saturday morning, Brian visited the clinic where the victims had spent the night, speaking to each one in turn as well as the clinicians who had examined them. Those who had been reported missing were allowed and encouraged to telephone their family or friends to assure them they were OK and were able to see visitors prior to being allowed to leave as soon as they were judged to be fit enough. Neither Diane Marshall nor Alice Bradshaw was among the victims, nor did any of the others know them.

On Monday morning, interviews commenced at ten. Brian and Scoffer, who volunteered to partner his boss for the interviews, had read the reports and were in the Interview Room awaiting the first of those arrested. At the same time, Gary and the rest of the team were examining the statements taken from the customers and arranging to interview them further at their home.

Brian and Scoffer's first interviewee was brought in accompanied by his legal representative. He was a portly, balding man in a cheap suit and so was his lawyer.

"So, Mr Mulligan. How long have you been holding these little 'soirées?"
"About six months. I saw an advert on the internet for a business opportunity."
"Give me the website address, please."
"It's been taken down. It doesn't exist anymore."
"You must have a record of it somewhere."
"On my phone."
"OK, we'll check that."

Scoffer left the room to organise for the phone to be taken from storage and sent to Forensics to analysis. The request was high priority. As soon as he returned, the interview resumed.

"And how were these evenings arranged?"

"Word of mouth. We'd send one of our trusty contacts to spread the word in the right areas. When they made contact, we'd tell them exactly what to expect and the price. Once they paid, we'd tell them the time and place."

"And, for the benefit of the recording, please state exactly what took place at these soirées."

"Girls were paraded in front of the audience."

"How were they dressed?"

"They were naked."

"Then, what?"

"A number was drawn and announced, and the ticket holder was allowed first go."

"What was that?"

"Whatever he wanted, apart from killing her. Though that once almost happened."

"We'll talk about that episode later. Please continue to describe what he would do."

"Generally, he'd have sex with her."

"Against her wishes?"

"None of them ever objected."

"Because they were drugged to the eyeballs?"

"I don't know about that."

"Well, let me tell you, all the girls were examined over the weekend. All of them had taken, or been forced to take, drugs. All of them had then been brutally raped, some anally. All of them we spoke to told us they were abducted and held against their will. They were drugged every night before being gang-raped and made to perform sexual acts against their will in front of a salivating audience. What do you have to say about that?"

"I was just trying to make an honest living."

"Well, your turn will come, Mulligan. When you've been sentenced, I'll personally recommend you be imprisoned among the worst sexual sadists we know. We'll see how you like it. Interview ended. Take this bastard back to his cell, and if he happens to trip and fall down the stairs, it will just be an unfortunate accident."

Scoffer could see the anger on his boss's face.

"Do you want me to take the next one, boss, while you take a break?"

"Yes, Scoffer. Thanks. I'll ask for a volunteer to sit in for me while I throw up."

He walked slowly back to the office, wondering silently why he still earned a living by having to deal with dross such as Mulligan. Lynn read the look on his face and volunteered to relieve him for a while. He accepted gratefully. But there was little respite; while having a coffee, he received a message from Teresa informing him she'd got the website address from Mulligan's phone. He went directly to her desk.

"Here it is, Brian. The appropriately named 'Perverts' Paradise'. A website indexing all known addresses, internet, that is, of every whorehouse, mobile or static, in the UK. I'm contacting them now to try to get their physical locations."

"That's great work, Teresa. Send them to me as and when you get them. By the way, any news of the girls we rescued at the weekend?"

"Almost all responding well to treatment. Some have already been released and united with their family. For others, it will take longer. They've suffered terrible trauma and there are a few who may never fully recover."

"Which makes me even more determined to catch those responsible. I can't walk away from this."

It was becoming clear to some of the staff, Teresa especially, that Brian was close to breaking point. It was her duty to report her suspicion to DCI Gardner, but she held back. Instead, she would pick the right time and discuss it with Brian. In the meantime, she tried to persuade some of the staff to take a little of the strain whenever possible from his shoulders. That wasn't easy; they were feeling the pressure too. Scoffer, though, seemed to relish the challenge. He was like a younger, less battle-hardened version of Brian, learning all he could from his master. There was no doubt he would make the grade.

# CHAPTER 15

He took the call late in the afternoon.

"Brian, I have some addresses where it's likely some of the abductees are located. Is it OK if I send the ones outside West Yorkshire to the NCA, so they can allocate units to investigate them?"
"Yes, Teresa. That's probably a good idea. We've enough on our plate. What about the local ones?"
"Five so far. Do you want to take them?"
"Not all of them. I'll pick one and you can send the rest to the NCA, please. I don't think we have the manpower to take them all, unfortunately."
"On their way."

He looked through the notes Teresa had compiled. Five local businesses, open seven days a week, from eight till midnight. Applications for membership by referral from a current member only. He selected the nearest one, in Leeds, before calling Scoffer.

"Do you think any of the scum you've interviewed today would be willing to do us a favour in exchange for a lighter sentence?"
"Depends on the favour, boss."
"I want someone to endorse our applications for membership of the clubs belonging to the Perverts' Paradise franchise."
"I know just the man. Leave it with me."

Scoffer went down to the cells for a quiet word with one of those arrested during one of Friday's raids. John Masham was the type Scoffer described as a sleazy-looking scrote. He was happy to do a deal if it meant he would be treated leniently with regard to sentencing. Under Scoffer's watchful eye, he completed the online application form, and in return received the password for entry at the nearby venue in Leeds for two people. Brian was ecstatic, even more so when Scoffer informed him of an added bonus.

"I watched him fill in the application, boss. I noted his online login password. I think I might be able to do another application in his name. If so, we can get four of us in on the same night."
"It's worth a try. Go for it."

Sure enough, Scoffer's application was accepted and another password for entry for two was issued.

"Well done, Scoffer. Would you like to pick the team?"

"I'd like Mick to have a chance, boss. He really enjoyed last Friday's sortie. We've been mates for ages. He'd love to join CID."

"OK, he's in. Anyone else?"

"Andy, I think. He's got the experience."

"Agreed. I'll contact Mick's boss out of courtesy. I'm sure he won't object. It's good experience for the lads in uniform."

"OK if I call Mick to let him know?"

"Only if he keeps it to himself."

"He will, boss. He's no fool."

"OK, wait until I've got his boss's approval. Then we'll meet to formulate a plan."

Teresa had done some research and had sourced a plan of the building they were due to raid. She marked the location of exits and access, noting the fire exit which opened into an alley. They would use that to let in an armed backup unit to maintain control when the customers realised they were subject to a police raid. She also pointed out there was a door leading from a small room, probably the office, to the alley at the back. Brian laid out his plan at a meeting with all four participants, before informing the armed squad of their part in proceedings. It was clear that all concerned were looking forward to the raid due to take place on Wednesday night.

Even Brian was looking forward to it. It was the type of operation he'd always cherished, since joining the Force, because, if the planning was meticulous, the chances of a positive outcome were high. The rush of adrenalin was what he craved, what made the job worth doing.

Driving home, he felt elated. He drank coffee while eating a salad. Earlier in the week, someone at work had made a remark about his waistline in jest. It struck home, so if he couldn't stay away from alcohol, he'd occasionally try to eat sensibly. He didn't really care about his weight, but he didn't want to outgrow the clothes he'd become comfortable in, especially the shirts which Sarah had bought for him.

Come Wednesday, Brian held a short meeting for the participants of that night's exercise. Satisfied that everyone knew his role, he allowed them all to finish a little early to ensure they were on time for proceedings to commence. They were all keyed up and raring to go.

They met in Leeds bus station and walked the short distance to the venue, a nondescript warehouse close to the river Aire. The entrance door had no handle, but there was a keypad. Brian punched in the code. Seconds later the door slid open to reveal a full-height turnstile. He went through, followed by Andy, whereupon the turnstile locked. Scoffer entered the second code, allowing Mick and himself entry. The four followed the corridor towards the source of the music, through a door into an open space where tables and chairs were distributed in front of a stage. They made their way around to the bar, careful not to obstruct anybody's view of the stage where a fat, bald man was having sex with a young woman. Nobody noticed them as all eyes were glued to the stage, except for those of a broken-nosed bouncer who was watching their every move from an alcove. His suspicions were aroused as the newcomers seemed to be spending more time looking at the audience and the surroundings than at the live sex show. He slipped back into the shadows and made a quiet call. Immediately, five more muscular men emerged from a door behind him and focused on the newcomers, and stood there watching, waiting to be called to action. A message crackled through the earpiece of the chief bouncer,

"Wait until they split up, then take them."

He whispered the orders to the others.

Meanwhile, Brian and his team were inching their way around the room, making mental notes of potential threats and advantages. They had already noticed the heavies and were prepared. They were all wearing body armour and Brian and Scoffer both carried tasers which they were trained to use. The chief bouncer received a second message and motioned his team to approach the four newcomers. When they were blocking the officers' progress and close enough to trade punches, Brian smiled and spoke quietly.

"We're from the Leeds Council Licensing Department, just checking you're operating within the terms of your licence. We'd like a word with your boss. We're not happy with the amount of people in here. Your licence is for no more than fifty. You're way over that. So, step aside, please, and show me where the office is."
"My orders are not to let you in."

"I'm afraid the law states you have to let us in, or else your licence to operate will be revoked. Now, let me have a word with your manager."

Broken nose spoke quietly into his microphone and waited for the response, nodding when it came through.

"You can go into the office. Only you. The rest wait here."
"That's not acceptable. We are a team. We all have different responsibilities. Michael is responsible for checking health and safety, Andrew's responsibility is hygiene, Joseph's is building regulations."
"And what about yours?"
"Mine is Human Relations."
"What the hell's that?"
"I have to persuade clowns and goons like you lot to get out of our way and let us do our job. Now, please step aside. We'd like to talk to your boss. All together."
"No. You're going nowhere. You can come back when we're closed and do your inspection. Then, you can all see the boss, together."
"OK, you're forcing my hand, here."

Brian pulled out his ID and held it in front of Broken nose's face. Enraged, he threw a punch which Brian expected and was able to parry before countering with a right hook of his own which caused his opponent's nose to fracture again, spraying blood in an arc as his head shook. Two other bouncers were incapacitated by taser darts, before the armed unit broke in through the fire exit. The three remaining bouncers seemed unsure how to react. They were unable to claim numerical superiority and each one of them came to the conclusion that they were fighting professionals and would lose their licences if they resisted. They meekly put their hands in the air, then behind their back so handcuffs could be applied. Scoffer called for a van to take them away while Brian announced that the show was over, but that the audience must remain where they were until they'd all been quickly interviewed and identified. Paramedics arrived to check over the woman who had been subjected to the sexual assault before Brian arranged for her to be kept in hospital overnight. A search of the premises revealed a locked room where six skimpily dressed young women sat patiently waiting to be called to perform. They were whisked away to safety. Faced with the threat of his office door being kicked in, the manager opened it so that Brian could go through for a quiet word before he was escorted to the police station. Once the members of the audience had been briefly interviewed, they were allowed to leave, except for the man who had participated in the show, who was placed overnight in a cell, pending a further interview.

Tired but triumphant, the team went back to HQ where Brian had arranged for drinks to be laid on for an impromptu party as the pubs had already closed. It was short-lived, though, when Brian, of all people, reminded his staff they had to work in the morning.

Before he left, news came through that all the raids carried out by the NCA were successful and indications were that Leeds was the hub from which the rest of the businesses were managed.

********

After a short meeting to talk about the previous night's successful outing, the business of interviewing started. Four pairs were selected so that four interviews could run concurrently in the four Interview Rooms. The chief bouncer and the manager were made to wait. Brian wanted to see how much information they could get from the underlings first. The man who was arrested while having sex on the stage was allowed to leave with a caution and a 'don't leave town' warning.

Brian and Scoffer started the ball rolling in Room 1, by introducing themselves and informing the subject of his rights. Brian wasted no time.

"Name?"
"Phil Burnett."
"How did you get the job?"
"A mate told me about it."
"What's his name?"
"Dave. You've arrested him as well."
"His surname?"
"Phillips."
"Did you know what went on at the venue?"
"Vaguely. I was told it was a sex club."
"How long have you worked there?"
"A month. It only opened a month ago."
"How much do you get paid?"
"£80 a night."
"Cash in hand?"

"Yes."

"No deductions for tax or national insurance?"

"No. We're classed as self-employed."

"So, you sort out your own tax returns?"

"Yes."

"We'll be checking on that. I'd be interested to see what earnings you actually declare."

"That's between me and my accountant."

"I imagine you all use the same accountant?"

"Yes."

"OK. If you don't answer honestly all my questions, we'll ask the Inland Revenue to look at your returns. I don't think you'd like that, so you need to be totally open with me. OK?"

"OK."

"Have you ever met your boss's boss?"

"No."

"Do you know his name?"

"No."

"Do you know how many clubs there are in this chain?"

"No."

"Well, there are five we know of in this area. It's highly likely there are many more dotted around the country."

"That's nothing to do with me."

"You're right. So, let's get back to your workplace. Tell me about the manager at your branch."

"What do you want to know?"

"Everything you know. His name. His boss's name, for a start."

"I don't know either by name. We're just here to keep control during the shows."

"Ever get any trouble?"

"Only last night, when you lot came in."

"OK. You've already wasted five minutes of my precious time, so I'm going to have you remanded in custody until you're a bit more forthcoming with information. By my reckoning, we should find time to have another word with you in about six weeks. We're a bit busy just now, so you'll have to sit in a cell and stew. Is that OK?"

His legal representative spoke up.

"You can't do that!"

"Yes, I can. And I will, and by the time you've gone through the process necessary to get him out, the six weeks will be up, and I'll say 'sorry, my mistake'. That's what will happen, unless he gives me something useful."

"Can I have a quiet word with my client?"

They left the room, and stood outside listening to the conversation through the speaker, and smiling when they were called back in.

"Right, what have you got to tell me, Phil?"
"My boss, the guy in charge at this club is called Dave Gorman. His boss is called Murphy. Eamonn Murphy"
"Any idea where we can get hold of Murphy?"
"No, sorry."
"So, what happens if Gorman's not around?"
"I dunno. He's always been here when we need him."
"OK. Let's try something else. Where do the girls come from?"
"No idea. Some will be local, I think."
"Don't piss me about. You know exactly what I mean. Where do you get them from? You don't advertise in the Yorkshire Post?"
"I don't know. They just bring them in a Transit van and take them away at the end of the show."
"Have you anything else you'd like to tell us?"
"No."
"Then you'll go back to your cell till we decide what to do with you. Personally, I'd like to give you a good kicking, but first we'll see what the working girls have to say about you."

Once the first round of interviews was completed, Gary and Andy interviewed the broken-nosed bouncer, while Brian and Scoffer took the manager, Dave Gorman.

"First question. Who's your boss?"
"I don't know his name."
"Right, this is not a very good start, is it? Why don't you just cooperate? There might be some benefit in telling the truth for probably the first time in your life. So, I'll ask you again, who's your boss?"
"I told you I don't know his name."
"Why not? All your staff know him."
"So, why bother asking me?"
"You've got a good point there. I think we'll just put you back in the cells and forget about you. Take him away."
"Charge me or let me go."
"Listen, Gorman. You might be the boss of the whorehouse, but I make the rules here. I'll get back to you when I'm ready."
"Give me my phone back."

"Sorry, we haven't finished with it yet. All in good time. Anyway, time spent downstairs in a cell will be a good rehearsal for you, when you get sentenced. You've got years in jail in front of you unless you start talking. Your choice."

Brian and Scoffer sat back, smiling, arms crossed, waiting. Eventually, with a sigh, Gorman conceded.

"Eamonn Murphy."
"And where can we find him?"
"No idea. He gets in touch with us for meetings."
"How does he get in touch?"
"Phone, mostly."
"Give me his number."
"It's on my phone."
"OK. What about an email address?"
"I can't remember it offhand. It's in my address book in the office."
"Where's the office?"
"Home."
"Give me the address."
"What do I get in exchange?"
"We'll come to some sort of an arrangement."
"I want it in writing."
"Tough. If you're withholding information, you get a longer sentence. If you help us, you'll get something in return. So, what's your home address?"
"The Manor, Manor Drive, Knaresborough."
"Is there anyone there at the moment?"
"My wife's probably in, unless she's out shopping in Harrogate."
"Mind if we go and take a look?"
"Don't leave it untidy."
"Make sure we have access to everything, office, drawers, safe, etc., then we don't have to break anything. Tell you what; ring your wife and tell her to expect a visit."
"You've got my phone."
"You can use this one. And no messing now. If she's not in, we'll break the door down. We'll have a warrant, and we'll tear the house apart if we have to."

He handed over his phone and watched, listening, as Gorman called his wife. She agreed to stay at home until the police had visited.

Brian called to arrange a forensic team to meet him at the address, suspended the interview and set off with Scoffer to Knaresborough. By the time he reached his destination, the forensics team was waiting outside.

"She won't let us in, boss."
"I've got a warrant. If she refuses, we'll break the door down."

While Scoffer waited in the car, Brian marched up to the door to be met by a fiery redhead in a foul temper and some choice language. He held up his hand to stop her.

"Any more language like that and I'll arrest you. Now, please step aside and let these gentlemen do their job. Your husband has already agreed to it."
"My husband's an arse."
"I couldn't agree with you more. Now step aside. Don't make things worse. This won't take long."

It took just over an hour, as they loaded bagged items into the van.

"That's it, Brian. We'll let you know the outcome asap."
"Thanks, lads."

And turning to Mrs Gorman, he smiled.

"Nice to have met you, Mrs Gorman. Have a nice day."

There had been no response from Forensics by six o'clock, so, naturally, Brian called for an update.

"We've got nothing we can trace immediately back to Murphy, Brian. We're still looking."
"OK, thanks. Let's hope it's better news in the morning."

On his way home, it occurred to Brian that he needed some shopping, though he'd never thought to make a list. He stopped off at the Aldi store in Idle, hoping that seeing all the items on the shelves would jog his memory. However, his logical mind couldn't apply itself where shopping was concerned and he ended up buying a bag of frozen mixed vegetables, a pork shoulder steak and a bag of potatoes, before adding a bottle of Shiraz to his basket. He loaded the bag into the car boot and, on a whim, set off up Idle High Street to call into the White Bear, also known affectionately as The Scruffy.

It was quite some time since he'd been in The Scruffy, but it hadn't changed. It still had the warm, welcoming, comfortable atmosphere he felt every time he entered. The staff and customers were cheerful and friendly and, as ever, the beer was good! And, for an hour, he was able to take his mind off his work. When he was in there having a quiet pint, he was Brian, not DI Peters.

The buzzing of his phone brought him back to reality. For a second or two, he deliberated whether to ignore it, after all he was off duty. But he had no choice; he had to answer. He was *never* off-duty. The concept no longer existed. He was forever on duty.

"Peters."
"Brian, it's Allen. I just thought I'd let you know we've found nothing of any use, so we're packing up for the day and we'll pick it up in the morning when we've had some rest. Sorry to disappoint."
"It's fine, Allen. We all need a break occasionally, otherwise we'd burn out. I'll talk to you tomorrow."
"Thanks, Brian."

He finished his pint and drove home, mindful of the fact that he'd had three pints, and praying he didn't get stopped for any reason.

# CHAPTER 16

The following morning, there was some good news from Forensics. The call came before Brian had even set off for work.

"We found an encrypted file on his laptop. We've only just managed to read the data and we've got an address for Eamonn Murphy, as well as a mobile number."

"Thanks, Allen. Email it to me at work, please. I'm on my way there now."

"OK."

"And, please put your team on standby. We'll arrange to visit his house asap and need your assistance."

"Will do."

The address was in Burley-in-Wharfedale and turned out to be a large, detached Victorian house in its own grounds with an electronic security gate barring entry. Being first on the scene, Brian pressed the bell, but could get no reply. He immediately called for a team to disable the electronics and force open the gate. The gates were open by the time the Forensics team arrived, but they were still faced with locked doors to the house. Brian's solution was clear.

"Break the door down."

Soon they were inside, ignoring the alarm which had been activated, until someone discovered how to disable it. Now they were able to explore the house in peace.

That peace was soon disturbed by a shout from upstairs as Brian was searching through a filing cabinet in the makeshift office.

"We've got a body!"

He dropped what he was doing and raced upstairs. In the master bedroom, where clothes had been scattered everywhere, the body of a naked man was sprawled across the double bed, his facial features all but obliterated by gunshot wounds through the back of the head. Allen Greaves was examining him.

"Someone's taken a lot of trouble to ensure he was dead. Three shots to the back of the head. I'm assuming it's Murphy, but we'll know for sure when we've got him on the slab and cleaned up. We'll take samples here for DNA comparison, and we'll be able to get hold of medical and dental records. I'll let you know as soon as he's been officially identified."

"I've no doubt it's Murphy. Someone knew we were coming."

"I'm sure you're right. Someone's been searching all the drawers and cupboards up here. You can see all the stuff strewn on the carpet."

"Have you got a time of death yet?"

"Some time last night. I can narrow it down once we've got him on the slab."

"OK, thanks. I'll just take a quick look in the dressing room."

That too was a mess. Someone had been searching for something specific. He opened a wardrobe to find everything in a heap on the floor. He picked up a jacket and searched the pockets. All empty. Other jackets had been similarly emptied of their contents, with the debris left on the floor. He was not surprised that there was no sign of any bank debit or credit cards, nor any cash, but it was evident to Brian that this was no ordinary housebreaking incident. They had been searching for something specific. Exactly what, as yet he had no idea.

He went outside and looked around the grounds, happy to see that SOCO were doing the same. He approached one of the team.

"Any idea how they broke in?"

"Not yet, no. No windows are broken or appear to have been interfered with. There are no prints. The back door is still locked and bolted from the inside. The front door was secure until we broke it open to acquire access. The signs are that whoever committed the murder was invited in or lived here."

"Have you found anything to indicate someone else lived here?"

"Yes. A wardrobe full of ladies' clothes and shoes. Makeup and stuff. No photos, though, which is strange."

"OK, thanks. I'll leave you to get on with it. I'll wait for the report."

He called at the nearby houses to see if anybody heard or saw anything unusual the previous evening. The problem was they were all large detached houses which were each set in their own grounds with a long drive to the front and the owners, not unreasonably, had not seen or heard anything out of the ordinary. Except one, whose security camera showed a dark coloured Range Rover passing the gates at 10.30 and passing in the other direction at 11.05 the previous night. The camera had captured the images side-on, so no numberplate was visible, and the vehicle windows were of tinted glass so no usable image of the driver was available.

He called Teresa to update her and asked if she could get someone to meet him at Gorman's house, thinking that Mrs Gorman might have guessed that he'd searched her house for Murphy's address and alerted someone to ensure Murphy wasn't able to talk to the police. Was it possible that Dave Gorman had asked her in advance to ensure the police never got the chance to speak to Murphy? He began to wonder exactly who the boss in the business was. Before ending his call, he asked Teresa if she could check whether Mr or Mrs Gorman owned a dark coloured Range Rover. He drove over to Knaresborough for another chat with Mrs Gorman.

When he arrived, he found Scoffer waiting on the road outside. Together they walked to the door and rang the bell. There was no answer. They walked round the property, looking in the windows but saw no sign of life. Brian checked the garage, hoping to see a dark coloured Range Rover, but it was empty. In despair he rang Teresa to get permission for them to enter the house, but Scoffer interrupted his call.

"Just a minute, boss. If you don't mind, I'll have a go at the window fastening."
"Think you can open it?"
"Possibly. I've done these before."
"I hope you haven't got a second job as a housebreaker?"
"It's just a skill I picked up on a training course."
"Burglary for Beginners?"

He grinned.

"Something like that."

It was an old house with old-fashioned security, and it took only a few minutes for Scoffer, with the help of two slim metal rods with hooked ends which he kept in the car, to lever the catch open. He pulled the window wide open in triumph.

"Ta-daaaah! Mind giving me a leg up, boss?"

With some grunting and swearing, Scoffer eased himself through the frame and on to the kitchen worktop, which thankfully was clear and dry. He turned so that he could get his feet on the ground before hurrying around to open the door to let Brian in.

"Thanks, Scoffer. Let's have a look round. You never know, Mrs Gorman might be in the toilet."
"Or behind a door with an axe."
"Good point. You go first."
"Thanks, boss."

They went from room to room. There were signs that someone had packed and left in a hurry – clothes strewn around, drawers left open.

"We'll need to get Forensics back. We don't have Mrs Gorman's fingerprints on file."
"Are you thinking we may match prints at Murphy's?"
"Possibly."
"But that won't prove anything. We don't know if the Gormans met Murphy socially."
"If you'd met her, you wouldn't want to know her socially. But we'd better put an APB out for her."
"I know it's unlikely, but we should check the size of the women's clothes and shoes we found at Murphy's and compare them to what's been left here. We can't rule out the fact that they may have been in a relationship."
"OK. Let's not rule anything out. What if Mrs Murphy's the boss?"
"Good point. She's bad-assed enough."
"Fancy running a sweep at HQ?"
"Not sure the DCI will go for that."
"OK. Let's just take it one step at a time and eliminate the suspects in turn."
"You're the boss."

********

Results started to come through from Forensics the next morning. As he received them, he updated the whiteboards. The first significant find was that Mrs Gorman's fingerprints were found all over Eamonn Murphy's house. This was followed by the fact that clothes and shoe sizes were the same in both houses, including nightwear. She was more than an occasional visitor. The big question mark hung over who killed Murphy. They couldn't rule out Mrs Gorman, but they needed to establish a motive. Brian had a theory: what if Dave Gorman was the boss? He and his wife ran the business. His wife kept Murphy happy while Gorman plotted to get rid of him once he had full control of the money. When they realised the police were closing in, they decided to eliminate Murphy before he talked and exposed Gorman and his wife as the real bosses. It was feasible, but somehow unlikely. Brian thought the idea was worth pursuing. He set up another interview with Gorman.

"Just thought I'd update you on the situation, Mr Gorman. Are you aware that Mr Murphy is dead?"
"Dead? No. When did this happen?"
"Last night. By the way, do you or Mrs Gorman own a Range Rover?"
"Yes, the wife has one."
"What colour?"
"Black. Why, is there a problem?"
"Maybe. Let's talk about you and your wife's relationship with Murphy. Has it always been simply professional?"
"Yes."
"How did you meet Murphy?"
"In a club, in Leeds. A few mates were having a beer and one of them knew him, so he introduced me to him."
"What was the name of the man who introduced him?"
"I can't remember. We'd all had a few drinks."
"What did you talk about?"
"I can't remember. We'd had a few drinks."
"So, after that, who contacted who?"
"I can't remember."
"Don't tell me; you'd all had a few drinks."
"That's right."
"Did he give you a business card, or did you give him yours?"
"Can't remember."
"So, after you'd come into contact again, did you decide to meet up?"
"I think so, but don't remember who suggested it. Or where we met."
"We're getting nowhere here, are we? Let's try a different tack. Did your wife ever meet Murphy?"
"Yes. Occasionally."
"In what sort of situation? Business? Social?"
"Both."
"So, your wife was involved in the business?"
"Not exactly."
"Yes, or no?"

"A bit. I mean, she was there at meetings, but just for moral support."

"So, she attended meetings about your business, the sex trade?"

"She was broadminded."

"Where did you first meet her?"

"I don't remember."

"Really? Most people remember quite clearly."

"Yeah? Not me, I'm afraid."

"Do you remember when you met her?"

"Not exactly. Roughly."

"The year?"

"2000 and something."

"Can you remember her maiden name?"

"No, sorry."

"Sounds like you've had a very close relationship."

"Mm, I suppose it does, when you look at it like that."

"One more question. What's your wife's first name? Surely you can remember that."

"Siobhan."

"We'll take a ten-minute break. Give your memory time to recover."

Brian stormed out of the Interview Room, banging the door shut after him. He was angry. He had asked straightforward questions, not difficult, yet Gorman refused to give anything away. What was he hiding? Suddenly it dawned on him. He called Teresa.

"Teresa, drop whatever you're doing. I need some information, urgently. I want to know everything about Gorman's wife, Siobhan. Get Ruth to help if you need it."

"On it now."

He stood in the corridor, drinking a coffee, waiting for a reply. It took only a few minutes.

"We've turned something up, Brian. I thought you'd like to know this immediately while we carry on with a full search of her history."

"Go on."

"Gorman's wife's maiden name is Murphy. She's Eamonn Murphy's sister!"

"Thanks, Teresa. Keep looking, please."

He took a deep breath, mentally rehearsing what he would say when the interview recommenced, then confidently strode back into the room.

"Why didn't you tell me about your wife's relationship with Murphy?"

"I answered your questions."

"No, you didn't! I asked if you remembered your wife's maiden name. You said 'no'."

"Memory lapse."

"Well, let me refresh your memory. Her maiden name was Murphy. Do you remember now?"

"Ah, yes, now I remember."

"And did you know she had a brother?"

"Now I come to think of it, yes."

"For the benefit of the recording, will you please state her brother's name?"

"Eamonn. Eamonn Murphy."

"The same Eamonn Murphy you worked with? The one you said was your boss?"

"Now you come to mention it, yes."

"Right now, I have staff poring over records, unearthing Siobhan's entire history. You could do yourself a huge favour by volunteering this information now."

"Let them carry on searching. I wouldn't like to put them out of a job."

"This interview is suspended at 11.25."

He switched off the recording.

"Go back to your cell and think carefully about want you want to do for the rest of your life."

Brian went back upstairs to talk to Teresa, who was hard at work with Ruth assisting.

"OK, ladies. Anything new for me?"

"Loads, Brian. Ruth and I are still turning up facts which shed new light on some recent events."

"Have you enough to give a presentation to the team?"

"Give us the rest of the day, please. I'll schedule a meeting for tomorrow morning in the Conference Room. We'll get the whiteboard set up."

"OK. Well done, both of you."

********

The Conference Room was full. Even DCI Gardner was present as Teresa arranged all the material before beginning. She showed an image of Siobhan Gorman on the screen.

"This is Siobhan Gorman. She is married to Dave Gorman who is ostensibly the manager of a club in Leeds which is one of several whorehouses, or sex clubs, run by a franchise called Perverts' Paradise. Gorman's boss is, or was, since he is now dead, a man called Eamonn Murphy. Murphy has a sister called Siobhan, the same Siobhan who is Dave Gorman's wife. Still with me? Good. We believe she killed her brother to stop him talking to us. We believe she, in fact, is Gorman's boss as well as his wife. Nationwide, we're trying to find her. She's done a runner. However, we've had a look into some of her recent business activities. She bought a removals company at the beginning of the pandemic, then applied for a bounce-back loan out of which it appears she bought six pantechnicons. Eamonn Murphy then bought another company, and took out a government loan to refurbish the vehicles and convert them into mobile residences, ie brothels.
Now, Perverts' Paradise runs dozens of sex clubs and brothels, mostly in the north of England. We're still working on discovering their locations. Some are static, others are mobile. As soon as we have the locations, we'll be working with the NCA to raid them.
Interestingly, a name has come up from an earlier investigation. Dave Crowther. He was apparently involved in prostitution and activities very much like the ones we're currently working on. We need to find him. My belief is he is the top man. Any questions?"

After a moment of silence, comments and suggestions came thick and fast.

"How the hell are we going to locate all these brothels, especially the mobile ones?"
"Through the power of the Internet. We're already tracing leads on the Dark Web. But it's not my decision how we proceed once we have locations. If we wait until we have, or believe we have, all of them, there may be a leak which results in us getting none of them. If we take them down as soon as we identify them, the rest may be shut down and become untraceable. The decision's not mine. I just supply the data."
"Thank you, Teresa. It's something we'll have to discuss with the NCA."
"Is there any reason why each area can't provide their own teams to take down their local sites in a coordinated attack nationwide?"

"That would be the ideal solution. I'll have to take it up with the powers that be."

"So, can we work on producing a list of venues we need to raid?"

"We're already on it. We'll need another twenty-four hours at least."

"OK. Please update me on progress tomorrow, Teresa. And everybody please note: all leave is cancelled for the next seven days."

The meeting was adjourned.

The following morning, a very stressed Teresa knocked on the DCI's door, and entered.

"You asked for an update on Perverts' Paradise, sir?"

"Yes, Teresa. Please, sit down. Any progress?"

"Some, sir. Everybody's been working flat out on it. We've identified six more static sites, around the north of England, and I have the locations where a further five mobiles are expected to be on Saturday night. There are a few more which have yet to post their whereabouts for the weekend's business, but I expect them to do so either today or tomorrow."

"Thank you, Teresa. Are any of the locations in our area?"

"Two. One in Armley, one in Chapeltown."

"OK. Please pass what you have to Brian. Ask him to work on a plan to take down those two. He'll have to co-ordinate the plan with the NCA, obviously."

"I think you can trust him to do the job correctly, sir."

"Of course, Teresa. OK, keep me informed."

Brian was on the phone when Teresa reached his desk. He was engaged in conversation with Alex at the NCA, so Teresa laid the report indicating the expected locations of the brothels in front of him. Seeing them, he changed the course of his conversation.

"Alex, Teresa has just brought me an update. Can you give me fifteen minutes to read through it, then I'll call you back?"

"That's fine, Brian. Can you ask Teresa to send me a copy, please?"

"It's on its way to your inbox already, Alex."

"Of course."

Brian read quickly through the report before sending a quick email to his team.

"Don't make any plans for Sat. night. We're needed on duty. More later. Conference room 2pm."

Next, he called Alex and between them they hammered out a plan for co-ordinated attacks on the venues Teresa had so far identified. The hope was that, among those they expected to arrest, there would be someone prepared to cut a deal by revealing some key details regarding the business hierarchy and some other so far unidentified locations. It was worth the gamble.

Brian and Teresa spent the rest of the morning contacting other divisions who would be expected to mount a raid on a target in their area. Armed support was also organised, and by 2pm his team was assembled in the Conference Room as Brian gave a presentation on Saturday night's planned assaults, including representatives of teams from other areas by video conference. By 4pm, all details had been discussed and agreed.

With the agreement of his team, Brian assigned his officers to the target sites as he thought appropriate for the job. Armley being the smaller of the two sites, Lynn, Andy, Scoffer and Jo-Jo would take it, whereas Brian, Gary, Paula, Louise and Ruth were assigned to the Chapeltown site. Each team had an armed unit for company. Forensics officers would be on call as soon as a site was under police control, and uniformed officers would be in the area as backup. Each officer taking part was fully aware of his role in the exercise.

At the end of the day, Brian drove down Highfield Road towards his home in Thackley, but without thinking turned left up Westfield Lane as he reached the junction. He immediately berated himself for his error and stopped, then decided to call in at The Scruffy for a drink. He tried to convince himself that had been his intention in the first place, but he somehow had felt compelled to drive past his previous home. He would have a pint, then decide what to do.

The pub was quiet. He ordered a pint and sat alone at a table, trying to relax. He had liked the pub right from his first visit. He felt comfortable and at ease and diverted his thoughts back to the upcoming exercise. Soon, he was enjoying his third pint and considered having more and leaving the car overnight, but sensibly dismissed the idea and left the pub, climbing into his car and driving purposely in the direction of his previous home. He pulled to a halt outside. It looked the same; only the curtains were different. He felt a strange desire to knock on the door, in the vain hope that Sarah or one of the kids would open it. He knew that was not possible. They were dead. Only the ghosts remained. He turned the car around and drove home, parked up and walked back to the Ainsbury for another pint. He needed company. And although it was busy and he recognised many of the customers, nodding a greeting, he didn't engage in conversation with anyone, simply taking his pint upstairs and sitting quietly in contemplation of things past.

Before he left, Nicky kindly ordered a takeaway for him to be delivered to his home. It arrived just as he staggered across the carpark.

On Saturday morning, he woke up late and shuffled into the kitchen to discover the mess he'd left the previous night. He went to the bathroom and promptly threw up. Lesson learnt, he thought. He spent the next few hours going over and over the plans for the evening's task, memorising every detail, and by two o'clock he felt well enough to have a light meal, without alcohol, for a change. He switched on his PC and checked his emails. Nothing of any significance, except a reminder from Teresa about the meeting time and place for the evening's foray. He smiled. He hadn't forgotten, but he knew unless he changed his ways, the day would come when many important things would simply slip his mind. He knew that time was not too far in the future, but he had some critical decisions to make, decisions which he couldn't keep putting on the back burner. He set his alarm for six o'clock and went back to bed.

The alarm woke him from his deep sleep, a sleep full of nightmares which he could never escape. As always, he shrugged them off, had a quick shower and a coffee and dressed for the night's event.

By 8pm he was at the rendezvous in Headingley waiting for the armed backup to arrive, while checking on the situation with the other groups. All were in place. He looked at his watch as the armed unit drew up. 8.10. Time for a quick briefing to ensure everyone was aware of their role. It was not necessary. Everyone knew what was expected. It was just a matter of killing time until 8.30, when the coordinated assaults were to commence. They set off at 8.20 towards Chapeltown, travelling in convoy towards their site, and pulled up around the corner from the gates to the industrial unit, watching as the time ticked round to 8.30 when

Brian shouted 'GO'. The armoured vehicle smashed through the entrance gates and pulled up in the car park, disgorging its crew of heavily armed officers while the other vehicles followed closely in their wake. Paula brought Brian's attention to a vehicle parked in an unlit area. It was a black Range Rover. He relayed the numberplate to HQ for confirmation, but in the meantime, they burst through the small reception area, which was now unmanned, and followed the corridor to a door at the end. On command, they stormed the auditorium where naked women were being paraded on a makeshift stage, while customers shouted bids for their services. There was panic in the room as the spectators ran for the exits only to be stopped in their tracks by armed officers. Brian estimated there were around fifty customers who were quickly rounded up and made to stand facing the wall as they were searched and then ordered to kneel on the floor whilst an armed guard watched over them. Brian collared the man who seemed to be coordinating the 'show', pulled him to one side and questioned him.

"Where's your boss?"
"In the office. At the back."

Brian motioned an armed officer to find the boss, while he handcuffed his prisoner. He looked round the room. Each officer was performing as expected. The girls were given blankets to cover themselves until transport arrived to take them to a safe place, and officers were combing every yard of the warehouse for evidence. As they reported back, Brian was informed the office was empty. There was no sign of Siobhan Gorman. The operation was wrapped up quickly after the 'guests' had been briefly interviewed and identified, and the girls had been removed to safety. As they stepped back out into the car park, they noticed the black Range Rover had gone.

Brian reported the conclusion of the operation to HQ, receiving a quick update on the results from similar sorties. He asked if there were any helicopters available to search the area for the Range Rover, but the response was negative. However, a nationwide hunt was authorised. As soon as Forensics arrived, everyone except Brian and Gary was allowed to stand down.

The operation was wound up shortly after 1pm by which time Forensics had completed their job, loaded up their transport with evidence and driven off. Brian was still receiving reports from

Teresa on the outcome of simultaneous raids. Overall, it had been a good night, with more than twenty operations around the country having been successfully concluded.

"OK, Gary. Let's knock off. Well done. It's been a productive night."
"It would have been better if we'd caught Siobhan."
"Maybe next time."

********

The mood of the officers the following morning was mixed. Overall, the operation had been successful, with thirteen mobile and static sites having been raided in the north of England, but there was disappointment that Siobhan Gorman had escaped capture. However, there were many interviews to be carried out with those identified as staff at the raided sites, which would keep officers throughout the area busy for quite some time. Certainly, in Bradford, the Interview Rooms were fully booked for days as officers took it in turn to conduct interviews whose main purpose was to uncover the identity of those at the highest level of the hierarchy and bring them to justice.

Gradually, as those at the base of the organisation were interviewed, names other than Siobhan Gorman began to emerge. These were added to the whiteboard:

David Black
Stephen Stainforth
Barry Whitehead
Angela Whitehead

As the names emerged, they were passed to Teresa for initial investigation and her findings relayed to Brian immediately.

"David Black was locked up for five years for running a protection racket in Leicester, where illegal immigrants were employed in the textiles industry. There is some evidence that he supplies female immigrants to the sex trade. Believed to reside in the East Midlands area.
Stephen Stainforth seems to have moved out, possibly to the Isle of Man, after being implicated in the same business as Whitehead. His whereabouts are unknown.
Barry and Angela Whitehead are siblings. Both served time for running brothels in the Newcastle area. Whereabouts unknown."

"Thanks, Teresa. I'll pass them to the NCA. We'll put out a nationwide request for information as to their whereabouts."

It wasn't long before the first piece of good news came through via a phone call to Brian.

"Good afternoon, DI Peters. I have some good news for you regarding one of the names which were flagged. We've just taken a man into custody for a driving offence. His licence gives his name as Barry Whitehead."
"Where have you got him?"
"He's in a cell here in Middlesbrough."
"For Christ's sake, don't let him go. Use any excuse you can think of but keep hold of him until we get there."
"No problem."
"We're on our way."

He turned to the team.

"Anybody fancy a trip with me to Middlesbrough?"
"I'm up for it, boss."
"Come on then, Scoffer."

They raced up the A1 with Scoffer driving as Brian gave directions while collecting updated information from Teresa regarding their interviewee on his laptop. More good news ensued after officers in Middlesbrough searched Barry Whitehead and found some correspondence on him bearing an address which didn't match the one on his driving licence. They quickly sent officers to the address and arrested his sister, Angela.

"Two birds, one stone, Scoffer."
"Could be a good day out for us."

The interviews went without problems. The Whiteheads both agreed to share everything they knew about the Perverts' Paradise business. Names, addresses, the lot.

Once Brian was satisfied the Whiteheads would be kept in custody until the operation was concluded, he and Scoffer returned to HQ, having already sent to Teresa a list of names, and addresses of properties to be raided. By the time they arrived at HQ, only Teresa was still at work.

"Working late again, Teresa?"

"Just ensuring the NCA has got all the details they need to sort out the raids for tomorrow. Pity there are none in our area."
"I think we've done our share, don't you? It's time we had a break. Anyone fancy a pint?"

Both Teresa and Scoffer reluctantly declined, leaving Brian to enjoy a solitary evening in the Black Rat. He was not surprised to be refused service after his third pint, as Alyson explained.

"Strict instructions from your friend Teresa, Brian. You've got a hard day tomorrow, I've been told."
"OK, Alyson. She's right. I need to leave now, or you'll have to throw me out at the death. I'll see you next time. Goodnight."

Sensibly, he went directly home, rummaging through the fridge for something to eat, before deciding on a cheese sandwich, washed down with a mug of tea.

# CHAPTER 17

The Conference Room had whiteboards everywhere. Each one bore the name of a different region or city as its heading, and underneath were the addresses to be raided, crossed off as information was received from the NCA. By the end of the day, a further seventeen sites had been shut down, with the added bonus that David Black had been arrested in Leicester and Stephen Stainforth had been traced to an address in Douglas, Isle of Man, from where his arrest was imminent.

Brian enjoyed a long phone conversation with Alex at the NCA.

"I'm confident we've shut down the entire operation, Brian. We're immensely grateful to you and your team for the effort you've put into this, and we'll make sure your DCI is fully aware of your contribution."
"Thanks, Alex. I'll pass your message to the team. They've all risen to the challenge of investigating some very difficult cases recently. I'm proud of them all."
"Would you also please make them aware we'll be recruiting again soon if anybody fancies a change of scenery? That includes both yourself and Teresa."
"Count me out, Alex. I think I've had enough."
"You'll be sorely missed, Brian. But I understand. Think about it anyway."
"I will. Thank you."

Brian turned his attention to the remaining open cases that had been on the back burner due to the recent caseload. He called a meeting to restore some focus to the team's outstanding investigations.

The main worry was the sheer number of car thefts which were still being reported.

"Gary, can you please give us an update on your progress with this?"
"No good news, boss. The last thing I heard was the NCA raided a chop shop in Oldham where they found a massive number of stolen vehicles and parts and then mounted a raid on a facility at Seaforth Docks on Merseyside. It seems there must have been a tip-off as the place was empty, totally cleared out, when they got there. However, they arrested a man called Shafique Khan, but

he's refused to acknowledge he had anything to do with it. He said he only rented the premises out and had no idea what it was used for. He gave a name of the person nominally running the business, but nobody's been able to locate him. So, I'm afraid it's a dead end at the moment."

"OK. As far as the investigation into the warehouse and the docks is concerned, that's NCA's business. It's out of our area. But car thefts are still being reported locally, and that *is* our business. So, let's make it our priority. Gary, I want you to lead on this. Pick a team to help you and see what you can find."

Gary collected the crime reports from Teresa and agreed with Brian that Jo-Jo, Paula, and Andy would join him in the initial investigation. Between them, they split the cases into two piles, one for the ladies, the other for himself and Andy, and set off to interview the owners of the stolen cars.

Brian was left with the problem of how to trace Siobhan.

********

Paula parked the car on the drive of a large, detached house in Ben Rhydding.

"Wow! What do you think of this, Jo-Jo?"
"I don't think I could afford the mortgage on the garden shed on my wage, never mind the tennis court and swimming pool. Let's go and see how the other half lives."

The door was answered by a young lady, the au pair, who was struggling to control two lively children in the absence of their parents who, apparently, were 'at work'.

"Could we please have their work address? We need to speak to them."
"Follow me".

She took them down a long path through a wooded area to the back of the house, where there was a secluded spot containing two new buildings – home offices.

"Mr Morris is in the first one, Mrs Morris is in the far one. Please knock before you enter. They are very busy."
"Thank you."

They watched as she dragged the unruly kids back to the house before knocking on the door of the first office.

"Enter."

They opened the door to find a man in his thirties, in jeans and T-shirt, sitting in front of a computer screen watching Youtube.

"What can I do for you?"
"We're from Bradford CID, Mr Morris. I believe you've had your car stolen?"
"Have you found it?"
"Not yet, sir. We'd like to ask you some questions, please."
"Fire away."
"Tell us about the car. Make, etc."
"Range Rover Sport. White, 2022 plate."
"Value?"
"Around 80k."
"Stolen a week or so ago?"
"Weekend before last. Have you found it?"
"Unfortunately, not yet, sir. Where exactly was it stolen from?"
"The garage. Well, the stables behind the pool."
"During the night?"
"Yes. About 1am. My wife heard a noise and looked out of the window. The garage door was wide open. She woke me up and I went to have a look. When I got downstairs, the front door was open, and the keys were missing."
"The car keys?"
"Yes. And the garage keys."
"Where were they taken from?
"A hook on the wall by the door."
"Not very secure."
"They were hidden under the coats. Someone would have to search for them."
"Or they knew exactly where to find them. Did you have any visitors in the weeks before the theft?"
"Of course! All friends. We have a lively social life."
"What about other callers? Tradesmen?"
"We had our internet upgraded for better reception in our workspaces."
"Who performed the work?"
"It was outsourced to some local company. Two men called one morning to size the job up. Then we didn't hear anything for a while, so we complained, and they sent someone else."

"Which company supplies your internet?"

"BT."

"May I ask, sir, was anything else stolen?"

"No. Nothing."

"One other thing. The men who came initially. Did they have a company name on the van?"

"No. It was just a scruffy white Transit."

"Thanks for your time. We'll be in touch."

They visited the homes of two other victims and were given a similar story. In both cases they'd needed something fixing and a couple of men in a scruffy Transit came to size up the job, told them they'd submit a quote, but they never heard from them again. They hired someone else to carry out the work.

Back at HQ at the end of the afternoon, they conferred with Gary and Andy who'd experienced much the same scenario.

"Rogue traders. But how are they getting the leads? Mr Morris dealt directly with BT, so someone at BT must have passed the message to the thieves."

"One of our interviewees was having a new kitchen installed and asked for quotes. They approached three different companies, but only two actually gave a quote. They never heard from the other guys, who turned up in a scruffy Transit. A white Transit, with no company name on it."

"OK. Get back in touch with the victims. Find out the name of the company who never got back to them. They must have advertised somewhere. My guess is it's the same company. And, if so, someone at a call centre may be passing them leads. I'll chase that one."

The following day, Andy commenced the difficult task of wringing relevant information from BT's Helpline, finding himself pushed from pillar to post until eventually he was put through to someone who was able to help.

"Sorry for the delay, sir. I've traced the initial enquiry. It seems it came by phone to our team and was dealt with by an operator who's no longer employed by us. It seems this person sent someone without recording who it was. A while later, we got another call from the customer complaining they hadn't heard anything, so we sent someone else. It sounds as if the person who

took the initial call sent some rogue team not authorised by us. I can only apologise."
"OK. Where can we find this operator who sent the rogue team?"
"Here's the name, and the address she gave us."
"And how long did she work for you?"
"A week. Then she said the job wasn't for her and left."
"Thanks for your help."

At the same time, Jo-Jo had spoken to the couple who'd phoned for a quote for a kitchen installation. The company who never got back to them had advertised their services on the noticeboard of the local supermarket. They were able to get a mobile number, and their trading name, Wilkins and Sons Kitchens. There was no answer when Jo-Jo called the number, nor was their trading name found in any directory. They were unable to trace them, so Gary sent Paula and Jo-Jo to an address the supermarket had provided, on the Ravenscliffe estate. There was nobody at home, so they tried the neighbour.

"Sorry to bother you. We're trying to get hold of your neighbour, Joan Watkinson. Do you know where we might find her?"
"I don't know anybody by that name. Sorry."
"So, who lives there?"
"Mandy Bryant."
"Do you know where she works?"
"No. She hasn't lived here long. She's hardly ever in."
"Anyone else live there?"
"A couple of men. I think they might be brothers, but I'm not sure. They never speak to anybody."
"Do they have transport?"
"Yes. A van."
"A white van? A Transit?"
"Yes."
"You don't happen to know the registration, do you?"
"No. Sorry. It's a 06 plate."
"Thanks for your help."

They discussed the situation back at HQ, before deciding to keep a watch on the house for forty-eight hours, in shifts. Gary and Jo-Jo drew the short straws and took up their position down the street from the house as soon as they'd finished their regular working day.

Forty-eight hours later, there had still been no sighting, but after a quick discussion, they decided to prolong their surveillance for a further period. Their persistence paid off when, in the early hours of the morning, a battered white Transit van pulled up outside the house where a woman got out before the van drove off. Paula and Andy decided to follow the van, Paula's decision being endorsed during a phone call to Gary, who in turn called HQ to request that on-duty officers drove past the house regularly during the night.

The Transit stopped at a row of lock-up garages in Eccleshill, where the passenger got out and opened one of the units to allow the van to drive straight in. The two men checked the garage was secured before walking away towards Undercliffe, with Andy discreetly following on foot at a distance. Once the two men had entered a house, Andy called Paula forward to join him in keeping watch on the house, while two uniformed officers were assigned to keep an eye on the garage.

Gary and Jo-Jo took over the surveillance at seven in the morning to allow Paula and Andy a break. They were soon called into action when the two men left the house and got into a waiting taxi. The detectives followed until the taxi stopped and the targets alighted and walked towards a disused warehouse. They stopped outside, the younger man looking round while the older man opened the side door. They slipped inside, locking the door behind them. A minute later, a flat-bed lorry pulled out of the front doors with a covered vehicle loaded and secured on the back. Jo-Jo called for backup while they followed the lorry towards the M62, Gary making phone calls to ensure access to the motorway would be blocked by police cars, while an armed squad raced to the site.

It was all over in minutes. As the van neared the access road to the motorway, they could clearly see the roadblock on the slip road. The driver stopped and prepared to reverse on to the roundabout, but his manoeuvre was blocked by a squad of police vehicles. Seeing the armed officer pointing weapons in their direction, the two men sheepishly climbed down from the cab, hands in the air.

Gary headed directly towards the flatbed, lifting the covers enough to recognise the white Range Rover. He checked the numberplate; it matched. The two men were taken into custody; the lorry impounded along with its cargo. He and Jo-Jo raced back to Ravenscliffe to arrest Joan Watkinson/Mandy Bryant, or whatever her real name was. She went with them to HQ without a fuss and was left in a cell so the officers could get a few hours' sleep.

Gary was back on duty at lunchtime, typing up his report and checking whether Teresa had yet been able to establish the prisoner's real identity. She had; it was Joan Watkinson, although she used several aliases, she was the wife of Gerry Watkinson, the elder of the two men in custody. Armed with that information, he walked down to the Interview Room with Jo-Jo. Their first target was Paul Watkinson, the younger brother.

"So, Paul, tell me about this enterprise of yours."
"I don't know what you mean. I just work for my big brother. He tells me what to do, and I do it."
"Like stealing cars?"
"I don't know anything about that. We're just repossessing 'em."
"Is that what your brother told you? You're repossessing cars? You're casing houses whose residents own expensive cars, you're breaking into the houses to steal the car keys and driving off to sell them. So, who are you taking them to?"
"I don't know! I'm only keeping my brother company."
"Well, lad, you'll be keeping him company in Armley for ten years unless you start talking. Your choice."

Gary could see the look of panic on Paul Watkinson's face. He was a ghostly white! Gary simply sat there, silent, staring at his prisoner until he broke.

"OK. What do you want to know?"
"Where you're taking the cars, and who is paying you to do it."
"I don't know who's paying. My brother looks after all that."
"So, who are you delivering to?"
"A place in Liverpool. I don't know what they call it."
"How many cars have you taken there?"
"I don't know. A dozen or so."
"What happens when you've delivered them?"
"My brother gets paid and gets a list of motors they want next time."
"All high-value cars?"
"Yeah."
"And what's your sister-in-law's part in all this?"
"She advertises us as tradesmen, so we get access to people's homes. Chance to weigh up the job."
"The job? You mean stealing their car?"

"Yeah."

"What else does she do?"

"Works at call centres and sends us out to houses instead of the proper tradesmen. And she takes orders for particular cars."

"So, how do you find out who owns these expensive cars?"

"She pays people who work in garages and MOT centres and showrooms and that for information."

"So, this place in Liverpool where you take the cars, you don't know its name?"

"No."

"Would you be able to take me there?"

"No."

"Why not? You've been there often enough."

"They'd kill me if I told you."

"Who would?"

"The people who run it."

"What's their name?"

"Ahmad. And Bashir. They're brothers."

"Iranian?"

"Something like that."

"OK. Anything else you want to tell me?"

"No."

"OK. Go back to sleep. We'll wake you when it's time to go to prison."

Gary and Jo-Jo left the Interview Room and walked down the corridor to the coffee machine. While Gary got the coffees, Jo-Jo made a call to Teresa to bring her up to date and ask if she could trace Ahmad and Bashir, knowing full well it would be highly improbable without a surname. Still, it was worth a shot. Gary returned with the coffees.

"So, Jo-Jo, who's next?"

"Mrs Watkinson, I think. She's the brains. The two men seem a bit thick to me."

"OK. Do you want to lead?"

"Love to."

Joan Watkinson was brought down, scowling. Jo-Jo decided to make her life even more of a misery.

"You're in a lot of trouble! You're facing a long prison sentence."

"You haven't proved I've done anything wrong, yet."

"Young Paul's just told us what you've been up to. Sending them out to do jobs they're not qualified to do, instead of sending proper tradesmen. Sending them out to steal cars and drive them to Liverpool. You're in charge of this little criminal gang. You're going to get the longest sentence."

"Wait a minute. That's wrong! I only do what Gerry tells me to do. He's the boss."

"Sorry. We've decided you're the one in charge. We'll be pushing for the longest possible sentence."

"That's not fair! Gerry's been nicking cars to order for years. Long before I met him."

"OK. Tell us your side of the story. From the beginning. How did you meet?"

"Outside the courts in Barnsley."

"What were you doing there?"

"I was just there as support for a friend who'd been caught shoplifting. Gerry was up for assault. We just got talking."

"Had a lot in common, did you?"

"I suppose so. We just hit it off."

"So, how long have you been partners-in-crime?"

"Just recently. This is our first offence."

"Really? I have evidence you were jointly convicted of fraud a year ago."

"We weren't guilty. We were set up."

Gary's phoned buzzed. He looked at the screen, grinned and stood up.

"I'll have to leave the room for a minute."

Outside the Interview Room, Teresa was waiting with a sheaf of papers.

"These are what Jo-Jo asked me to look into."
"Thanks."

He took one look at them, grinned and went back into the room, placing the papers in front of Jo-Jo. She glanced at them and picked up the interview.

"So, you were saying this is your first offence."
"That's right."
"What about the house in Menston about six months ago?"
"I don't know what you're on about."

"Let me refresh your memory. You were working at a call centre in Leeds. You took a call from a Mr Martin, who had a problem with his central heating. You told him you'd send an engineer to look at it. But, instead, you sent Gerry and Paul. When they got there, they saw a Ferrari on the drive. They had a look at the central heating, made up a story about needing a part and said they'd be back in a couple of days to fit it. But they lied. They came back the same night and nicked the Ferrari. It was only when nobody came to fix the central heating that Mr Martin put two and two together and found that the call centre could find no record of his call."

"I don't know anything about that."

"Strange, because a similar thing happened a few weeks later when you sent your friends Laurel and Hardy to give a quote for some re-wiring at a house in Harrogate, where a nice shining Bentley Continental GTS was parked outside. And guess what? It got nicked during the night. Do you need any more examples?"

Joan Watkinson sat, looking down. She was spent.

"Can we make a deal?"

"That depends. What's in it for us? And what do you expect in return?"

"I'll tell you everything I know, as long as you accept that I was forced to do it. Gerry used to beat me up."

"Have you any evidence to back that up?"

"No."

"No trips to BRI for treatment? No visits to the doctor?"

"No. He wouldn't let me go. He terrorised me."

"This is bollocks, and you know it. The only way you'll get away with a lighter sentence is if you tell us the truth so we can catch the people who are buying the stolen cars from you. Now, you can go back and stew in your cell for an hour and think about it. Interview over."

They conferred in the corridor.

"What do you think, Jo-Jo?"

"I think she's making it all up. I think she's the boss."

"So do I. Let's have a word with Gerry. Let's tell him she says he's the mastermind and see how he reacts."

"I want to hear him say the names of the guys in Liverpool. If he confirms what his younger brother said, we can check them out."

"OK, let's talk to him."

The interview was brief. Once he was told what his wife and brother had confessed to, he did all he could to convince his interviewers he was just a stooge. His wife was the boss. She set up all the thefts from taking the orders for specific cars and locating them by paying dealerships and garages for information, to fishing expeditions by sending bogus tradesmen, himself and his brother, out to see if there were any desirable cars in the area and casing the premises. All he and his brother did was steal the cars and take them to the chop shop in Liverpool. They were all charged and remanded in custody.

Gary and Jo-Jo reported their progress to Brian, who congratulated them.

"I want you two to take the credit for this, so take it to the DCI and tell him you'd like to organise a raid on the Liverpool site. You'll need backup from the NCA, or they may want to take it over. It's your choice whether you want that to happen. Personally, I'd like you two to be in at the kill. It's a bonus to have something like this on your record. I'll let you make the decision what you want to do. Well done, both of you."

They walked up to Teresa's desk beaming with pride and thanked her for her part in the operation so far. Next, they had the opportunity to outline their plans to DCI Gardner who listened with interest.

"So, we have Mrs Watkinson's mobile, which she uses to arrange the deliveries. We'll send a message to tell them we've got a Range Rover for them and agree a delivery date. Then we get backup from the NCA to accompany us. We'll need to take Joe Schofield since he's the only one who's got the required HGV licence."
"OK. Set it up with the NCA. Check first with DI Peters. He'll spot any flaws in your plan if any exist."
"Thank you, sir."

# CHAPTER 18

There was great excitement as the flat-back set off from Bradford in the morning, except instead of a Range Rover sitting under the cover, there was an armoured vehicle containing six armed officers. Jo-Jo followed in a backup vehicle with officers, including Alex from the NCA. The two vehicles swapped messages throughout the journey until the moment they pulled into the yard where delivery was to take place. As Scoffer pulled to a halt, he saw two men approaching the cab. He was prepared when one of them asked.

"You're not the usual guys. Where are they?"
"Both off sick. Covid. That's why the last delivery was cancelled."
"Drive into the warehouse. You can unload in there."
"OK. You two must be Ahmad and Bashir."
"Yeah."

Scoffer drove slowly into the warehouse and pulled up. He and Gary jumped out of the cab and motioned the men to look at the vehicle before they unloaded it.

As they approached, the tarpaulin was thrown back, and they found themselves outnumbered by armed officers who ordered them to kneel on the ground with their hands behind their head. They complied. Four more officers slipped quietly into the warehouse and emerged soon after with three handcuffed men in overalls. Gary cheerfully phoned HQ to notify the operation had been an unqualified success, before handing over the prisoners to the NCA. Both officers were in high spirits until Scoffer asked the question.

"How do we get back home?"
"We'll have to ask these kind men with the guns if they can give us a lift."
"You ask."

********

When they arrived back at HQ, Brian was waiting to greet them.

"Well done, you two. You've done a great job. Gary, will you write it up, please?"
"Of course, boss."
"Thanks. Can I have a word with you, Scoffer?"

"Yes, boss."

Brian waited until Gary had gone before starting the conversation.

"I've got a job I'd like you to take, Scoffer."
"No problem, boss. What is it?"
"It seems there's a gang on the Holme Wood estate handling stolen goods. The local kids are nicking stuff, either through housebreaking or thieving from shops, and selling them to this gang in exchange for drugs. I want it stopped. Think you can handle it?"
"I'll give it my best. Do I get a partner?"
"How about giving Ruth a go?"
"Yeah. Ruth seems keen to learn."
"OK. Get your heads together and make a plan how you want to tackle the job and then we'll discuss it further."
"OK, boss. Thanks."

Scoffer and Ruth together went through all the reports they had, making copious notes and working out a strategy to bring a halt to the enterprise. They realised that they didn't have the full story; what happened to the stolen goods? How were they disposing of the items?

After some thought, they made a list of the recent items stolen from households. They included jewellery, small electrical items, household appliances and CDs. Where insurance claims were recorded, there were often accompanying photographs and detailed descriptions of the items stolen. They split the list, and each checked social media and local second-hand sales sites to see if any of the items were logged there. They were immediately successful.

"Here, Scoffer. On Gumtree, there's a watch identical to one stolen four days ago from a house on Tong Street. It's a man's Seiko. They're asking £400 for it."
"Make an enquiry. You're very interested but need to see it first."

During the course of the afternoon, they identified six items, recently listed as stolen, now on sale online. They made arrangements to view each item within the next two days, using different names and email addresses. They insisted on seeing the items at the seller's home rather than in a pub, as the seller suggested.

"I've got a feeling, Ruth, that all these items are for sale by the same person, even though we've been given different names and addresses."

"The thought crossed my mind, too. The way all the different items are described is too similar. The background in all the photos is the same. OK, it's just a pine table, but there's the same cigarette burn in the top corner on all of them. This is the work of a fence."

"OK, let's talk it over with the boss."

********

Brian was impressed at their thoroughness.

"OK. Assuming you can be absolutely certain the first item is the result of theft, what do you do next?"

"Make an arrest and get Forensics to search the house for other items."

"OK. And what do you need for that?"

"Authorisation to proceed?"

"Yes. You need a search warrant. Go ask the DCI. Tell him I've authorised the sting."

"OK. Thanks, boss."

"Good luck."

The DCI duly authorised the operation and search warrant. Scoffer informed Forensics and he and Ruth set off to visit the address they'd been given, a scruffy-looking semi with a van parked outside.

"OK, Ruth. The story is we're looking for a watch for my brother's 30th birthday. He's into bling. Once we say we'll take it, we ask if he's got any other well-priced watches, or ladies jewellery. We'll see where that takes us. OK?"

"Sounds like a plan."

They were surprised when a woman opened the door to them.

"Oh, is Barry in? We've come to see him about a watch."

"He's out. I've got the watch. Come in."

She led them into the kitchen where piles of cardboard boxes were stacked in a corner. Scoffer gestured towards them.

"You moving?"

"No. We're just short of space to store stuff."

"Oh. So, can we see the watch?"

She opened a drawer and took out the watch, laying it on the pine kitchen table. Brian noticed the cigarette burn in the corner of the table. He picked up the watch and inspected it. There was an inscription on the back.

"Who's Geoff?"

"Pardon?"

"Who's Geoff? His name is inscribed on the back."

"Oh, it's Barry's brother. We're selling it for him. He needs the money."

"I'll give you £350 for it."

"He's asking for £400."

"£375. Final offer."

"Done. Cash only."

"OK. Anything else while we're here?"

"Such as?"

"Ladies jewellery."

"Just a minute."

She rummaged through the cardboard boxes until she found the one she was looking for. Removing the lid, she took out one at a time a selection of necklaces, earrings, rings, watches in gold, silver and adorned with precious stones. She laid them carefully on the table.

"Anything you fancy?"

"I like this ring. Are the diamonds real?"

"Absolutely."

"How much?"

"A grand."

"Too much. I tell you what I'll do. I'll take it back to its rightful owner and ask how much she paid for it."

"What do you mean? It's mine. I bought it."

"You bought it all right. From the local thieves. How much did you pay?"

"That's none of your business. I bought it. That's all you need to know."

"You bought it from the local kids, who stole it in a burglary at a house in Bierley. I have a photo of it here."

He took out his phone and showed the photo.

"I bought it in good faith. I didn't know it was stolen."

"I don't believe you. Now, if you'd like to give me the names and addresses of the lads you buy from…."

"Not a chance! Look, I just sell this stuff. It's my boyfriend, Barry, who brings them home."

"Where is he now?"

"Down at the Cross Keys."

"OK. I'll tell you what happens next. You'll be charged with handling stolen goods. A car will take you to the station and SOCO will search your house while you're out. If you'd like to give us a photo of your boyfriend, it would greatly help your defence. So?"

She flipped through pages on her phone.

"Here. This is him."

"I'll just take a copy. Right, we'll stay with you until the car arrives, and we'll talk again later. Thank you for your help. By the way, what's your name?"

"Sandra."

"It's been a pleasure doing business with you, Sandra."

She just scowled at him as the doorbell rang. Ruth let the team in, and Sandra was taken away while Forensics searched the house. They left them to it and headed towards the Cross Keys where they found Barry propping up the bar.

"Go and chat him up, Ruth. See if he's got any bargains."

"OK."

She strode confidently across the room and sat on the stool next to Barry. She smiled as he turned towards her.

"Hi. Are you Barry?"

"Yes. Who are you?"

"Ruth. I was just talking to your Sandra. She said you might have a wedding ring for me."

"I might. But why are you buying your own wedding ring?"

"It's not for me. It's for my sister. She's marrying a horrible man who won't even buy her a wedding ring. How miserable is that?"

"How much do you want to pay?"

"As little as possible."

He put his hand into his jacket pocket and fished out a handful of rings, spreading them on the bar.

"Any of these take your fancy?"

"How much is this one?"

"£75."

"Too much. Have you any under £50?"

"What about this?"

"Aw, that's nice. Can I try it on? She takes the same size as me."

"Try it, then."

"Thank you. She'll be so pleased to get it back again."

"What do you mean?"

"I'm not paying for it. It already belongs to her. You stole it. I'm calling the police."

"Wait a minute! I didn't steal it. I bought it."

"Who from?"

"Does it matter? It's yours for £25."

"I've told you already. I'm not paying for it. It's evidence. So, tell me where you got it, or I'll arrest you."

"You're police?"

"What do you think? Now, you've got a choice here. Either you tell me where I can get hold of the kids who are doing the burglaries, or I assume it's you. Your choice."

"I want to see my lawyer."

"I haven't even taken you into custody yet! These kids; where are they?"

"They meet down at the play area in the park after tea. About eight. Then they decide which streets they're targeting, or which stores."

"And when do they bring them to you?"

"About eight in the morning. On their way to school."

"They actually go to school?"

"Well, some of them do."

"OK. You're coming with us. Finish your pint."

They dropped him off at HQ, in a nice little cell while they went for a cuppa to decide their course of action. They agreed on a plan but had to have it approved by DI Peters.

"I've a feeling he'll like this, Ruth. It's the sort of thing he'd do."

Brian was impressed but had reservations.

"I love the idea. My only concern is what happens if they change their modus operandi? We're allowing them to commit acts of burglary and only arresting them when they're selling on the stolen goods. What happens if some of the items are missing? What if they sell them to someone else?"

"Sorry, boss. I hadn't thought about that. But if we tail them all night and try to arrest them in the act, what happens if they split up? If they work in small groups, it'll take a lot of manpower to watch all of them. They'll probably realise they're being observed and abandon their activities."

"That's possible. But we need to balance that against the possibility that a householder gets injured during a burglary. Or killed. However small the possibility, we can't risk it. Think about it. How would you feel as a householder if you found out the police had allowed a burglary to be carried out with their full knowledge, and it had resulted in an injury, or, worse still, a death?"

"OK, boss. We get the point. We'll try to borrow some manpower to keep an eye on these kids. See if we can catch them in the act as soon as they effect entry."

"OK. I'll sanction that. I love your first idea, but the possibility of collateral damage is unacceptable."

They drove over to the meeting site and found a patch of higher ground from where they could observe proceedings. Back at HQ, they were able to persuade Louise, Andy and Jo-Jo and a few Uniforms to act as innocent bystanders, dog-walkers and the like. They were all in position before 8pm as a few young boys drifted towards the rendezvous. A tall, ginger-haired lad seemed to be in charge, sorting the boys into groups of four and allocating the targets before they dispersed in their little groups. Silently and inconspicuously, each group was followed at a distance by an officer or two. Messages passed between the officers regularly until the targets were identified. Andy, hiding in bushes, could see one group preparing a burglary. One boy, no more than ten years old, stood by the gate to a house, keeping watch, while three other older boys crept around the back. Andy called for backup and immediately ran towards the house. Startled, the young boy screamed as Andy knocked him to the ground and ran to the rear where a boy was clambering through an open window. Andy grabbed him by the back of his waistband and threw him on to the path just as a PC arrived to hold him down. Andy tried to climb through the open window but wasn't agile enough, but then heard a clamour from the front of the house where the two boys who had entered now tried to escape via the front door. They were too late as they were dragged to the ground and pinned down by officers. Andy ran to the front to find the grinning officers kneeling on the lads, holding them down. He called for a van to take them away but stayed behind to explain what had happened to the aged householders in bed watching TV who were disturbed by the clamour. Over his phone came the news that three other groups had been arrested a few streets away.

Once the news was relayed to Teresa, she gratefully crossed it off her whiteboard. That left one unsolved case.

********

Lynn turned her attention back to the case she'd been investigating, without much progress, for some time. The female murderers had been quiet in recent weeks and the investigation had ground to a halt. But not for long. The very next day, late in the afternoon, she took a call from Teresa.

"Lynn, a body has been found in a hotel room in Halifax. It may be linked to the cases you were looking into. Brian asked me to send all the info to you, so you could see if there were similarities."
"OK, send what you've got. Have we got an officer free to accompany me?"
"Andy's available."
"OK, I'll take him with me."

They drove quickly to the venue, an upmarket hotel regularly used for events such as weddings, anniversaries, and business functions. As such, the turnover of guests was high, with the majority booking in for one night only. They were expected and the manager showed them immediately into a private office, before apologising profusely.

"I hope you will understand that our guests don't expect the police at our door. We have a reputation to maintain as a top-class venue for business and leisure events."
"Don't worry. We'll be discreet. We'll just ask questions after we've seen the crime scene. First, have any scene-of-crime investigators arrived yet?"
"Yes. There are four men currently in the room where the body was found."
"OK, we'll go there after we've asked you a few general questions."
"Fire away."
"Who were the guests?"
"A couple. A man called Preston. James Preston. And his partner, Helen."
"Helen Preston?"
"I don't believe they were married. Mr Preston signed in for them both as Mr and Mrs Preston, but I noticed she didn't wear a

wedding ring. But we're not that old fashioned. Lots of unmarried couples use our services."

"Could you describe Helen?"

"I can do better than that. We have CCTV cameras dotted about the place. A member of my staff is copying the relevant bits for you."

"Thank you. So, how long did they book in for?"

"Two nights. They arrived yesterday."

"And you discovered the body today?"

"Yes. They didn't come down for breakfast, and we had a 'do not disturb' note on the booking. It was only this afternoon when one of our staff noticed their car had gone that we became suspicious."

"What time did it leave?"

"One-thirty, according to CCTV. We only noticed it had gone at about three, so a member of staff went to the room to see if they required anything. There was no answer. He checked again at four-thirty. Again nothing. Not a sound, so he let himself in. That was when he found the body of Mr Preston."

"Tell me, do you often enter rooms when guests haven't appeared during the day? What about honeymoon couples? Or lovers looking for some private time away?"

"No, not at all. It was just, in passing, that one of our kitchen staff mentioned he'd noticed the female guest leaving through the fire door."

"What time was that?"

"Approximately one-thirty."

"Didn't he challenge her?"

"No. She put a finger to her lips and giggled. He just thought she was slipping out without her partner noticing. He thought it was some sort of game. We often get lovers having illicit affairs. We get used to odd behaviour."

"OK. Do you have the car's registration?"

"Yes. We ask for it when they book in. I'll get it for you."

"OK. We'll go to the room. We'll pick up the CCTV footage before we leave."

Forensics were almost finished by the time Lynn and Andy entered the room. It looked unused, except for the body of a naked man draped across the bed.

"Hello, you two. You're just in time. We're finished here. Just waiting for the black bus to take the body to the lab."

"Cause of death?"

"Poison, by the look of it. I'll be able to confirm as soon as we get him on the slab."

"Have you got prints?"

"Yes, and DNA. I'm almost certain they'll match what we have from previous recent cases."

"Any other evidence to link the crimes?"

"His wallet and bank cards are missing."

"Like the others. We'll get card details from Reception before we go. Anything else, Allen?"

"Not for now. You'll have the full report, hopefully, by tomorrow morning."

Before leaving, Lynn picked up a copy of the CCTV images and Mr Preston's bank card details. She passed the card number to Teresa so that she could put a trace on its use since.

"I think we'll find she's been on a spending spree again. We'll see if it leads us anywhere."

"If it's like the other cases, she'll spend wildly for a few hours, then dump the card."

Back at HQ, they put a 'stop' on the card and requested they be informed immediately if anyone attempted to use it. They were not surprised to find it had already been used in a number of outlets in and around Halifax. Lynn called in a favour from the Halifax team to call at the outlets and pick up any CCTV footage available.

The following morning, the report came through from Forensics. The victim, Mr Preston, a 26-year-old accountant, was poisoned after having sex. Cyanide, again. Lynn was faced with the unenviable task of informing his next of kin. She drove with Andy to Denholme, where his parents lived. This was a part of the job she disliked the most. Parents never suspected their child would have been murdered. It was heart-breaking to tell them and often better to leave out some of the more prurient details. Sometimes, she felt it was better to tell them simply that their child had been murdered and that enquiries were ongoing.

"Do you know if he was involved with anyone? Any girlfriends?"

"We knew he'd started seeing a woman. He seemed quite fond of her."

"Did you meet her?"

"No. She seemed to be very busy. He told us she ran her own business and went away for days at a time. He said he would go with her if it could be arranged. Why do you ask? Is it anything to do with her?"

"It's a possibility. Did he tell you he had any plans to go away for a day or two?"

"He'd booked a few days holiday for the beginning of this week. He didn't say whether he was going away. Is that what happened?"

"We found his body in a hotel room. We're not certain yet of the cause of death. All I can say is we're treating the case as murder. Do you know how he met this woman he was seeing?"

"He said it was through the internet."

"Does he have a computer here?"

"Yes. It's in his bedroom."

"We'll need to take it, if that's OK. We may be able to discover evidence which hopefully leads to an arrest."

"Take it, by all means. We don't use it."

"Thank you. We'll give you a receipt and return the computer when it's been examined. We'd like a look at his room, now, please."

They found little of any use apart from a small notebook which seemed to contain login details and passwords for various sites.

"We'll take this. It will save a lot of time searching through his data."

By the time they'd returned to HQ, Teresa had been informed by the NCA that a similar murder had taken place the previous day in North Wales and that details would follow. All indications were that it was the work of a copycat. She passed the information to Lynn on her return.

"That's all we need! We've enough on our plate examining Preston's computer, and to cap it all, it looks like all his passwords are encrypted."

"Let me have a look."

"Be my guest."

It took Teresa less than ten minutes to decipher the code.

"Look at his notebook. On the front page he explains how to decrypt the passwords. At the top of the page is this:

L + 2, N + 3, S +1.

This is the key. L means letter, N is number, S is symbol. So if the password is given as ffbxPEed793*&%, it translates on the qwerty keyboard as hhmvSTtg026(*^. How simple can that be? Using a standard qwerty keyboard it's straightforward. Login uses the same format. Let's try it. Go to the signing in page for Facebook."

Lynn applied the transcription method as Teresa had specified and Facebook opened. She went straight to Messenger and scanned through the list of contacts. One caught her attention immediately. It showed the face of an attractive woman with short blonde hair and wearing sunglasses. Her name was Helen Lusty, also known as Circe the Enchantress.

"Let's see what we can find out about this sorceress."

She scrolled through the messages and their replies, taking notes along the way. Initially, Helen had made contact by asking a specific question relating to a photo Preston had posted. It was all innocent to start with, but became increasingly friendly up until the point where one thread caught her attention when Helen had typed

"I'd love to spend time alone with you in a big bed. Away from everyone we know. Just us 2."

The immediate response caused a cascade of messages.

"OK. Where?"
"Any nice hotel away from it all."
"I know a nice place. Fancy Halifax?"
"Never been."
"You'll love it."
"You'll have to make it worth my while."
"I will."
"Wear the swimming trunks in your pix. I want to see if it's real."
"It's real."
"Will it satisfy me?"
"Oh, yes."
"Make sure hotel knows we're not to be disturbed."
"Can't wait."

There followed instructions about where he could pick her up, how long they would be away for, and a demand that he mustn't tell anyone about it beforehand.

"It's easy to see how men are likely to get caught up in it. I guess she must pick her victims carefully by following their lives on social media. If she has any doubt at all, she probably stops the conversation dead. I imagine she uses this method regularly to initiate a conversation. Can we find out if the other victims we're aware of were snared by the same method?"

"I'll make some enquiries for you."

"Thanks, Teresa."

Meanwhile, CCTV from shops in and around Halifax had been forwarded by the local force. They clearly showed images of 'Helen Lusty' in different shops, buying items, often expensive jewellery and paying by card. Though she did her best to ensure she avoided looking directly at the CCTV cameras, occasionally her face was clearly visible. It was the same woman suspected of the murder of the man in Haworth. Her hair was styled and coloured differently, but it was unmistakeably her as Teresa had proved by running it through a facial recognition program.

"A 90% probability. That's enough evidence for me. We can put these images out to see if anyone recognises her."

"I'll contact the T & A."

"No, Lynn. Perhaps we ought to review what we've got about the copycat first."

"You're right, Teresa. As usual. Let's do it. Can you get all the stuff together?"

"Leave it to me."

# CHAPTER 19

When Teresa had collated all the data regarding the copycat's crimes, she placed it all in one folder and put it on Lynn's desk.

"OK, Andy and I will go through these first before we look at the most recent one."

They were still collating the data early in the evening before they decided to call a halt to the day's work. Andy was clearly worn out by the afternoon's work.

"I don't know about you, Lynn, but I'm going for a pint."
"I'll join you, if that's OK."
"No shop talk?"
"Definitely not."

It was raining heavily when they left HQ and drove to a pub they'd frequently visited without the knowledge of their colleagues. Here, they were two people just enjoying each other's company.

********

Lynn's alarm woke them. They lay together holding each other close, before Lynn broke the silence.

"Come on. We'll be late for work. Put the kettle on while I get showered."
"I'd rather stay here all day."
"Sorry. We've a job to do. We'll talk about this later."

The subject would remain closed until the end of the working day. In the meantime, they had to focus on the job in hand. Teresa, it seemed, was the only one who noticed anything different.

"You two seem to have a good working relationship. You've got the makings of a good team."

She noticed the faint blush as Lynn smiled in return.

"Don't worry, Lynn. It's nobody's business but yours."

Lynn picked up the work on the copycat's historical crimes, while Andy looked at the details of the latest one reported. He was astonished by the similarities shared by both perpetrators, not only in their methods, but also in their looks. He compared CCTV images of the two women side by side.

"Are we absolutely sure these are two different people, Lynn?"
"Absolutely. If you look closely, the one on the left is left-handed. The one on the other screen is right-handed. My guess, though, is they're identical twins."
"Looks like it. Let's see what other similarities they share."
"Apart from murdering people?"
"Apart from that, yes."
"How many pseudonyms does she use?"
"I've counted six so far. One for each murder."
"Have we checked any of the victims' computers?"
"No."
"Can we get hold of them? Or at least get hold of their Facebook login and password?"
"I'll ask."

By early afternoon, Teresa had arranged for the laptops belonging to two of the victims to be picked up and brought to HQ, along with a list of login and password information for various applications.

"Isn't it odd that passwords were put in place to prevent others from accessing confidential files, yet so many people keep a written list of all of them in a little book in a drawer somewhere?"
"Human nature, I guess. We need so many different passwords, we run out of ideas unless we use the same one all the time, in which case there's little security."

They soon had both laptops side by side and were examining the various strings of text on Messenger. Andy found the first suspicious string of dialogue and asked Lynn for her opinion.

"Have you got a contact called Valerie Haller on Messenger?"
"Just a minute. Yes."
"Read some of the dialogue. Tell me what you think."
"OK.... Christ! Where have we seen this sort of stuff before?"
"On Preston's computer. Helen Lusty. It's practically identical. They must be working together. Everything about them is identical. Their appearance, their modus operandi, the things they buy with the victim's cards. Are we absolutely certain they are different people?"
"DNA and fingerprint evidence tell us they're different, but closely related."

"So, how do we find them? Is there a national database of twins, or something?"

"Let's start by Googling their names. You take Haller, I'll take Lusty. You never know your luck."

Surprisingly, Google turned up a couple of entries but neither seemed promising until Lynn noticed the link.

"They are both characters in the same play, but one of the names was different. Instead of Valerie Haller, it was Valhalla. As in the Norse mythology, the hall of slain warriors."

"I don't really see a link there. Who wrote the play?"

"Just a minute. Some guy I've never heard of. Bruce Battler."

"Let's Google him."

"Nothing of any use. No mention of anything other than the fact he wrote the play. This is a dead end."

"OK. Let's see if they have any friends in common on Facebook."

They soon realised the information in their profile was practically the same. Same interests, etc. Same date of birth.

"They must have collaborated on this. They *must* be twins. They're so alike in everything they do. Is it possible they were separated at birth and brought up in different environments?"

"It's as good a theory as anything. There must be a national register we can examine."

"Let's have a look. Here we are. The General Register Office."

"Looks like we'll have to make an official request for information."

"Ask Teresa. She'll know."

"And if not, she'll find out."

Teresa had the answer before the end of the working day.

"The information will be sent by post, but I was given it verbally when I said it was a matter of life and death. Wait till you hear this. I explained the problem and we discussed various options. The lady on the phone was really helpful. So, we tried using different parameters to filter the results. We started with date of birth, assuming they'd both given the correct date on Facebook. Then, we applied the filters 'removed from mother' and 'separately adopted'. Finally, we applied 'identical twins'. That gave us five results. Checking the names they were given, only one pair were christened Valerie and Helen. Their adoptive names are Helen Lester and Valerie Hebden.

I've since gathered a little more information about them. Their mother was a heroin addict whose twins were adopted separately and grew up separately, but accidentally met at university, bonded, and gradually learnt the truth about themselves and each other. After university, they drifted apart. Each, though, had the killer instinct, which somehow developed separately, and they only discovered they were alike in that respect recently once the crimes became public knowledge. It was only then that they got in touch with each other again. We now know enough to find them. I'll get on it as soon as I get back to my PC."

"That's great work, Teresa. Anything we can do to help?"

"Try the Electoral Rolls. From the area where the crimes took place, I think it's a good bet that Helen lives in the Yorkshire area, and Valerie lives in Wales. Start with those and work outwards."

Andy expressed a thought.

"I've had an idea. Why don't I set up a fake Facebook page and try to make contact with Helen?"

"Do you think it'll work?"

"If I make myself an ideal target, there's a good chance."

"OK, let's think about it. She seems to pick good-looking men, with a stable career, successful, not short of money, unattached…."

"That's me to a T."

"Let's give it a shot."

"Run it past the boss, first. If he agrees, we'll set up a profile she won't be able to resist."

"Could we do the same with the one in Wales as well?"

"Let's see how this goes, first."

"I just thought maybe we could do both at the same time. I mean, it's possible they talk to each other immediately after each murder. They probably know each other's schedule and if one fails to check in after a murder, the other may get spooked and do a runner."

"Do we have any evidence they are in contact with each other regularly?"

"We could try to find out."

"Let's see what the boss thinks, first."

********

Brian was happy to give his endorsement to the plan but asked them to wait until he'd talked it through with DCI Gardner. He wasn't sure the DCI trusted his judgment enough to place the life of one of his team in peril. He needn't have worried. Gardner agreed immediately.

"I think it's a good plan, Brian. Cover all your bases before you put it into action, as you always do."
"Thanks for putting your trust in me, sir. We won't let you down."
"I've no doubt. This will fit well in the Hall of Fame."
"There's another thing though, boss."
"What's that?"
"The possibility of setting up a simultaneous sting in Wales to catch her sister at the same time."

Gardner though for a while before giving his decision.

"It's a no-go, Brian. It would take a long time to work out the details to coordinate the two stings. That's if I could convince the bosses in Wales that we could make it work in the first place. I think we should go ahead with our plan, and, when it's finished, look at the Welsh killer and pass our expertise to the Welsh Force. Unless you can persuade the NCA to take over the lot, it's too big for us to coordinate. Let's concentrate on our own case, Brian."
"Very well, sir."

Brian was in good spirits when he assembled the team to give them the go-ahead.

"We've got the go ahead for our case, but the DCI thinks we should leave the Welsh case to their Force. I agree. I wouldn't want another Force coming to us and taking over our cases. Approaching us afterwards and passing on tips is fine, but a joint operation would take too long to coordinate. So, let's deal with our case. Sort out what you plan and keep me informed all the way through. I'll be immensely proud of you when you've pulled it off. Go. Start planning. The sooner we catch this woman, the better."

Brian left them to organise who would do what, and when. He was happy to let them work without his interference; they would learn more from it than from blindly following someone else's instructions.

By the end of the following day, Teresa had set up a Facebook page for Andy, who was to be Andrew Thomas, a freelance graphic designer, who at the age of 28, and single, ran his own online business 'Thomas Graphics'. There were images, doctored by Teresa, showing him sunbathing in the Caribbean, sightseeing in Tokyo, as well as carefully-crafted video clips of him giving a lecture in front of an audience of businessmen at a New York convention.

His profile stated he was looking for a fun-loving companion to join him, all expenses paid, on some of his trips.

Teresa also created a false LinkedIn profile and inserted his name into various sites to increase his online presence. Then she posted short entries to Facebook with responses from female 'friends' she'd fabricated. Then, they sat, monitoring the site for a time until Teresa considered they were ready to begin the game.

Lynn and Teresa sat either side of Andy as he typed into Helen's Messenger,

"Hi, you look as if you like to enjoy yourself. I'd love to meet you for a drink (somewhere public). What do you think?"

They sat patiently for an hour. No response had appeared, but Teresa was unfazed.

"She'll be doing some research into Andrew Thomas. When she's certain you're genuine, then you'll get an answer. Be patient."

Eventually, they packed up for the day, after Andy had posted another photo supposedly of him working out in the gym, but actually using digital jiggery-pokery to look as if it was him.

On Monday morning, as soon as Teresa logged on and opened the Facebook page, she saw the indication that a message had been posted. She clicked on it while calling Andy and Lynn to come to her desk. The message read,

"Where are you based?"

Teresa took the responsibility of responding, in vague terms.

"West Yorks. You?"
"Same."
"Like to meet?"
"Maybe. Depends."
"Depends on what?"
"I'm sure you could afford a nice meal and a couple of drinks, while we get to know each other."
"I'm OK with that. Where would you like to go?"

"There's a nice restaurant in Ilkley."

"Too far to drive home after I've had a drink."

"Well, how about we stay over?"

"Is that where you live?"

"No. I mean why don't you stay in a hotel?"

"I'd be lonely on my own."

"I never said anything about being on your own. I'm very good company when it comes to intimacy."

"Anywhere you prefer to stay?"

"Craiglands is nice. Can eat there, too."

"OK. You want me to book a night?"

"Why not make it two. Friday and Sat. would be nice. Then we can enjoy some time together, just the two of us. How's that sound?"

"Good. This weekend?"

"OK."

"I'll do it now, and let you know when it's done."

"Looking forward to this."

"Me too."

Teresa closed the communication and turned to her audience.

"So, how are we going to play this? Do you want me to actually book a room?"

"I think so. Then we'll meet. I'll wear a wire and we'll see where it takes us."

"Stop before it goes too far. It's not a pleasure trip. This is work."

"I know. I want to gather as much evidence as I can. I want to ask about places she's visited to see if they tally with any of the murders. If it starts getting hairy, I'll say a particular phrase we agree means you burst into the room immediately."

"OK. I'll book the room. I'll have a private chat with the manager to tell him it's a sting and that we'll be bugging the room."

"OK, then we'll talk a bit more on Messenger."

They left Teresa in order to discuss how Andy should respond to Helen's questions and how to guide the conversation so that Helen talked about herself and the places she'd visited, hoping to gather information to tie the information she gave to specific dates and venues, without making it obvious he was manipulating the conversation. Teresa's phone call interrupted them.

"You're booked for this weekend. The manager is fine with what we're doing. He just asks that we pay for any damage."

"I hope there won't be any."

"Me too. Do you want to come up and I'll contact Helen to confirm?"
"On our way."

Andy tried not to make it obvious, but his heart was pounding at the thought of being at the centre of the sting. It would be his most significant role since he joined the Force, and he was nervous about it, but at the same time determined to ensure he acquitted himself well. It would be a real feather in his cap.

When Andy and Lynn arrived at Teresa's desk, Brian was waiting for them.

"I've no intention of interfering with your plans. I'd just like to hear them."

They quickly went through what they'd planned while Brian listened carefully. At the end, they asked him to comment.

"I like what you've decided. The only thing I would suggest is that we get more people involved at the scene. I suggest we get officers masquerading as staff, helping on Reception, serving in the restaurant, that sort of thing. It gives us more control if anything goes wrong."
"That's a good idea, boss. I'm sure we could all fit in a couple of hours training before the weekend. I'll put it to the manager and see what we can organise."
"OK. Sort it out among yourselves when you'll go for training and what roles you'll take. Just make sure someone's available on callout in case there's a major unexpected event over the weekend."

When Lynn and Andy had returned to their desks, Teresa questioned Brian.

"Are you alright, Brian?"
"Yes. Why do you ask?"
"Because normally you'd lead a project like this."
"They all need the chance to prove to me and to themselves they're fully capable of performing without having me watching on."
"I understand that, but normally you would relish an exercise such as this."
"It's time I took a back seat."
"You're not thinking of retiring, are you?"

"Well, it has to happen sometime. I'd rather know that the team can function fully without me. Let them prove themselves. They don't need me on their back for this. I've got faith in them."
"OK. Just checking."

Once Brian had gone back to his desk, Teresa thought over what he had said. She wasn't convinced. As she saw it, he was losing his desire to lead the team and wondered if there was anything she could do to rekindle the spark he used to have. She decided to devote more time and effort into tracing Siobhan Gorman.

# CHAPTER 20

By the time Friday came around, the team were ready individually and collectively for the evening's operation. They had all rehearsed their roles and how they would interact with each other and with the permanent staff. After a short afternoon meeting, they were allowed to leave early to give them time to get ready and in place for their evening's work. Scoffer lightened the mood by doing an impression of Manuel from Fawlty Towers before leaving HQ.

Andy was waiting at the Bus Station as agreed at 16.50 when the bus from Leeds pulled in. He recognised her immediately, even though she was wearing a long ginger wig. She stood out from the crowd. She was stunningly beautiful and elegantly dressed. For a second or two, Andy was prepared to forget he was on duty until he heard his mobile ping to indicate a message had arrived. Lynn.

"Here you go, Andy. Don't forget why we're here."

He smiled and walked quickly towards her.

"Hi, Helen. You look even lovelier in the flesh, so to speak."
"You can decide that later. First, would you mind if we pop into a shop? I've left my favourite perfume at home."
"There's a beauty parlour just down the road, I think."
"I know. I googled it on the bus."

Helen soon selected the perfume she wanted. No surprise, it was the most expensive. She put her card in the machine and seemed surprised when it was rejected.

"Silly me. I've forgotten my PIN. Would you mind paying? I'll pay you back."
"No problem."

Andy tried not to look annoyed when he realised the cost. He didn't fail to notice her watching closely as he entered his PIN. Fortunately, she couldn't see the name on the card.

"There you are."
"Oh, thank you, Andrew. Now, I need a drink. Where would you recommend that's got a bit of style and intimacy?"
"I don't know, really. I've only been here a couple of times. Shall we make our way to the hotel and maybe have a drink in the bar?"
"Or, in the room?"

"Your call. So, how's your day been so far?"

"So far, OK. But it's bound to get better now. Is your car nearby?"

"Yes. In the car park just over the road."

"Good. I don't want to carry this luggage around with me."

"It's a big suitcase for a couple of nights."

"There may be one or two surprises in it for you."

"I'll look forward to seeing them."

"Patience, dear boy. All things come to those who wait. I assure you it will be worth waiting for."

"I'm sure it will. So, let's get your stuff into the car and take it to the hotel."

They had a drink in the hotel bar, which was empty apart from a couple of ladies, off duty policewomen, across the room. Andy played his role well, answering all Helen's questions as he'd been coached by Teresa and Lynn. He was sure Helen had come to the conclusion that he was quite a naïve young man and therefore was an easy target for her game. It wasn't going to be as easy as she'd imagined though; that was obvious to Andy as he saw many of his colleagues passing through in their guise as hotel employees. He'd even given Scoffer a small tip when he'd served their drinks in the bar. The look on Scoffer's face was one of total surprise when he realised the tip was a mere five pence!

Helen asked politely if Andrew would get her another drink, so that she would be totally in the mood for what was to come. Andy obliged, naturally, when she'd whispered in his ear,

"I get so horny when I've had a couple of drinks."

So far, the game was playing out exactly as the team had imagined, and shortly after Andy had seen someone entering the Gents, he excused himself.

"Excuse me, please, Helen. I need to go for a pee."

In the Gents, he exchanged a few words with a fellow officer. The game was going exactly to plan. Andy returned to the table, only to find Helen had already finished her drink and just concluded a phone call.

"Hurry up, Andrew. I'm ready for you. Shall I go up and get naked?"

"Let's go up together and get naked."

"Finish your drink."

"Do you want to take one up with you?"

"I've got something in my bag for upstairs."

"What is it?"

"An aphrodisiac! You'll have an erection like you've never known."

"They don't call me 'donkey dick' for nothing."

"Come on. I can't wait to see it."

They went up to the room. Helen locked the door and began to strip to her underwear.

"You too, Andrew. Don't be shy."

"I might need the aphrodisiac first. I'm a bit nervous."

"OK. I'll get it."

She rummaged through her suitcase, eventually pulling out a small bottle without a label.

"This will give you the biggest and hardest erection you've even imagined."

"What is it?"

"I got it in Marrakesh. It's a blend of herbs and spices. It works fast! I watched a man drink just a little and in five minutes he had a dick like a stallion. Just a small glass should be enough. Pass me one, please."

He watched as she poured a small measure before passing it back to him.

"You must down it in one, Andrew. It will only take a few minutes. Just down the lot and lie on the bed."

"You're sure it's safe?"

"Of course. Drink it."

"I'm not sure. What if I have an adverse reaction?"

"For Heaven's sake, Andrew! Just drink it!"

"No."

"Why on earth not?"

"I'm frightened."

"There's nothing to be frightened of. Just drink it for fuck's sake!"

"No. I'm frightened I'll turn into a policeman."

The door burst open immediately. Six officers raced in and restrained Helen, ensuring they got the drink safely out of her hands so that Forensics could examine it.

Lynn completed the formalities.

"I'm arresting you on suspicion of murder…."

They threw a blanket over Helen to preserve her modesty and took her down the stairs and out of a back door where a police car was waiting to whisk her to Bradford HQ.

Scoffer patted Andy on the back, congratulating him on the way he'd played his role.

"You did really well there, mate. Not so much 'Andrew Thomas'; more like 'John Thomas'."
"Thank you, bartender. Can I have the tip back, now?"
"I put it in the charity jar. Claim it on expenses."
"That reminds me. I need to go back to the room. I've forgotten my perfume."
"Perfume? You don't wear perfume!"
"No. I had to buy her a bottle. Bloody expensive, too. I want to make sure I get the money back."
"I'd keep it for the next woman you take out if I were you. It certainly got this one horny."
"I can't wait to find out what's in the aphrodisiac she tried to get me to drink."
"I think we both know what was in it."

They were right. Examination in the lab proved it was a poisonous substance which would have killed Andy in minutes, as it did with her previous victims.

The clock was ticking now that Helen was under arrest. The feeling in CID was that she would report back to her sister when her assignment was completed. It was probable that her sister would go into hiding if she didn't get feedback on the operation within a certain timeframe. They had to act fast!

********

Pint in hand, Brian was perched on a barstool in the Black Rat, a big smile on his face as he followed proceedings via messages sent to his mobile. He had taken no part in the actual operation, being happy to delegate it to his team in whom he had total confidence. Besides, he was certain this siren would not be able to influence the professionalism of his team, even though, as he had been informed, she was strikingly attractive. He didn't care much. His life had boiled down to this. A good pint was all the company he needed. This couldn't go on. This lack of enthusiasm would be noticed before long. He had to make a decision about which course his future should take. He took a long drink from his glass while he thought about it. And when his glass was empty, he ordered another.

\*\*\*\*\*\*\*\*

Helen Lester refused to talk during her interview. No incentive, such as a lighter sentence would cause her to change her mind. Teresa understood why.

"She's not going to rat on her sister. It's as straightforward as that. She won't cooperate while her sister's at large."

Gary had a solution, though.

"What about her phone? Can't we send a message to her sister saying mission accomplished, or something similar. And then open a dialogue to ask what she's up to and if it's possible to meet."

The team thought it was a workable plan. Teresa, though, introduced a note of caution.

"We need to be careful we don't tip her off that something's wrong. It wouldn't surprise me if they have an 'alarm code' – an innocent phrase which has a totally different meaning. Before we do anything, I'd like to analyse her phone, so when I send her a message, I can avoid alarming her."
"You're right, Teresa. When you communicate, use words or phrases she's used in the past."
"While I'm calling her, we could try to trace the signal to her phone and possibly work out her whereabouts."
"You can do that?"
"Yep. It's just a nifty piece of software. A bit illegal, but I'm sure I can do it, and if necessary, we can apply for a Court Order in retrospect."
"OK, go for it. If you can unlock the phone, that is."
"No problem. Brian's friend at the university showed me how. Just takes a minute or two…. There we are. Just give me a minute to read the messages and print it all out…."

Five minutes later, they were gathered around Teresa's workstation as she explained what she was planning.

"We're fortunate that the press hasn't got word of our escapade earlier, so I'm just going to message Valerie, or Val on Messenger and tell her in the sort of language Helen uses. Here goes."

She typed.

"Hi Val. Total success today. Spent over 3K on his card and driven away in his car. Instructions left at hotel not to disturb us in room till lunch tomorrow. Coming down to see you. Be there tomorrow eve. How's your plan going?"

And the immediate response.

"All set for tomorrow. Imperial hotel, Llandudno. Lovely rich man called Edward Sands will rue the day."
"Good luck."
"I'll msg you after. We'll meet. Usual place."

Teresa sprang into action.

"I'll call the Llandudno police and tell them what to expect. As long as they stop Val and Mr Sands getting into the hotel room, we'll be OK."
"Agreed."

Teresa spent almost fifteen minutes on the phone convincing the North Wales police she was not making a hoax call, before being put through to the DCI, who listened carefully and asked for the case notes to be forwarded before making his decision. Teresa was becoming increasingly frustrated so took the decision to inform DCI Gardner.

"Leave it with me, Teresa. I'll sort the buggers out."

Gardner's voice could be heard across the room. He pulled no punches, ending his argument with the words

"If you don't get a team in place to split this woman from her innocent date before they get into the bedroom, you'll have the murder of an innocent man to explain to the press. Get this woman arrested and keep her in custody until we get down there."

The Llandudno force immediately made plans for the next day's sortie, while Gardner asked for volunteers to drive to North Wales in the morning. Lynn, Andy and Scoffer were given the job.

However, their plans were in tatters when Teresa made an alarming discovery. She took it straight to the DCI.

"Sorry to bother you, sir, but we've got a real problem."
"What is it, Teresa?"
"Val's pulled out."
"Why? What's happened?"
"She sent a message to Helen's phone. It sounded innocent enough, but she's spooked and gone into hiding."
"Sit down and go through the events with me, please, Teresa."
"OK. She sent Helen a message a short while ago. It simply said, 'How are you?' I replied, 'OK'. Then, about fifteen minutes later, she asked again, 'How are you?' Then, I realised, her initial call was simply to elicit a particular reply. Evidently, I should have replied with a specific phrase, rather than 'OK'. I didn't know the code word, so I started looking back at previous conversations they'd had. There was nothing. I couldn't find it in any of the strings of type. Then I realised, the query must be meant to elicit a reply by other means, such as a phone call. And by then, she'd realised there was something wrong and sent a cryptic message. C U 15th. U know where. That's it. We've lost her."
"OK, Teresa. I'll tell North Wales CID. Let's see if we can trace her some other way."
"I'll get straight on it, sir."

********

Working late into the evening, Teresa finally made a breakthrough. She called Brian but got no response. She tried Lynn instead.

"Lynn. I think I may have stumbled upon something concerning the copycat murderers. There's something in their past I missed first time round, but it's highly significant."
"Let's hear it."
"OK. When they were separated at birth, both had significant problems adjusting to life with their foster parents in their early years. Both, independently, at the age of ten, were referred to a child psychologist, a Doctor Moira Haversham. According to the official reports, their behaviour improved dramatically and eventually, after six years of treatment and psychiatric care, their treatment was ended. On the face of it, both girls appeared normal, but in fact they still both reported to the Doctor on a regular basis. They weren't to know but the Doctor was writing a paper about them and had made them so dependent on her over the years that

they would do whatever she asked. I believe she was the one who turned them into killers, for her own benefit. She was the first to know whenever one of the girls was planning a murder. She was the first to know when it had been committed. I got this information from Helen's phone. It's not a theory. This is real. It's possible this Doctor is the person who put the children on the course they took. And it looks like she did it simply to publish a book about their psychological problems – problems she'd helped to foster."

"Have you got her address?"

"Yes. She's in Manchester."

"OK. Send it to me. Does the DCI know?"

"Not yet. He was on the phone earlier, and I couldn't get Brian either."

"OK. Brian's off duty but try him again. I'll try to talk to the DCI."

"Oh, and another thing; Helen took a call from someone just before she was arrested. I've traced it back to Manchester; it belongs to Dr Haversham."

Lynn was able to discuss the situation with DCI Gardner, who spoke to his counterpart in Manchester and arranged to have Dr Haversham arrested. He asked Lynn to drive to Manchester to conduct the interview. She was able to get Andy to accompany her but was still unable to contact Brian before they arrived at their destination.

The interview was brief as Dr Haversham denied any involvement in the murders. In fact, she would not acknowledge having any contact with either of the murderers 'for as long as she could remember'.

"We have evidence you made a phone call to Helen Lester shortly before she attempted to commit a murder in Ilkley. Do you remember that?"

"I have no knowledge of that. In fact, I haven't contacted either twin for many years, since I dealt with them in a professional capacity."

"OK. You're staying here until you tell us the truth."

"You can't keep me here. I've done nothing wrong."

"You are suspected of being complicit in an attempted murder. You're staying here until we say you can leave. Oh, and we'll be taking your phone with us."

"You can't do that!"

"We can. We're only borrowing it. We'll give you a receipt."

On the drive back, she called Brian to ask for permission to use his phone analyser. She was still unable to contact him but would use it anyway. She knew where he kept it and he had always said any of his team could use it anytime. Besides, it was late. It would have to wait until the morning.

*********

Brian was at his desk early the following morning, looking fit and ready to pick up the reins. When asked, he simply told his colleagues he'd been busy and didn't want to be interrupted, but now, he was free to listen to their progress. He congratulated everyone on their work, asking them to continue until the cases were concluded. He would not interfere. They didn't need him. To some, it felt like they were being abandoned. To others, it seemed like an endorsement of their abilities. However, word soon reached Teresa that Brian seemed to be dissociating himself from the job. She went to see him.

"Morning, Brian."
"Morning, Teresa."
"Could I have a word with you in private, please?"
"Of course. Conference Room? Or would you prefer an Interview Room?"
"The Conference Room will be fine, Brian."

She didn't mention the fact that people could listen in to a conversation in the Interview Room simply by flicking a switch on the speaker outside the room.

"So, what would you like to talk about?"
"I'm worried about you, Brian. You seem distant, or at least that's what your team have noticed."
"I think it's time they were given the chance to prove they don't need my opinion on everything. They don't need to consult me all the time."
"But that's why you're the DI. Your job is to guide your team so that they know they're making the right decisions."
"They're capable. Certainly, the more senior ones. Besides, I'm keeping tabs on them."
"They weren't able to contact you last night when important decisions had to be made."
"I'm entitled to time off, too, Teresa."

"I know. I also know you're going through a bad patch. And I know what the cause is. We all do. And we sympathise. We just want to help you."

"You can help me by not bringing minor problems to my attention. My team are quite capable of making the correct decisions. In fact, I'm going to ask for a meeting with the DCI to discuss promotions for some of the staff. They deserve it."

"Brian, this isn't about them. It's about you. Why don't you book some more time with your counsellor? It's obvious you're struggling."

"Maybe you're right, Teresa. Between you and me, I think I've had enough."

"Why don't you talk to DCI Gardner? Be frank with him. Ask for a couple of weeks off. Go away somewhere quiet and relax, and then see how you feel when you come back?"

There was a long silence as Brian considered his response, until finally he told the truth.

"I think you're right, Teresa. My heart's not in it any longer. My team deserve my support and they're not getting it. It's time for a change. I'll talk to the boss."

# CHAPTER 21

DCI Gardner was sympathetic to Brian's situation and suggested a walk in the City Park. It was a sunny day, warm enough to be out without a coat and with a slight breeze. They sat on a bench facing Town Hall and talked.

"When I first was offered the job here and came down to look around, I sat on this very bench and immediately decided to take the job. I knew that any time work was stressing me out, I could just come out here and sit for a while. And I still do. So, any time you can't find me when I'm on duty, it's quite possible I'm out here. You need somewhere like this, Brian. Not a pub. Somewhere out in the open."

"I know that, sir. Sometimes, I just can't cope. And sometimes, not always, alcohol helps. It stops me from feeling like I need to kill somebody to even things up. I know you can't understand, sir. God forbid it ever happening to you, but until then, you have absolutely no idea how you would feel. And what you would do to try to cope with everyday life. Don't forget that bastard wiped out my whole family. My wife, two kids. And left me with nothing but deep pain and anger."

There was silence for a short time before Gardner spoke again.

"I don't know what to say, Brian. I admit that, never having been in your shoes, I don't fully understand the impact it must have had. All I can do is try to sympathise. You mean a great deal to the people who work here. Everybody has the highest regard for you and will be devastated should you decide to leave. However, it's your choice. You must do what you think is right for you. And should you ever want to drop in for a chat, you'll always be very welcome. But I sense your mind is already made up. Now it's just a matter of picking the right time to do it. Am I correct?"

"Yes, sir. I just don't want to let anybody down. The people here have given their all for me. I need to repay them."

"You already have. Look how they've improved under your tutelage. They're all competent officers. They all make good decisions. They work well as a team and some of them will go on to greater things and all that is down to the way you've nurtured and guided them. You should be proud, Brian. You can leave with everyone's blessing if that's what you wish to do."

"It is, sir. I have it in writing. It's been in my pocket for a couple of weeks. I just can't go on any longer, so here it is, sir."

"I accept it with sadness, Brian. Now, how do you want to handle it? Do you want me to announce it in front of the team or do you just want to go quietly?"

"I've been thinking, sir. I should tell them individually, but I don't think I can without bursting into tears. So, how would you feel if I recorded a short video to play after I've left the building?"

"A good idea, Brian. But someone is bound to see you emptying your desk drawers."

"Not if you call them into a meeting in the Conference Room so I could sneak out. Then you could play the video."

"OK. If that's what you want, I'll honour your wishes. When do you want to do it?"

"A Friday afternoon, I think. Then everyone could just go home afterwards and think about it over the weekend. And by Monday morning they'll have forgotten all about me."

"I doubt that will ever happen."

"Give them time, sir. They'll be OK. There are a couple of natural stand-ins for my job, and some very promising recent additions. I think I've left you something to build on."

"You have, Brian. And the Hall of Fame will be a daily reminder of some of the high points of your career in CID. I want to personally thank you for your hard work and dedication. You can be proud of your achievements here."

DCI Gardner extended his hand and Brian shook it. Without a further word, they stood and walked back to HQ. There was nothing more to say.

********

When Brian walked back into the office, he could sense a change in the atmosphere though nobody spoke. He sat at his desk, surreptitiously slipping some personal items into his briefcase when he thought nobody was looking and placing files in their folders before putting them back into their respective cabinets. Teresa sent him a message.

"Can you come up to my desk, please?"

He did as she asked.

"What's up, Teresa?"
"I know you won't like this, Brian, but I've got an awful feeling something's wrong."
"What makes you think that?"

"I saw you leaving the building with the DCI earlier."

"What's wrong with that? We needed to have a chat, and some fresh air at the same time. Nothing for you to worry about."

"Promise?"

"Everything's fine, Teresa. Finally, everything's clear in my mind."

"As long as you're sure."

"Couldn't be surer."

A little over an hour later, Brian shut down his PC, locked his drawer and pulled on his jacket. He picked up his briefcase and his keys, said 'goodnight' to everyone and walked out of the office. Outside, it was warm, and the sun was shining. He felt the weight being lifted from his shoulders as he made his way to the car. There was to be no stopping at the pub tonight. He intended to drive straight home and take a ready meal out of the freezer. He intended to stay in and have an early night. And for once, his willpower held out.

********

He was back at his desk by 08.30 the next morning, greeting his team with a smile and a cheery 'Good morning' when they arrived. Lynn was the first to engage in conversation.

"Good morning, boss. I hope you don't mind but I borrowed your phone analyser yesterday. I took Dr Haversham's phone and wanted to see what communications passed between her and the copycat murderers."

"You may use it any time, Lynn. Did it help?"

"Immensely. But I haven't finished. Can I borrow it again today?"

"Of course. So, where are we with the case?"

"It seems as if this psychiatrist is responsible for the way the twins turned out. They were referred to her from an early age, and I believe she groomed them to commit murders. I've already got some compelling evidence from her phone, but I need to check something else."

"Have you established her motive?"

"It looks like she's planning to publish a book about the twins' behaviour, without admitting she's responsible for the way they turned out. She brainwashed them, in effect."

"And can you prove it?"

"I think so. North Wales police intend to arrest Val as soon as they find her. I think once we get the twins together, they'll tell us the full story, or, at least, implicate her as the driving force behind the

murders. I'm checking her history at the moment. There must be some incident in her past which has triggered her psychosis."
"Do you need any help, Lynn?"
"No, boss. Andy's with me. We're doing OK."
"I wouldn't expect anything less, Lynn. You're both very capable, and work well together. I'm proud of you. All of you."
"Thanks, boss."

Lynn walked away with her head in the clouds, stopping only at Andy's desk to inform him how they'd be tackling the day's workload, starting with checking Dr Haversham's phone.

It wasn't long before Andy made the initial breakthrough.

"Lynn! Look at this. I think I might have found the trigger for Haversham's actions. When she was a child, it appears she was raped. It took more than a week before she told her parents who initially didn't believe her, but eventually took it to the police. Although she identified the man who'd raped her, he was never charged due to lack of evidence. Shortly after, her father died in mysterious circumstances. The coroner said he'd drunk some poisonous substance and ruled it 'death by misadventure'. There was a suspicion he'd been deliberately poisoned, but it couldn't be proved. I think this may be the incident which set her on the path of murder by proxy. She recruited the twins to kill to gain revenge for her rape and I think it's a possibility she poisoned her father because he didn't believe she was raped."
"I think you're right, Andy. Good work."
"That's not all. Take a look at this. We've got her. She's got a banking app on her phone. It shows regular payments for treatment. I've just traced two of the accounts. They belong to Helen and Val. So, I looked back through Haversham's financial records, and it seems that the twins have been paying for private treatment with this so-called psychiatrist since they turned sixteen, when NHS funding stopped. Since then, they've been killing to fund their treatment!"
"And she's been encouraging them to kill men to avenge her rape."
"Yep."
"Brilliant! Let's get it all written up so we can present it to the DCI. I'm sure we've enough to get the DPP interested."
"OK. But shouldn't we tell the boss, first. Out of courtesy, if nothing else."
"Of course. He's still our boss."

Brian sat patiently as they presented their findings, before breaking out in a big smile.

"Well done, you two. This is great work. You've nailed it. I knew you could do it. You've certainly justified my faith in you. When you get a conviction for all three of them, it will go on the Hall of Fame. You've made it!"

They walked back to their desks beaming with pride and the good news got better when they heard that Val had been arrested in Llandudno.

********

There was a buzz around the office as the news spread. Spirits were high. Everything was going well until Brian took a call from the front desk.

"Sorry to disturb you, sir. There's a gentleman here who believes he's found a body."
"A dead body, I presume?"
"Yes, sir. In Heaton Woods, sir."

The words struck a chord with Brian.

"I'll be right down."

He remembered a case of a serial killer months ago, which was never quite closed – there were still two missing persons, presumed dead – whose corpses had not yet turned up. The mention of Heaton Woods brought back the memory of a woman he'd interviewed who said she'd escaped being murdered in those woods. He'd take the man's statement to see if there was a link.

He introduced himself to the man in Reception and motioned for him to join him in a nearby room. He asked the man's name.

"Ronald Higgs."
"And how can I help you today, Mr Higgs."
"I was just telling the man on the desk. I think I've found a dead body."
"Where?"
"Heaton Woods."
"OK, tell me the whole story. Why were you in the woods?"

"I often take the dog for a walk there. I live in Heaton, and my father died six months ago, and we had to take his dog, Boson."
"Boson?"
"Yes, it was one of dad's jokes. He used to be a physics teacher. He was really into particle physics and when the theory of the Higg's Boson was proved in 2012, he named his lurcher after it."
"OK. Please go on."
"Well, Boson's been off his food for a few days, and then he started being sick and listless. We can't afford Vet's bills, so we just bought stuff from the pet shop that they recommended. Anyway, we woke up yesterday morning and he was dead, poor bugger. So, I put him in a sack and took him up to the woods. I went well off the path, looking for an area where he wouldn't be disturbed and started to dig him a grave."

He paused, embarrassed, before continuing.

"And it was then that I found some bones."
"Did you know they were human?"
"Pretty much, yes. As soon as I found the skull."
"Why didn't you report it then?"
"I panicked. I thought I might get blamed for it. I just covered it up and ran. I took the dog with me and put his body in the shed."
"OK, so, then what?"
"I told the wife when she came home from work. She said I should have told the police straight away."
"She was right. You should. So, why didn't you?"
"I just told you; because I thought I'd get the blame. The wife told me you could tell how long it had been dead. She watches those mortuary programs on TV. She said they'd know it wasn't me because we lived in Bridlington until a year ago."
"Anything else, Mr Higgs?"
"I'm not in trouble, am I?"
"No. You've done the right thing by coming here. Now, could you direct me to the spot where the body lies?"
"Oh, yes."
"OK, just sit tight for a few minutes while I get a forensic team to join us. I'll be right back."

He called Allen Greaves, told him the story and arranged to meet near the spot. Then, he checked his team's workload, and seeing that Jo-Jo and Paula had some slack time, asked them to take the case.

"Be aware that we never found two of the bodies we expected from last year's murder cases."

They took a car with Mr Higgs guiding them where to park to gain easiest access to the site of the makeshift grave. Allen and two of his team were waiting from them.

"OK, Mr Higgs. Take us to the spot, please."
"Follow me."

Once there, they started to dig and soon had unearthed the decomposed body of a female. Paula immediately informed Brian.

"It's an open case again, boss. They're just getting the dogs to see if they can find another body anywhere nearby. I'll let you know."
"OK. Take Mr Higgs home but tell him he must dispose of the carcass of his pet dog in accordance with council guidelines. His best bet is probably to contact the RSPCA. They should be able to help him."

A further half-mile into the woods, a second body was found, again a female. The dogs were deployed again at various spots without further success, at which point Allen called them off and allowed his team to give their full attention to the dump sites, where they remained into the evening until they'd removed all the evidence for further examination back in the lab. Again, Paula phoned Brian to inform him of the situation before they knocked off for the night. There was nothing they could do until the bodies were identified. She left a message for Teresa to retrieve the case notes regarding the missing persons, hoping they matched the corpses.

By the time Paula started work next morning, an email from Teresa awaited her.

"Our notes state that Simon Hartley only confessed to one body buried in Heaton Woods and as yet not found. Known only as 'Anne' (surname not known), apparently a prostitute. Died 1999. Hartley's only other attack in Heaton Woods on a prostitute - a Miss Watkins - who managed to elude him and survived."

Paula called Forensics to see if they had managed to identify either body.

"We're still working on it, Paula. We've managed to extract some DNA from the one we call Anne, but the trouble is we have nothing to compare it to. It's your decision whether to put out an appeal in the local paper to see if anyone can identify her from the few details we can provide, such as height, and name 'Anne'. And don't forget, 'Anne' might be her working name, just a pseudonym. Now, regarding the other body we lifted, I'm not confident we'll get anything. The body is really badly decomposed. It's possible we'll get some DNA from the bone but again, what do we compare it to? Both bodies were naked, so there's nothing to help there. Apart from the fact it's been in the ground for a very long time, probably too long for it to have been one of Hartley's victims."

"Thanks, Allen. I'll talk to Brian. He can make the decision whether we continue or not."

She asked Brian for his opinion, and as she expected, he suggested she contact the T & A regarding an appeal. He wasn't optimistic.

"We can only try, but it's a long shot after all this time. We can't commit resources without a break. They'll just remain as cold cases."

"I've another idea, boss. It might just help if we play on his weakness."

"What are you suggesting, Paula?"

"Let me talk to Hartley. See if I can get anything else about Anne out of him. We know he has a soft spot for blondes."

"OK. Anything's worth a try. Take Scoffer with you. I don't want you alone with him, even in a prison interview room."

The interview was scheduled for the following morning. Paula drove with Scoffer over to Armley where they signed in and were escorted to the room set aside for a private interview. Hartley's face lit up when he saw Paula.

"Hey, you're looking good. In fact, you're beautiful."

"Thank you, Simon. How are you? Are they treating you OK?"

"Not really. The females who work here are all hard-faced bitches. Never smile. Not like you. You're gorgeous!"

"I try to look after myself. After all, you can never get enough sex, can you?"

"I'll make it up to you when I get out."

"I'll look forward to that. But, for now, I wonder if you could do me a favour?"

"Anything, darling. What is it?"

"I'm sorry. It's work. They've told me I have to get some information from you or else I'll be demoted, moved to Traffic, maybe. All I need is a little favour from you. I'll make it worth your while when you get out. That's a promise."

"What do you need?"

"You killed a prostitute called Anne and dumped her body in Heaton Woods. Do you remember her?"

"Vaguely."

"Well, we've found the body and I've been told I have to identify her. Can you help me?"

"How?"

"Is there anything about her you really liked? Did you take any souvenirs, or anything like that?"

"Actually, I think I did."

"What was it?"

"She had a photo. Herself and her mother, I think it was. A Christmas photo."

"Do you still have it?"

"No. It was with my belongings. The police took everything. I don't know what they did with them. They might have chucked everything away. They might have given them to one of my surviving relatives. I don't know."

"Anything else?"

"I took some jewellery from some of the ladies I knew. It's possible I got a keepsake from Anne. I don't remember. It was a long time ago. Anyway, if you find what you're looking for, do I get something from you in return?"

"Oh, yes."

"Then, I'll look forward to seeing you again. They have private rooms here, you know. You could ask for one next time."

"What a lovely thought. Anyway, I can't stay. I'll see you soon. 'Bye."

Once they'd left the room, Paula was visibly relieved.

"God! He gives me the creeps. If you've got something useful, I'll be happy to go back and tell him what I really think of him."

Back at HQ, they went through Hartley's file. He had a daughter. Jean, with his first wife, who divorced him. They both considered it most likely that she would become the keeper of his worldly possessions, even though she hated him. Paula contacted her and arranged to call on her during the afternoon. When she arrived with Scoffer, Jean's initial question was,

"What the hell has he done now?"

"We're trying to source his belongings. We believe he may have passed them to you when he was imprisoned."

"Well, *he* didn't, but the police brought a bag of stuff. They said he couldn't keep it in jail and would I look after it for him."

"And did you?"

"I thought about chucking it all in the bin, but then I thought they were probably his keepsakes from his activities, and I looked forward to throwing them back at him if he ever got out of jail."

"Could we look at them, please?"

"I'll go and get them."

She returned with a large shopping bag full of items, including jewellery, photographs, hand-written notes, and ornaments. She spread them out on the dining table and left them to it with the words,

"I'll be in the kitchen if you need me."

They set to work, separating the pictures of blonde girls from the rest and taking snaps on their mobiles to send to Teresa so she could compare them to images on the various databases she had access to.

Next, they looked at the items of jewellery, mostly cheap rings and earrings, with the occasional necklace. One stood out. It was a cheap necklace with a small silver coloured pendant in the shape of a heart. Scoffer nudged Paula as soon as he read the inscription.

"To my darling daughter Anne."

"Put it aside."

He soon found a bracelet inscribed 'Anne'. Again, he passed it to Paula.

Having examined the jewellery, they turned their attention to the notes. One caught their eye. It read,

"Dear Anne,

I'm sorry to have to tell you this, but I've had a visit from the police. They informed me you were arrested for shoplifting yesterday. I'm so disappointed in you. I know we don't have much, but I've never stolen anything, and I never expected you to, either.

You need to stop seeing that Simon. He's bad for you. I know it's my fault you've become a pro, but I don't know any other way to make money. Just be more careful who you have sex with.
Mum."

"Bag these, Scoffer. There may be prints on them somewhere. And if they were both on the game, they'll probably have a police record."

With Jean's approval, they took the items and dropped them at the lab before returning to HQ and filing their report.

********

It took a full two days before the results came back. Allen Greaves explained to Paula.

"The note yielded two different prints which are on file. They belonged to Jackie McGrath and her daughter Anne McGrath. Anne's prints were also on the pendant and the bracelet. In addition, Anne's prints were on many of the other items, along with those of others we have been unable to identify. And as we expected, Hartley's prints are clear on many of the items.
Both Jackie McGrath and her daughter Anne McGrath had charges on file for soliciting.
I think it's safe to assume the body is that of Anne McGrath and that she was killed by Simon Hartley."

Unfortunately, they were unable to explain the circumstances surrounding Anne's disappearance to her mother as Jackie had died of lung cancer in 2020. There were no other living relatives.

# CHAPTER 22

Paula and Scoffer paid another visit to Armley the following morning on the off chance that Hartley would disclose some information about the other unidentified body. It was a waste of time. He either knew nothing, or decided to keep it to himself, knowing they couldn't pin it on him without his confessing to yet another murder. Disappointed, they drove back to HQ.

"What do you think, Paula?"
"I genuinely don't think he knows anything about it. He's nothing more to lose by confessing. In fact, admitting to another murder would raise him another notch in the list of all-time prolific killers. It's a dead end. All we can do is put out another appeal in the T & A."

The Forensic examination of the body was unable to establish a cause of death as Allen explained in an accompanying note.

"There is no evidence of injury or trauma to the body. We can find nothing. We are unable to identify the body, so have no medical records to examine. We'll have to send the body away to have the bones carbon dated. We don't have the equipment here. Leeds will do it for us, but I think it's far too old to be one of Hartley's. There's nothing we can do. Sorry."

********

Val had been escorted to Bradford and was waiting in Interview Room 1 while her twin Helen was in the room next door. Lynn and Jo-Jo were conducting the interview with Helen, while Gary and Louise were interrogating Val, who was refusing to cooperate.

"We've checked your phone, Val. You're probably not aware but we can recover messages you've deleted, so we're fully aware of what you and your twin sister have been up to. We'd just like to know why. Why have you been murdering people? People you haven't even met before. People you've just communicated with online. Why?"
"I don't know what you're talking about?"
"Was it just for the money? To pay your psychiatrist's bills? Or was it because your sister was doing exactly the same, and you just wanted to be like her?"
"No comment."

"Or was it because your psychiatrist ordered you to do it?"

"I don't know what you mean."

"Of course you do! Since you had sessions with her as a child, she's been grooming you to kill. Did you realise that? She's done exactly the same with your sister."

"I don't know what you're talking about."

"Revenge for rape. That's what it's all about, isn't it?"

"I haven't been raped."

"No, but your psychologist has. In all the sessions you've had with her, she's drummed it into you, and your sister, that all men are evil. They just want to rape you. So, she's conditioned you over the years to pick up men and kill them. And you've taken your victims' money to pay for your sessions with this maniac psycho, so she can reinforce the message every session. She's just been using you all these years. We want to make her stop. We want to put her in prison so she can't have any further influence over your life. You and your sister can become normal people. You don't need someone to control your every thought, your every move. You can be free of her influence. Just tell us how she's manipulated you and Helen all these years."

"No comment."

In the room next door, Gary and Louise met the same resistance from Helen. They conferred in the corridor.

"I wonder if we could get them to agree to hypnosis?"

"Maybe. If we could convince them that it might mean a lighter sentence."

"Is there any other way?"

"Maybe we could tell Haversham they've blamed her for everything and see if it leads her to come clean."

"Shall we take it to the boss?"

"I think he'd agree it was the best course of action."

"Me too. Let's interview Haversham again."

"Just a thought, but it might be better if we get Haversham over here."

"So the twins accidentally catch sight of her?"

"Mmm. I wonder what would happen."

"Let's find out."

They made the arrangements, and all went for a coffee. They chatted about recent events regarding Brian, all agreeing that he needed time off, but unanimous in their belief he still had a role to play in CID. Scoffer spoke up.

"He's been brilliant with me. Always had an answer. Always ready to point me in the right direction if he thought I was astray. He's taught me a lot. I've got a lot of admiration for him."

"I think we all feel the same, Scoffer. If he ever leaves, I'll be devastated."

"I think we all will."

********

When Haversham was brought in, they deliberately walked her past the cells in which the twins were being held. She was surprised to see them but said nothing and simply strolled past towards the Interview Room where Lynn and Gary were waiting with her legal representative. After the formalities were completed, Lynn made her opening gambit.

"We've just been reading up on your history. It explains a lot about why you've become who you are. It explains it but doesn't justify it."

"What are you talking about?"

"Using your position of trust to influence the judgment of two young unfortunate twins who'd had a hard start to their young lives."

"They were unhappy and confused. I helped them."

"You twisted their minds. Just because you felt you'd been badly treated, you used them to get your own back."

"I did nothing of the sort."

"You did! You made them hate men! Just because you were raped as a child and the rapist got away with it. Just because your father didn't seem to believe you, you poisoned him. You had all this anger inside you, and you found the perfect vehicle to express it when these two innocent young children were entrusted to you. You nurtured a hatred of men in them. You persuaded them to kill innocent men simply because they were *men*. You persuaded them to steal from their dead victims to pay you for your help. You corrupted them and made them murderers. For your satisfaction. They were so fooled by your act, that they believed their innocent victims deserved to die. Because that's what *you* thought. That was the view you indoctrinated them to believe. All men are evil! Isn't that right? You were acting out your rage and hatred of men through them. Isn't that true?" Just because you had a distorted view, you thought everybody else should share it. Isn't that right? And you chanced upon two young, impressionable twins who'd had a difficult start to life, and you thought you'd use them to get your revenge on men. Not *their* revenge. *Your* revenge. Isn't that true?"

"YES, IT'S TRUE!"

They were stunned by the fury of her response but delighted to hear it and encouraged her to proceed.

"You used them, didn't you? You trained them to kill, to satisfy your desire for revenge?"

"Yes. They were young. They needed to realise how evil men were before they grew up and fell into their grasping arms. They had to know they would become victims unless they learned how to outwit men, lead them on, and then dispose of them. They learnt well. I'm proud of them. I'm proud of how I was able to teach them to stand up for themselves, to prevent them becoming victims."

"So, you encouraged them to murder?"

"Yes. And I'm proud of it. Look at the type of men who turned up to meet them simply for their own pleasure. For sex. Well, they got what they deserved. These are intelligent women. Not the playthings of sex-mad men."

The air was thick with her fury. Lynn and Gary sat quietly until she calmed down. Then Gary spoke the words he was aching to say.

"Moira Haversham, I'm charging you with being complicit in the murders of several young men, in that you brainwashed two young, troubled women into committing murder. You don't have to say anything...."

She was handcuffed and taken down to a cell, from where she was visible to the twins. They simply laughed at her plight.

********

When Gary and Lynn returned to their desks, their joyous mood soon dissipated when Teresa reminded them they still had two missing persons to be found – Diane Marshall and Alice Bradshaw.

"Right, Gary. Back to it."

# EPILOGUE

Finally, it was the end of a long hard week. He walked into his apartment, took off his tie and pulled the cork on a bottle of malt, pouring himself only a small glass. He had things to do. He opened a drawer and took out the envelopes, opening them one at a time and reading the letters, checking that none needed any last-minute correction. They would do. It was not ideal, but it would do. He sealed each one in its addressed envelope and put them on the kitchen worktop while he went looking for stamps, rummaging through the kitchen drawers. Having found some, he affixed them to the envelopes and placed them back on the worktop while he sipped his whisky.

He looked around the apartment. It was clean and tidy, and the bins and cupboards and fridge had been emptied so that the place wouldn't stink when he'd gone. He would miss this place. It had brought him some peace. Time alone to ponder his future. It had served its purpose. Time to move on. He emptied the glass, washed and dried it, and put it back in its rightful place in the cupboard. He picked up the carrier bag, having checked its contents and put the envelopes inside. Finally, he put on a coat and walked out to the car.

The air was still and warm, with just a few light clouds. The forecast for the weekend was fine and dry, not that he was too concerned, but there was plenty traffic on the roads leading to the coasts and the Dales as people headed away to enjoy a weekend break. Brian, though, was only heading for Ilkley, to pay his respects. On the way, he stopped at a post-box to post his letters.

He pulled into the car park close to the Cow and Calf rocks and climbed to his favourite spot, looking out over the town and Wharfedale beyond. Here, he felt at peace, with his family. He pulled from his carrier bag an unopened half-bottle of whisky, removed the seal and took a long swig. He smiled, at peace with himself and the world. He pulled out his phone and flicked through the songs until he found the one he wanted and pressed 'Play'.

"You meet me in the night with tears falling down
Come let me dry them for you
I wish I could tell a story, chase away all those ghosts
You got inside of you…"

He sat quietly, his eyes closed, letting the memories return as the song played. The song Sarah used to sing to the kids at bedtime. The song he played for them at their funerals. The song which had come to mean so much to him.

And when it ended, he played it again, and again as tears filled his eyes.

"Now I know it can feel like you're slipping away
At night you'll get lost in that deep dark place
We'll let the night come and do what it may
Together we'll find the courage, we'll find faith
Until you awake
I'll stand by you always, always, always..."

He took another drink, lost in thoughts of how life could have been so different; how the ones he loved were so cruelly wrenched away from him, and how, finally, he had realised that life without them simply wasn't worth living. He'd tried so hard, succumbing frequently to heavy drinking to ease the pain, but it wouldn't go away. He'd avenged their deaths by killing their murderer, but it didn't bring them back. Nothing could bring them back. So, he would join them instead. It was the only viable option. The only way to bring an end to the pain.

He sat there until darkness fell, listening to the song over and over while drinking the whisky. When the bottle was empty, he dug into the carrier bag for a different bottle, with a label in Chinese, which he'd purchased on the Internet. He opened it and prepared to drink, holding it up in the air and whispering.

"This is for you, darling. I'll be with you soon. Kiss the kids for me and put the kettle on."

He took a long swig from the bottle as the music continued to play. Soon he began to feel dizzy, and his heart was beating fast. He started to feel sick and short of breath with pains in his chest. He knew it was working. It wouldn't be long now. He laid back, staring at the stars, then closed his eyes. He'd posted letters to his parents and to many of his friends and wondered what their reaction would be when they read them. He'd tried to explain how he felt. He knew some would understand, but others wouldn't. But it was *his* life. *His* choice. And to him, it was the right choice. He needed Sarah and his kids. He missed them so much. He had to be with them. And soon, he would be. He could already feel their presence, sense their love, and was being drawn towards them.

Then he heard a loud noise.

"Brian!"

His eyes remained closed, but his brain strained to recognise the sound. It was a voice. A human voice. He felt himself being lifted and pushed onto his side. He felt something in his mouth and retched violently. Water was being forced into his mouth and making him vomit. Something, a coat, or similar was pulled over his body to keep him warm and he was aware of the sound of someone talking, almost hysterically. He heard and recognised his name being called.

"Brian. Brian. Stay with me. Stay with me. The ambulance will be here soon. Stay with me, please."

Someone was holding him, tightly. Keeping him warm. He recognised the voice, but even with his eyes open he couldn't focus on its owner. His eyes kept closing. He was tired. Unable to focus. But the voice continued to call his name as he tried to concentrate on identifying its owner. He knew her.

He could hear the sound becoming louder. A siren. Then voices. Then footsteps approaching.

"Hold on, Brian. Help's coming. Just hang on. Stay with me."

Then he lost consciousness.

********

He woke to a dazzling light. Heaven? He could hear voices. He heard someone speak.

"He's awake."

He opened his eyes. It wasn't how he'd imagined heaven. It was more like a hospital. It was a hospital! He could see people busily checking monitors and equipment. The voice again.

"Relax. You're going to be OK. Thanks to your friend."

He tried to speak, but his mouth was burning, his throat parched. He closed his eyes and tried to sleep but a voice pleaded with him to stay awake. This time he vaguely recognised the voice and tried without success to speak. A hand gripped his, firmly.

"I'm here, Brian. It's Teresa. I'm here. You'll be OK. I'll stand by you. Always."

Then everything went blank again.

Hours later, he woke again. He could hear a beeping sound. A monitor had captured the change in rhythm of his heartbeat. He looked to his left. In the chair at the bedside, Teresa sat, dozing, but woke quickly as she felt his hand move against hers.

"Brian, just relax. A nurse is on her way."

In fact, two nurses were hurrying towards the bed. They checked the monitor, recorded his vital signs and altered the flow of fluids in and out of his body via the catheters. Teresa whispered to one of the nurses.

"Is everything OK?"

She nodded in reply. Teresa breathed a sigh of relief and squeezed Brian's hand as if to reassure him she was still there. In response, his eyelids flickered, and he fell asleep once again.

********

He slept through the rest of the night, as did Teresa who had been asked to leave the ward and sit in the corridor. She slept fitfully and was back at his side as soon as she was allowed. She was there when he woke and recognised her. They smiled at each other, and Teresa gestured for a nurse to come over.

"He's awake. Can he have a sip of water? He's trying to speak."

The nurse lifted his head gently and placed a cup to his lips. He sipped a little of the fluid and turned his head aside. His voice hoarse and rasping, he uttered the words,

"Hello, Teresa."

Teresa burst into tears, squeezing his hand. She wiped her tears, smiled and replied.

"Hello, Brian. Welcome back."

"Why am I here?"

"You had an accident."

"Am I OK?"

"Yes. Yes, you're OK."

"What happened?"

"We'll talk about it later. Get some rest."

He smiled at her.

"Thank you for being here."

"I'm always here for you, Brian."

He drifted off to sleep. Silently, Teresa got up from her chair and went out into the corridor to make her phone calls.

"Good morning, sir. He's awake and out of danger."

"Thank God for that, Teresa. Are you staying with him?"

"With your permission, yes, sir."

"Stay as long as you need, Teresa. Keep me posted."

"I will, sir."

Her next call was to her partner, Nikki.

"Hi, Nikki. Are you OK?"

"Yes. How are you?"

"Tired."

"How's Brian?"

"He's conscious. It looks like he'll be OK."

"Thank God. When are you coming home?"

"I don't know yet. We'll have to wait to see what the doctor says."

"OK. Keep me informed. I'm missing you."

"I miss you too. We'll talk later. 'Bye."

It was true. Teresa missed her partner terribly, but at the moment, her place was at Brian's side. He needed her more than ever before. And she would be there for him.

She lay on the bench in the corridor and slept for a few hours until a nurse nudged her awake.

"He's awake. He's asking for you."

She freshened herself up in the Ladies before taking her seat by his bed. He smiled.

"Hello, Teresa. You look tired. Are you OK?"

"Fine. How are you feeling now?"

"Foolish."

"Don't be. I understand. I'm sure I'd have done the same in your shoes. But don't worry. Sarah and Daniel and Samantha will still be there for you when your time comes. There's no rush."

"I was just speaking to the nurse. Apparently, you found me unconscious at Ilkley. How did you know where I was?"

"I've been working with top-class detectives, remember. Some of their skills obviously rubbed off."

"Tell me what happened."

"I'd been trying to call you but got no answer. I emailed and texted. Again, no response. I was a little worried, so I called your favourite pubs. The Black Rat, The Scruffy, The Ainsbury; none of them had seen you. So, I drove up to your flat and noticed your car wasn't there. I asked a neighbour if she'd seen you and she told me she'd seen you driving off late in the afternoon. I went into the flats and rang your doorbell and hammered on your door. No response. So, I looked through your letterbox and in the hall I saw an empty box. It was a box which had previously held a half-bottle of whisky. I couldn't tell the brand."

"It was Glenlivet."

"Well, as soon as I saw that, I guessed there could only be one place you had gone to. And then I remembered it would have been Sarah's birthday. So, where else would you have gone?"

"You would make a great detective."

"Well, anyway, I drove over here, calling your phone while the rest of the team were calling the pubs and other places you might have gone. I knew where you were, Brian. Logically, It's the only place you would be."

"You deserve a promotion."

"Just promise me you won't do it ever again."

"I can't promise, Teresa. You know that."

"I understand, Brian. But you have so much to give. So many people have come to rely on you."

"They've all proved lately that they don't need me. They're all quite capable without my help. They just needed time and opportunity to realise it. They'll be fine. It's you they need. Your work must be piling up with all the time you're spending here."

"It's not a problem. Ruth's covering for me. She's very capable."

"We'll see."

"If you don't come back, I'm joining the NCA."

"Well, it's a good move for you. I'm sure you'll be happy there."

"I'd be happier if you joined me. By the way, I have some good news for you."

"What's that?"

"Siobhan was arrested last night. Silly bitch left her car parked on a double yellow line and when they checked the number, her name flashed up. She's locked up in Hull at the moment."

"So, there is a God. I'm glad. I didn't really want to leave any cases open."

"You haven't! Siobhan's done a deal already. She's told us where we can find Dave Crowther in exchange for a reduced sentence. And on top of that, Gary solved two missing persons cases."

"Good for him. Which were they?"

"Diane Marshall and Alice Bradshaw. The two cases were linked."

"Tell me more."

"Well, Gary called on Mrs Bradshaw out of courtesy and to ask if she'd heard anything from her daughter. She hadn't, but during the conversation, she brought out some photographs, the latest ones she had of her daughter when they took a holiday in Greece late last year and showed them to Gary. He recognised two other people in one of the photos. And guess what?"

"Just tell me."

"They were Mr and Mrs Marshall! It turned out that they were all on the same flight from Leeds/ Bradford in seats across the aisle. They had a conversation and found they were all staying in the same resort, in the same hotel. Once they'd settled, they started spending time together, all four of them, going on trips, eating out together. The trouble was, neither Mr Marshall or Mrs Bradshaw realised how close Diane and Alice had become. Gary later discovered that they'd continued seeing each other once the holiday was over, and despite the age gap, it seems they fell in love. So, once he told me the story, I did some digging, and eventually discovered what had happened."

"And?"

"When they went 'missing', they were actually on a flight together back to Greece. So, it's out of our hands. There doesn't seem to have been any coercion. We managed to trace them and asked the police over there if they'd call on them to check the situation. Their report suggested the two were a very happy couple hoping to settle together over there and had no intention of returning to their old life in the UK. Gary's informed Mr Marshall and Mrs Bradshaw who seem to have accepted the situation. End of story."

"I thought we had a taxi driver in the frame. Choudhary."

"We've spoken to him. By chance, he was the one who picked them both up to take to the airport, but they missed their flight, so they called him to take them to a hotel, but instead went back to his flat where they all had consensual sex and he took them to the airport next morning."

"That's it, then. Job done."

"Well, when you get out of here, take some time to think about what you really want. You've still got so much to offer, and so many people relying on you for help, for advice."

"I'll think about it."

"Make sure you do."

There was a moment of silence before Brian spoke again.

"I'm sorry."

Teresa burst into tears.

# THE END

## Previous novels by Ian McKnight

### Premonition (Dec 2017)

A fast-paced crime thriller centred on a terrorist plot to explode a bomb in Bradford City Centre and the CTU's attempt to thwart it.

### The Devil Finds Work (Oct 2018)

A routine investigation into a girl's death from a drug overdose escalates into the search for an international drugs smuggler in a fast-moving tale of corruption.

### Games People Play (Oct 2019)

DI Peters and his team investigate a series of murders while dealing with cases of missing persons, when they become aware of an international human trafficking ring operating on their patch.

### Unfinished Business (Jul 2020)

The discovery of an amputated foot leads DI Peters on a trail of crimes involving Climate Change Activists with a hidden agenda, international drugs smuggling; a serial child abuser; corruption in local government, and a computer hacker terrorising and blackmailing innocent victims.

### The Pandora Program (Jun 2021)

The team chase people smugglers enslaving immigrants and uncover a paedophile ring.

### Retribution (Dec 2021)

DI Peters finds his family slain after a brutal attack, the first of many, and must hunt down the killer and his paymaster in this fast-moving and emotional tale of revenge.

The Ray Light trilogy: **(2017)**

### Losing Lucy
### Light Years On
### Light At The End Of The Road

A philandering widower seeks to rebuild his life following the death of his wife. A hilarious trilogy full of twists and turns.

### The Forkham Predicament (Nov 2020)

A madcap comedy set against the background of a pandemic.

All available from Amazon, in paperback and Kindle.

Printed in Great Britain
by Amazon

20985056R00149